BEAUTIFUL POISON

BEAUTIFUL POISON

The Phantom Series Book 4

LAURA C. REDEN

Beautiful Poison

The Phantom Series Book 4

Copyright © 2022 by Laura C. Reden

Laura's Book Count 11

Paperback: ISBN 978-1-954587-45-8

Hardback: ISBN 978-1-954587-32-8

Ebook: ISBN 978-1-954587-29-8

Dyslexic Edition: ISBN 978-1-954587-58-8

Edited by Sandusky Editorial Services

Cover designed by Laura C. Reden

Cover Images:

© Adobe Stock / serikbaib

© Adobe Stock / Dan Kosmayer

© Adobe Stock / Mr.Vander

© Adobe Stock / VectorART

© Adobe Stock / tilialucida

© Adobe Stock / Pixelbuddha

© Adobe Stock / kichigin19

© Adobe Stock / Patrick

© Adobe Stock / Wings

Interior Images:

© Adobe Stock / andreiuc88

© Adobe Stock / serikbaib

© Adobe Stock / kostiuchenko

CONTENTS

BEAUTIFUL
POISON

4

LAURA C.
REDEN

Change was on the horizon. It wasn't something I saw, like a storm front blowing in from the south, but more something I felt from within. The summer was coming to an end. Most of my friends had died in one horrific nightmare or another, and the ones who remained were trying everything to get back home. It was only a matter of time before they found a way. Or died trying.

When the calendar had one unmarked day left, that's when it would happen. I had to imagine that my body was healing somewhere in the Decord City hospital. The swelling in my brain must have decreased by now, and they wouldn't keep me on the meds forever. Nor would this limbo I'd been in last forever. If that wasn't a clear enough message that my time in Baylor was ending, I had Layla sneaking me reminders. *You don't belong here . . .*

I've often heard that when one door closes, another opens. I suppose that means I should be looking at the end of summer like an opportunity. But it didn't really matter if I died at home or in Baylor, because either way, I'd suffer. There would be no happy ending for me. I couldn't live two lives forever. I put off the decision any way I could.

Thankfully, I now had some control over my unconscious thoughts, and could secretly reset the days as often as needed. Today was one of those days. It never gave me an extra day on the calendar, but it pushed the Summerfield State Fair back, and that's all I really needed. Now that I had a little taste of wolf's blood, and the power that came with it, I knew the next time I saw Layla would be the final showdown. That girl was crossing over, one way or another. And when she did, I'd agree to meet my destiny.

Since the car accident, I'd been dreaming of the crash. I'd see it on the news or browse past it in the newspaper. Though at the time, I hadn't known it was *my* accident. That *I* was in the car. I didn't even recognize the car, let alone remember the night it happened. But when I discovered I was still alive somewhere in this world, I stopped having those dreams. Maybe the idea became too painful to relive. Or maybe I would be too inquisitive and search for answers beyond the bounds of my dream state. Either way, the rules of this consciousness were breaking down, and things were getting weird, even for Baylor.

When I had that dream again, I knew it wasn't like any time before.

I stood under the overpass. Gran was by my side. The night was misty, and the fog was dense. Seemingly in slow motion, we watched as the blue sedan with tinted windows flew overhead. Gran's hand tightened around mine, and I took notice of how cold her skin was. Even in the afterlife, she was frigid. Though I doubted she could feel it. Her skin was paper-thin, and even though I could feel her veins across the top of her hand, I knew there was no blood pumping through them. Maybe that's why she was so cold? It was the little things like the temperature difference between her and me that stood out in my mind. I always thought of us as being similar here in Baylor, but actually, that couldn't be further from the truth.

She had definitely passed on, and I was the opposite of that. I assumed I was in transition, but the way my gran looked at me said I was only here temporarily. I couldn't imagine my life resuming back home after a full summer in Baylor. What used to be surreal was now quite natural. I imagined that going back to my previous life would be dull and somewhat depressing. It didn't mean that I enjoyed everything that happened to me here—quite the contrary. But at least it had always been engaging. I couldn't fathom working at the art gallery for peanuts per hour, plugging numbers into a spreadsheet and talking to the random customer about paint strokes. What was the point?

I had fought off skinless monsters of the mist, conjured a tornado of crows, and swam with familiar but vile shapeshifters. I had become a human beehive and grown ten feet tall. It wasn't glorious work, but it was exciting. And I held on to the hope that I could make more beautiful things here, given the time. Now that the fear of Walker's rejection wasn't in the forefront of my mind, maybe I could have that dream. Or a proper date. Was that too much to ask of a girl in a coma? I didn't think so.

I contemplated my existence as it was, and as it could be, while I watched the undercarriage of the four-door sedan plummet to its demise. Glass shards exploded into the sky like confetti as the car smashed into the street. The front of the car compressed like an accordion, and the remaining intact windows burst like fireworks. The car stood on end, perpendicular to the road, before teetering over. It landed flat on its roof, the metal frame bent like a tin can. The fog lights flickered in the nearby condensation, illuminating the moist air and the particles of glass and debris.

Before, I'd only been vaguely aware of the yellow fabric pressed against what remained of the driver's side window. Now that I knew it was me pressed against the window, I recognized the blouse as one of my favorites. I obviously chose that top for my eighteenth birthday celebration. I used to love how it contrasted with my dark chestnut hair and thought it made me stand out in the usual sea of black tops. I winced, wondering what my funeral would be like.

The sympathy in Gran's eyes met mine. I'd had this dream so often that I now recognized the sadness that flashed across her face as different from before. Because all the times before, my gran had shown no emotion. Her green eyes had been no more than the distant fog of cataracts, her voice as cold as her skin. But as we stood under the overpass now, her eyes were a brilliant green, just like they had been when she was alive. Yes, change was on the horizon.

"We should go," she said, just like she always had. She coaxed me to leave the scene with a tug on the arm. But this time, I didn't move. I was lucid, and I finally knew what that meant.

"Not yet." I shook my head and watched as Gran's face creased with worry. She didn't want me to see this. Nobody should have to see their own death. But I had seen it many times before, though this was the first time I'd seen it with open eyes. *I* was in that car. And I wanted to know why. I wanted to see myself. Talk to myself. Could I do that?

I slipped my hand out of Gran's weak grasp and walked toward the car. A small protest choked in her throat as I stepped out of the shadows. The night was silent but for the settling of the car that groaned in the distance. I cracked my knuckles as I approached the car. I didn't want to see myself beaten and battered, but I was still curious. I'd already seen a version of myself in the hospital that I hadn't recognized, and I knew this would be far worse. Dark hair covered my face, and for that, I was thankful.

I kneeled next to the upside-down door, trying to look inside. An unsettled feeling washed over me. This was harder than I imagined it would be. The unexpected urge to protect the girl dressed in yellow came over me, and I reached out instinctively. I tried to grab hold of her shoulders—my shoulders—and shake the girl awake. I tried to swipe her hair out of her face. I called out to her.

"Wake up!"

My hands were useless as they passed through her.

"Wake up!" I yelled. She couldn't hear me.

I searched frantically for ways to get her out of the car, but I couldn't even grasp the door handle. My help was of no use to the girl now, for she was in reality, and I was anything but. I was a phantom. An apparition. Just a projection inside her delicate mind. I withdrew my hands, staring at them. My breath billowed out in front of me. How could I be so alone? How could *she* be so alone?

"Gran! You've got to do something!"

Gran stood several strides away, averting her gaze from the accident. Her eyes drooped with sadness and the admission of helplessness. But I was not as easily persuaded.

"You *have* to help her!"

"I am, dear."

But she was just standing there. "Then do it! Help her!" I thrust my hand toward the motionless body. Why was she so calm at a time like this?

"It's not as straightforward as it looks."

"You're not doing anything! I can't grab hold of her. Help me pull her out!" I turned my attention back to the car, trying again to scrape my way in.

Gran placed a feeble hand on my shoulder. "That's not how you help her now."

I knew it was true, but I wasn't ready to accept it yet. What was done, was done. There was nothing that Gran or I could do now. I sat down with my head in my hands, watching my breath cloud between my bent knees. I half-heartedly listened to my gran's words while I tried to come up with ways I could stop the accident from happening in the first place.

"Listen, this accident already happened, and we can't fix that now. But if you wish to help her . . ."

"We need to! We need to help her . . ." I cried. That was me in there. A version of me I couldn't quite recognize, but it was still me, nonetheless. That was *my* beating heart strapped inside. I didn't always like the girl, but I loved her.

"Oh dear. You're not going to like what I have to say . . ."

"Just say it!"

"The only way to help her now . . . is to *go home*."

I flinched back. That was the last thing I expected her to say. I looked up and met Gran's gaze. She knew how I felt about it.

So it was my life, or hers . . .

The girl in yellow lay still, but not peaceful. There was something behind her closed eyelids that wreaked havoc on my soul. I knew the things she'd have to endure, and I didn't want that for her. Yet, I wanted to continue this life I had found in Baylor. It was different for me than it was for her. I loved her, but how much? Would I give my life for her? The girl I used to be?

"We should go." Gran held out her bony hand. She helped me rise, and together we walked away from the wreck. How could I feel like two people at once?

As I looked back over my shoulder, I felt the familiar tug in my heart. I was walking away from something I shouldn't. I knew that. Yet, I did it every time. Steam climbed into the black night and the sedan's fog lights illuminated the desolate distance. It was eerily quiet; no sirens on the horizon. I wondered how long it would be before somebody would find me.

"What happens if I don't go home?"

"You mean, if you stay here?" She wouldn't meet my eyes.

"Yeah, if I stay."

"She can't live without you. She would die. And everybody you love would have a piece of them die too."

I sighed heavily. I could have done without the last part. Clearly, it's not what I wanted. I never wanted to break my mom's heart. It seemed like there was no good option for me. It was the first time I wished the void would take me away.

As we returned to the overpass, my eyes trailed upward, taking in the surroundings I'd never paid attention to before. The bumper of a car jutted slightly over the broken guardrail. I wasn't entirely alone. That must have been the car that hit me. I never noticed it before, probably because I had never ventured out from the shadow of the overpass. I'd never even considered the fact that I wasn't in the accident alone. Had I hit them? Had I hurt a family? A sick feeling twisted in my gut. I couldn't live with myself if I had.

"Do you see that?"

Gran looked around aimlessly.

"Up there," I said, pointing to the car. "Did I hit them? Or did they hit me?"

Gran's brows furrowed and her lips pinched. Her hand dropped from mine, and she faded into the darkness. Her green eyes held mine until there was nothing left of her.

"Gran?"

I spun around, surprised I was still in the dream without her. I looked into the darkness, knowing that's where the dream usually ended. A black space that led into the void. A portal from one dream to the next.

"Gran?" I called out one last time.

Seemingly impossible, it was even quieter now that she was gone. Darker too. This was definitely a world I didn't want to live in without her. Where did she go when she left me? My heart rate sped up. I wanted to run straight into the void, but my feet wouldn't move.

A shadow of a man appeared out of nowhere and stood on the overpass. I hadn't wanted to be alone, but the presence of this stranger scared me even more than my solitude. I feared for my safety, even though I knew he couldn't hurt me. Perhaps what I feared most was that he would hurt the *other* me. The vulnerable one.

I shot a quick glance toward the girl in yellow and was alarmed to see another shadow emerge. A tall, lanky figure stood just outside the shattered window. It was as if an invisible human being was standing there, and their shadow had distorted behind them. My heart raced, and I had the undeniable feeling that I was seeing something I shouldn't be. Something no eyes should ever see. Who was it? *What* was it?

Was it the Grim Reaper? Was he coming to extract me? Had I solidified my choice, and my life was now coming to an end? Was I going to have to watch?

It was difficult to pry my eyes away from the figure by my car, but I had to see what the other shadow was doing. Conflicted, I forced a quick glance to the overpass and sucked in a quick shallow breath as the figure disappeared.

Where had it gone? I spun around, fearful it was coming for me, but I couldn't find it. A black shadow lost in the darkness.

Slowly, I stepped backward, inching my way toward the void. I would have to turn and run. If only I could build up the courage. I wasn't sure what was happening here, but I wasn't safe without my gran. I was ready to wake up in the cabin. And this time, I wouldn't scream. I wouldn't shove my head into my pillow, feeling like I was trapped in a web. A nightmare. No, this time I'd welcome it.

When the second shadow figure reappeared, it was by my car. The two figures stood side by side. A meeting of sorts. One was slightly bigger, taller, and lankier than the other. But they were equal in darkness and depth. I didn't know what exactly they were, but they were two of a kind. I watched in terror, waiting for something to happen.

Side by side, the figures walked away from the car. The shadows grew smaller the farther away they got, and my heartbeat gradually slowed as the threat moved on. It surprised me to see the yellow fabric still pressed against the window of the car, and I was unsure if the Grim Reapers had taken me with them. Much like the time I had found myself both between the walls of the cabin and inside the real-life operating room, I felt the distinct feeling that I should not have been allowed to witness what I had. Somebody or something was breaking a lot of rules with me.

I needed to get out of here before the feeling swallowed me whole. I turned away from the shrinking shadows and the birthday girl who lay tangled in her seatbelt, and I ran straight into the black void. The temperature dropped into an icy bath of nothingness, and I knew I would soon sink into my days spent at Baylor Lake.

CHAPTER 2

The sun had settled behind the treetops long ago, and the sky was quickly losing the last of its color, giving way to nightfall. I readjusted my seat on the stiff bench of the canoe, stretching my back for just a moment. Walker paddled mindlessly. Spending time with him was my favorite pastime, but it hurt me tonight, knowing he was in pain. His scar had been an open wound since the day he'd admitted to having feelings for me, and he tried to hide it—rather conspicuously—behind a baseball cap. I didn't pry. I knew what it meant.

He wasn't completely over Layla, and being with me was somewhat of a painful choice for him to make. It hurt me too. It hurt to know that he'd given me part of his heart, but not all of it. How much had he given me, though? And how much was reserved for Layla? That part I didn't know. I didn't think I wanted to. I wished I could be content knowing that my feelings for Walker were reciprocated, but from the moment he told me, I only wanted more. I feared my longing was a bottomless pit that would never be satisfied. It felt that way tonight as I watched Walker's pensive gaze. I wondered which of us he was thinking of.

He'd said it was wrong for us to be together. There were a hundred reasons that might be true, but I didn't know which one he was thinking of when he said it. I contemplated asking him, but I wasn't ready to hear the truth.

"It's a nice night," I said, breaking the ice. Walker blinked rapidly, as if waking from a stupor. He examined the night sky.

"Sure is," he agreed.

It wasn't really, though. Actually, it was quite average. The stars weren't even out yet. Walker's fresh wound was bothering him, and he was preoccupied with thoughts from beyond the canoe. And if I had to be honest, I was too. There were several trees on fire on the north side of the lake. At least, I thought it was the north side. I sometimes got turned around and only had the glow of the flames to orient myself with.

The fires had started the night of the balloon crash. The night I'd turned into my enemy—the wolf. A ten-foot tall, hairy, bloodthirsty beast. The night that greed coursed through my veins and all that mattered was that I got what I wanted, when I wanted it. Despite the rain, the patch of smoldering wet grass never died. I didn't think much of it at the time, but ever since, I'd been seeing fires come to life in the most uncanny of places. Trees were on fire, pinecones were glowing with embers, and sometimes even patches of the sky were catching fire. As if the blue sky had a piece, invisible to the human eye, cut out and soaked in something flammable, then hung back up for everyone to see. It had been odd to see flames licking up the backside of a low-hanging cloud. But that wasn't the most disturbing part. The part that bothered me most was that nobody else had noticed. Nobody mentioned that the world around them was burning down. Nobody saw it but me.

I glanced at the small grouping of trees from what I still thought was the north side of the lake and wondered why Walker hadn't seen it. He was a ghost, after all. Couldn't he see the things nobody else could? Maybe it was just me making it all up in my head. Maybe it was the idea my gran had put in my head; that I'd be going home soon. I certainly could see how that fear would make the world crumble around me. But it wasn't just the fires; it was little things too. Like Walker wearing the flannel that he'd given me. The same flannel I *knew* was strewn across the foot of my bed at this very moment. I wore it often, and I'd intentionally never given it back to him. Yet he wore it now, as he stared absentminded into the abyss. Why?

Had the world I created for myself become too much for me to hold without dropping pieces here or there? Was

I losing little bits of dream-mapping that should be obvious? Like the sky isn't flammable. Like Walker's flannel was now mine, a gift I held dear to my heart. Would I forget about gravity, because I was more focused on the script that Layla had snuck me on the train? Or because I had added too many manifestations to remember them all clearly? Would I begin to drop parts of my dream like marbles falling out of a brown bag with a soggy bottom? And would the whole collection of marbles fall at once, bouncing out of my grasp, causing total mayhem? Or would it be a slow unnerving process that unraveled before me?

"What did you mean when you said that we were more alike than I realized?" I asked, trying to distract myself from my bag of marbles.

Walker straightened his back and paddled the canoe with longer and stronger strokes. But no answer came.

"It seems like things are changing. Little things. Do you think I'm transitioning into your world? Do you think it's a slow change over time? Or does it happen all at once?" I waited for an answer, but grew impatient while he chose his words. "Is it like a whoosh of freedom that captures your soul and sets you free?" I squinted into the night, trying to imagine it.

"No. Not quite."

"What was it like for you? Could you feel it?"

"Not really."

"Can you explain it? I want to know when it happens to me." I ruffled my hair as I peeked at the glow of burning trees.

"Wilde . . . I don't think we should let that happen." His voice was small and pained, like he had changed his mind but didn't know how to say it.

"What do you mean?"

"I—"

"I thought we agreed I was going to stay here!" Immediately I heard the betrayal in my tone. He didn't want me. He never had.

"I want you to stay!" he exclaimed. "But it's selfish. I think we both know the best thing for you would be to go home. You have a chance to live your life. Why wouldn't you take it?"

"But I *am* living my life. I'm living it right now. Here, with you."

"You know what I mean. It's not the same thing, Wilde. You have so many people counting on you to make a recovery. I would never forgive myself if I let you stay with me."

His words sank in, leaving a chill on my arms and shoulders. I rubbed the goosebumps away, but the rejection remained, not so easily removed. "With all due respect, Walker, it's not your choice. I don't need your permission to stay here."

"No, you don't. You're right. Can I ask you

something?" He rested his arms across the paddle as he took a break.

"Okay."

"What is it you like about this place? Hasn't it been somewhat awful?"

That was a fair question. I could see why he and Gran hadn't seen the appeal. "I feel like I'm getting to know myself here. I'm growing into something I could never be back home. You don't know what it was like for me to be—"

"Ordinary?" he interrupted.

I thought about his assumption. No, it wasn't ordinary that I detested. It was far worse than that.

"Behind." I let the word float between us. Was that the right description? Had I been left behind in life? "I felt like I was always in a race that I could never win. I always felt one step behind everyone else. It was a constant feeling of not being good enough. It weighs on you, you know?" I shrugged, hoping he understood.

"Yeah, I get that."

"But here, I . . . I'm—"

"Powerful?" Walker guessed.

While that was true—I had been powerful in the wolf's guise—that wasn't what drew me to Walker's world.

"No. It's not the magic, though that is a nice perk. It's more about having the option to choose who I want to be. I don't have to be behind here. I don't have to be dyslexic. It's as if I can choose which life I want, and it's always within my grasp if only I work hard enough. It's not like that in the real world."

I thought silently about what his world meant to me, and my heart swelled with the opportunities I saw in my future. I stood up, suddenly full of excitement. "I can swim to the bottom of the lake if I want. I can freeze the water and walk on top of it. And I bet I could climb the night using a ladder of stars, given the time and practice."

"You probably could," Walker laughed.

"I can't do that at home."

"You certainly couldn't." His smile faded, and I thought maybe he understood.

"I can't shed who I was and start anew." I shook my head, looking for a way to explain myself. "If earth was a cage with intricate brass bars holding us within, then the afterlife would be . . . limitless, I suppose."

A splash sounded not too far away, pulling my attention in the direction of the burning trees. It was too dark to see what had caused it.

"But you're not in the afterlife. What if it's different from what you expect? Are you really willing to give up everything for a place you've never seen?"

I sat down like a deflating balloon as the excitement withdrew. "What do you mean? This *is* it, isn't it?"

Walker looked away, and even in the dark, I could tell he was hiding something from me. "You are in a dream state. Not the afterlife. They are completely different dimensions."

"I know that." I knew they were different, but how different could they be if we could see each other?

A loon sang its long, mournful call into the night and sent a chill down my spine.

"Your gran is in the afterlife, and she is barely around. She can hardly communicate with you. Where do you think she goes when she's not with you?"

I'd thought of this before, but couldn't come to a plausible conclusion. "I don't know. But you're here with me. So it has to be similar, right?" Walker sighed heavily, keeping his secrets locked behind pursed lips.

A splash came from the middle of the lake, drawing our attention away from the debate. We craned our necks, trying to get a better look at the dancing fish, but it was far too dark to see where the lake's surface kissed the night air.

"All I'm saying is, everybody's reality is unique to themselves. Don't believe all that you see." Walker refocused on me.

"Ahhhh!" A guttural scream ripped through the night, and water hammered frantically.

"What the hell?" Walker said beneath his breath. I couldn't see anything, but it sounded awful.

"What is that?" I asked.

"I don't know." Walker picked up the paddle and started moving us toward the screams.

"What are you doing!?" I asked, alarmed.

Another gurgling scream echoed off the bordering forest. This time I could make out a girl's voice, afraid, and clearly in danger. What was she doing all the way out here, in the middle of the lake?

"Are you all right?" Walker called out.

I searched desperately in the dark water, looking for anything that resembled a girl in danger. I hated the part of me that wondered if it was a trap. If my mind was playing tricks on me. Or if we shouldn't save her life, in hopes of protecting our own. A loon called out again, reminding me just how haunted the lake could be when the sky was this dark and the nightmares came out to play.

We bumped against searching hands, and I could hear the girl panting from pure exhaustion. Walker leaned over and instinctively pulled the helpless girl into the canoe, splashing water across my face. The girl trembled in fear and what looked to be confusion. I watched her shoulders rise and fall and her hands quake with adrenaline.

I looked at Walker with the same confusion that the girl wore. His dimples were piercing, even through the tight clench of his jaw. The stubble from his unshaven face caught the glimmer from the peeking starlight. When had the stars had come out? It was really quite something, just how many there were. It didn't seem at all something that would accompany such a frantic event.

"Hello?" Walker asked.

The girl trembled as she tried to regain some sort of control. I wiped the water from my face and noted the swirling unease in my stomach. Something wasn't right. It was wrong. Very wrong.

"Hello?" Walker repeated himself.

"Ya-yeah. Yes," the girl stammered.

I recognized her voice and leaned over to get a better look at her face. She brushed the wet hair from her eyes, and I almost fell off my bench.

It was me. I sucked in a sharp breath and grabbed the edge of the canoe to brace myself while my world spun out of control.

"What the hell were you doing all the way out here? We must be miles from the nearest shore." Walker was seemingly unaware of the misprint.

The girl before me perched on her elbows, and I flinched back. I didn't want *it* touching me. I had no clue how there were two of me sitting in the canoe. I had to get Walker's attention, but I didn't want the girl to look behind her and see me. I felt something terrible would happen if her eyes met mine.

I waved my hand overhead, and Walker's eyes ticked up. "That's me!" I mouthed, pointing in an exaggeration.

Walker's back slowly straightened. His eyes flickered between me and the girl. A terrified look stretched across his face, and the girl tensed. She crab-walked an inch backward, bumping into my shins.

She was as real as I was. The past me and the present me had just collided with the slightest touch. I sucked in a sharp breath, and she spun her head to see me.

For just a moment, our eyes met. It was like looking into a mirror and seeing your past self come to life. It was like knowing yourself, but not being able to trust it. Like wanting to protect the vulnerable, but equally craving to heave it off the life raft and let it sink to the bottom of the lake. It was love and hate, all wrapped up in one.

Her eyes were my eyes, and we were both horrified to be looking at one another. I knew the look she gave me. I could read her face well, but I couldn't feel her emotions. Perhaps mine were too loud to feel someone else's.

Something in my brain told me this wasn't right, that there shouldn't be duplicates of me wandering around Baylor Lake.

The girl faded.

I watched her fear-filled eyes disappear into the night. She left nothing but a puddle of water behind. And even that shrank as it evaporated. The puddle dried, and I reached down to touch the once-soaked wooden planks. *I couldn't trust my mind any longer.*

"What was that!?" Walker asked, more afraid than I'd ever seen him.

I looked at him in shock. "It was me!"

"But why? Why were you just in the middle of the lake?"

"I don't know. It's like it was some sort of weird replay from the first night we met!" I glanced into the water, looking for myself out there, but only saw the reflection of the brilliant stars twinkling above. I remembered that. That the stars had come from nowhere that night, and it had been the most beautiful night I'd ever seen. It was like that now. I eyed Walker's flannel and wondered if he would have given it to my wet, distraught self if I hadn't interrupted.

"Were you thinking of the night we met or something? Did you manifest her?"

"No! I don't know why that happened. It shouldn't have happened!" I said, thinking of the trees on fire. The sky shouldn't have been burning the other day either, yet it was. I knew Baylor had been a breeding ground for mischievous phenomena, but this was different. This was almost like the system was breaking down. Like the very connections that allowed this world to come together had begun to falter.

So, it was true. My time here was ending. I wasn't meant to dream forever. I looked up at the tranquil sky and felt the pending doom wrap around me like a weighted blanket. The Milky Way was tinged pink and teal, and golden embers twinkled from bright to dim in a never-ending waltz.

"You might just get your wish," I muttered.

"Which one?" he huffed.

"I don't think I'm allowed to stay here much longer." I tried to swallow through the tightness that clenched my throat.

"Oh."

My chin began to tremble, and Walker crossed the canoe and wrapped his arms around me. I rested my head on his shoulder and hid my tears beneath a curtain of my hair. "I just don't have the strength to go home."

"I know it will be hard. But I promise you, it will be worth it."

"How? I don't want to leave you . . ."

"I know. I know."

The weight of Walker's body felt ten times heavier as the thought sank in. I brushed my foot over the dried puddle. It was hard to think that I was in two places at once. Three, if you counted the version of me that was in the hospital. It took tremendous effort on my part to conjure three from one. Separated were the body and the mind, and the mind into halves. I felt the exhaustion of it all. I was tired.

As my body grew stronger back home, my mind grew weaker here. Wires were getting crossed, and the past was commingling with the present. I would never get my underwater tea party and endless celebrity golf tournaments. My summer at Baylor Lake was ending just as my relationship was beginning.

"Just promise me one thing?" Walker asked.

"What's that?"

"You won't leave without saying goodbye."

"I'm *not* leaving. Not without a fight, anyway."

"Just promise."

I clenched my teeth. It felt like I was conceding defeat if I agreed. But I knew he needed to hear it, so I said it for him. "I won't leave you without saying goodbye."

When I came back to the cabin that night, the lights were out and everybody was asleep. I desperately needed to talk to Emma about seeing my double nearly drown. I had to sort out my feelings, because I both wanted to harm the girl and simultaneously save her. I didn't exactly understand it, but I had a theory; the dream was crumbling, and what little understanding I had before was now gone.

I hesitated in front of Emma's door, contemplating waking her, before I hung my head and strode across the hall. I crawled into bed and lay awake for what seemed like an eternity. Maybe it was. I found an edge of the blanket and fiddled with the fabric while staring at the shadows in the corner of my room. When I got restless, I headed to the bathroom to splash cold water on my face.

I closed my eyes and dipped my face into a small

puddle of cool tap water in my cupped hands. The chill did wonders to orient me. I blotted my cheeks with a towel and stared up at myself in the mirror. I was nothing more than the dark shadows I had seen in my bedroom. I could make out the outline of my jaw and, most of all, my dark hair. I searched for discerning features but found none. No features to say that I was, in fact, Kinsley Wilde. For all I knew, I could be looking into the eyes of my double.

I flipped on the light switch and took a long, hard look at myself. My hair was tousled and chestnut brown, my lips pouty, and my eyes dark. Soulless though? I looked deeper. I searched for the green fleck in the bottom right corner of my eye. For a moment I panicked, leaning closer to the mirror until I was nearly pressed against it. That's when I saw it. The small memento from my gran. I leaned back, my heels touching the floor once again, and I sighed a breath of relief.

I was still myself. At least for now. My whole world might come crumbling down, but in this moment in time, I knew who I was. That should be enough to let me sleep. I flipped the lights off and staggered back to my bed, unbearably weary. I tucked myself in for the tenth time that night and closed my eyes, hoping there would be no more interruptions in the world of my making . . . at least, until I woke.

I wasn't so lucky. In the faraway distance, I heard a sound. Music? A quiet melody that I couldn't quite put my finger on. I recognized it from somewhere, but the more I focused on the notes, the quieter it became, fading out until almost disappearing. As I began to drift off to sleep, it would grow louder again. I played the guessing game for quite some time before one of the quiet lulls finally put me to sleep.

When I went down for breakfast after a restless sleep, replaying the melody in my head like an addiction, it was already evening. Late evening. Noah was outside stacking wood for a bonfire, while Gunner dug a hole nearby. Scarlett May was draining a pot of noodles for what I assumed was spaghetti, and Emma was finishing a book on the couch. I felt a little insecure joining them this late in the day, but nobody seemed to notice my absence. Sometimes their oblivion could work in my favor, and this was one of those times. I slipped into the conversation as if I hadn't just woken up, and my worries about missing out dissipated quickly.

"Is Sampson coming over tonight?" I asked Scarlett May, as I checked on the breadsticks I'd seen her slip into the oven.

"No. I don't think so. I couldn't get a hold of him."

"Is Walker coming over tonight?"

"Nope. Not tonight. We have plans tomorrow night, though. I'm going to take him on our first date."

Scarlett May threw the potholder down and stared at

me in surprise. I laughed and covered my face with my hands. "What?"

"What!? You didn't tell me you guys were dating!" Honestly, I didn't think she'd care. But now that Kimber and Trinity were gone, I supposed I should include her more often. I shrugged apologetically. Emma jumped from the sofa and joined us in the kitchen.

"Well, it's still really new. We kind of admitted to having feelings for each other at the Baylor Balloon Festival. We've talked little about it since, so I wanted to take him out for an official date. I thought it might help solidify things."

The truth was, we had talked little about it, but I didn't like where we'd left things. I felt nervous about Walker changing his mind on me, and I wanted reassurance. I wanted to show him what we *could* have if I stayed. I wasn't sure how to plan the date, but I knew I had to blow his mind. He seemed to have liked the missiles flying from the movie screen at the drive-in, so I wanted to make some grand gesture again.

"What are you going to do on your date?" Emma asked.

"I'm open for suggestions. I've never planned a date before. The only thing I can think of is a picnic, but it seems kind of silly." I turned off the oven and took the breadsticks out. They were perfectly browned and smelled of butter and garlic. My mouth watered.

"You guys could go swimming in one of the remote coves around here. Take the golf cart?" Emma suggested.

Scarlett May moaned. "Come on. That's *so* boring!"

"What? She could wear a cute little bikini and bring strawberries and wine coolers. It could be great!" Emma chirped. I briefly wondered if that's what she had planned to do with Levi before he broke her heart.

"No, no, no. What you need to do is get a bunch of candles from the store. Light them in a trail from the dock all the way to your bedroom—"

Noah walked in dusting his hands and scowled. I shrank in his presence. "Candles? For what?" he asked, swiping a breadstick from the hot pan.

"Uhh—" I muttered.

"Kinsley is taking Walker on a date! I'm teaching her how to do it right, so she'll get lucky," Scarlett May said, with a smug look on her face. I smacked the oven mitt across her arm and she flinched. Then I scrunched my eyes shut, not wanting to see the disappointed look in Noah's eyes. When I opened them, the look was even worse than I had imagined. It only lasted a moment before his mood shifted into something icy.

"You should take him swimming," he said.

"See! That's what I said!" Emma exclaimed.

"Take him to the three boulders and practice jumping off the rope swing," he continued, his denim blue eyes turning to glaciers. Both Scarlett May and Emma turned away, lips pursed. My stomach sank as I thought of Ethan dropping from the rope swing and never surfacing.

Was that what he wanted? Did Noah want Walker to jump off the rope swing and drown, like so many others had? I knew Noah wasn't a fan of Walker, but did he really want him dead? My mood lightened when I realized Walker already was dead. There was nothing Noah could ever do to hurt him. The joke was on Noah, and he didn't even know it.

"Or you could take him to the Summerfield State Fair. Maybe you guys could have your first kiss on the Ferris wheel! That would be . . ." Emma piped in, trying to temper the room. It worked, somewhat, to dispel thoughts of Ethan, but Noah was still gritting his teeth. He grabbed the lighter fluid from the kitchen counter and went outside. As soon as the door slammed shut, the three of us let out the breaths we'd unconsciously been holding.

"On second thought, Emma is right. The Ferris wheel *is* really romantic. You should do that. And then the second date could be the candle thing." Scarlett May mixed the spaghetti sauce with the noodles and threw a pair of metal tongs into the bowl.

I had thought a lot about that Ferris wheel. I'd seen it the first night I drowned. Maybe my destiny was waiting for me at the top of that large sparkling wheel, and all I had to do was ride it with Walker. Perhaps it would be a kiss at the stroke of midnight. Maybe a lightning bolt from a summer storm. The electricity would strike the metal of the wheel, and I would transition into eternity. A butterfly emerging from its chrysalis. I yearned for the possibilities of something great but feared the more likely outcome. Our first date would be our last.

I dished up a plate of spaghetti, covered it in Parmesan cheese, and threw a garlic breadstick on top while mulling over the possibilities of my soon-to-be future. The state fair was only two days away—assuming I didn't get cold feet and add more rising suns to the summer. As it was now, I had forty-eight hours to figure it all out. It hardly seemed like enough time. Emma dished up plates for herself and Noah. Balancing the two as she opened the door to the patio. Scarlett May followed, talking about how wonderful it would be to fall in love at the fair, and I knew she was thinking about Sampson.

"Do you think he's going to win you one of those big stuffed animals? The ones that are so gigantic you have to carry them on your back?" she swooned.

"Or maybe he'll say something like you owe him a kiss if you can't pop a balloon with a dart," Emma said, before abruptly clearing her throat at the sight of Noah. The three of us stiffened as he shook his head. Emma handed him a plate of spaghetti, and we took our seats around the campfire. It must be lonely to be the only guy left. It was too bad he and Walker couldn't be friends. Though that would be incredibly awkward for me.

"Actually, I wanted to talk to you guys about the state fair." I redirected the subject away from Walker. "I have a theory. Hear me out, okay?" I asked, before shoving noodles in my mouth.

Nobody said a word; instead, they eyed each other nervously. Theories in Baylor have proven to be useless, and they usually ended in crippling disappointment. I could see it on their faces now. They didn't want to get their hopes up.

I covered my mouth as I spoke. "I think that I've been getting these signs, or premonitions, about the state fair. Little signs here and there. And I think it means there will be another red door present."

This had everybody's attention. "You mean, like the one we tried to find at the bottom of the lake?" Emma asked warily.

"The portal?" Noah demanded, his fork frozen just in front of his mouth.

Of course, I already knew there was going to be a red door at the state fair. Summer was ending. The calendar was nearly filled with X's. And the dream was crumbling like a house of cards in the wind. The three of them would go home to their families if it was the last thing I did. But I hoped I'd have time to ride the Ferris wheel with Walker and live in eternal happiness. It seemed like a tall order. Gunner placed his paw on my knee and licked his lips. We would have to get him home, too. I ripped off the corner of my breadstick and tossed it for him.

"Yes, the portal. I've seen more than one before, and I think there are even more out there. We just have to find them."

"We just find it, and then we can go home?" Scarlett May looked at Emma with a wrinkle in her brow. She appeared to be questioning the ease of it all. "What about Layla? I thought we had to find her?"

"The only reason I'm stuck here is to find her and get her through that door. Just like you guys. I mean *us*. My, um, my gran told me she's having trouble getting to where she needs to be, just like we are. And that red door isn't just a portal home. It can take us anywhere. Anywhere we really belong, that is." I wondered what would happen if I fell through the portal. I wasn't sure what side I would end up on. Would the portal spit me out with the living, or recast me to the afterlife?

"Your gran?" Noah asked. I swallowed a lump lodged in my throat. *He caught that.*

"I've sort of been in contact with her." I shrugged, eyeing the dirt beneath my feet. Noah sighed, frustrated with the amount of information I'd been withholding. He ran his hands through his shaggy, sandy hair and tipped back in his chair, causing the front two legs to lift from the ground.

"Why is Layla stuck here?" Emma wondered.

"Who cares? We just need to find the door and shove her through it," Noah said sharply. He was done with me and this entire summer. And I didn't blame him.

"I'm not really sure why she's trapped here. I think she's relying on all of us to help get her home. Wherever that may be."

"Is Walker going to come with us?" Scarlett May asked through a mouthful of spaghetti.

I'd never thought about him coming home with me. I'd only imagined me staying here with him. Was it possible? Could he come home to Clover and exist among the living? Could I date a ghost? I guess I already knew the answer. I had been dating him all summer long, or at least trying to.

Nobody would see him back in the real world, though. And I imagined that would weigh heavily on our relationship. It would probably put me in a mental hospital. It would only be a matter of time before my mom caught me talking to myself, or worse. I shuddered.

I frowned, and Emma looked at me sympathetically. She was the only one who knew that Walker and Layla were ghosts. I never dared to tell Scarlett May or the others that Walker had been the Butcher of Baylor Lake. I imagined if I had, this summer would have gone differently. For starters, I wouldn't be getting dating advice.

"Yeah. Walker and I are going through the portal, too. He's dying to get back home," I said, lying through my teeth. I saw Emma's brows furrow, but she said nothing. The other two bought it easily enough, and we dropped the subject as Gunner came back begging for food.

My gaze rested on the orange flames flickering between the logs in the campfire. I couldn't tell the truth because they would surely lose hope. And right now, hope was all they had. And they weren't the only ones. I had hope for them getting home, too. I really wanted to find the door and get them through it. But when it came time, I planned to skip away, holding Walker's hand.

I wondered if Layla would go willingly or not. I imagined it both ways. She'd either give me a hug and tell me thank you, and the feud would finally be over, or the war I saw in my dreams would begin. Either way, I had to be prepared for the worst. I had to assume that she would stab me in the back, given the chance. And by the look Noah had on his face as he stared absentmindedly into the fire pit, I might have to watch my back around him, too.

My eyes met Emma's which seemed to convey a sadness. She knew I wasn't telling the whole truth. I bit my lip and felt the guilt wash over me. I knew she would miss me when I didn't return home. I thought about my family and then quickly pushed the thought away, burying it in butter and garlic.

"We'll have to bring this guy, too," Emma mumbled.

Everyone watched Emma feed Gunner. She held a single, long noodle above his nose. As the noodle swayed, my focus was drawn to the forest. Layla crept between the trees. I felt my heart rate rise but remained still and kept my composure. It was the first time I had seen her since the lightning strike, but I'd known she'd be back. A girl like her wasn't so easily dissuaded by a little magic. The first thing I noticed was she no longer wore the crimson cloak. That fairy tale had ended. Had a new story begun? I wondered if she'd heard us talking about her. Did she want to pass on? Was she happy to have us looking out for her, or did she only care about ruining me?

"Ouch!" Scarlett May yelped and shot out of her chair. A burning hot ember flew out of the fire pit and slammed into her bare shoulder. She batted at the sparkling coal, swiping it off her arm.

"Whoa! It burned a hole right through your chair!" Noah said. A red glowing circle ate through the fabric and began to spread outward.

I checked back with Layla, but she had made herself scarce during the commotion. Emma was assessing the burn on Scarlett May's shoulder, while Noah just stared at the chair. The taut nylon continued to burn, though there were no flames. The tiny embers fed until they consumed the entire thing. When Scarlett May was ready to sit back down, her chair was nothing more than metal legs and two long posts where the back had once stretched between. The trees weren't on fire tonight, but that didn't mean the flames had been extinguished.

We spent the evening talking around the campfire, and I was well aware it was one of our last nights together. It made me miss my family of misfits to think of them gone. Scarlett May sat in my lap, and we wrapped a blanket around both of us. Inevitably, the blanket caught fire from another rogue ember, and Noah put the campfire out with a bucket of lake water. We all went to bed early, but I couldn't turn in before taking one last glance out my window. Layla was sitting at the edge of the dock. What was she doing so close to the cabin?

It hurt my heart to see her hunched back and dangling legs. The girl was a broken soul. It was hard for me to understand how someone so powerful needed help from someone so wounded. I was a nobody in this world. I didn't even belong. And she made sure I knew that.

But still, I couldn't stand to see her in pain when it was just the two of us. I knew she lived an invisible life alongside Walker, which seemed to be a torture of the worst kind. I couldn't imagine looking into his golden eyes and having him see straight through me.

I decided right then to go to her. I slipped a hoodie over my head and stepped into my slippers. But when I opened the patio door, the ghost was gone. There was nothing but thick fog wafting over the dock and the smell of campfire lingering in the air.

CHAPTER 4

I was anxiously awaiting Walker's arrival for our first official date. I sat on the dock, my legs hanging over the edge and my bare feet barely skimming the top of a wet paddleboard. I'd rented two of them in a watersports rental shop in town earlier this morning. While I was worried about falling into the haunted water, I wanted to recreate the night of the Fourth of July. It was the first time I had experienced the magic that Baylor had to offer, and I longed for that curiosity and excitement again.

Then, it had been nothing more than a simple thought of wanting the night to last forever. And it was that one fleeting thought that had brought on the serene glowing lake, the elegant white swans, and the fireworks that fell like blazing streamers from the sky. I could only imagine what my feelings for Walker would do on a day like this. I secretly hoped that we would swing from the stars and bask in the clouds. Nothing was too far from reach in a place like this, with a guy like that.

I rummaged through my old backpack as I waited impatiently. Stuffed at the bottom were two thin towels I grabbed off the back railing on my way out. On top, I'd gently laid our lunches in a clear Ziploc bag. I had prepared two sandwiches and added a couple bags of chips, sodas, and a bag of fresh strawberries to share. It wasn't the most romantic lunch, but I was hoping to make up for that with the water show.

How I was going to manifest it, I wasn't sure. But I had seen various water shows on TV. Massive fountains with shooting water in intricately timed spurts, streaming over and under each other in a beautiful design, and lit by colored lights that cut through the night. I hoped all I had to do was tap into my emotions for Walker and think about the fountains I'd seen on TV, and then they would appear just as beautiful as, if not better than, I had imagined. I zipped up the backpack and double-checked the smaller pouch on the front of the bag. It contained a tube of sunscreen and a very old lip balm. Could that expire?

The door slammed behind me, and I turned to see Gunner running out of the cabin. Nose to the ground, he followed an invisible trail that led him to the dock. Once he spotted me, he came running.

"Hey, boy!" He pushed his nose forcefully under my

arm, begging me to scratch behind his ears. I did as he asked, and he bowed his head, leaning into me for more loving. I giggled just as Walker glided around the cove. With my thoughts trained on Walker, my hand slowed. I watched my future come toward me, brighter with each stroke. Gunner wouldn't have it, though. He pushed into me with all his might, his tail painfully flogging me in the back. "Okay! Okay! I love you too," I said, giving him my attention once more.

"Hey, Wilde. You look nice."

I smiled, more embarrassed than I should have been. It certainly wasn't the first time I'd tried to impress Walker, but I had taken more care than usual with my appearance today. Which is precisely what he noticed first. I had put on a lip stain that usually dried my lips out, but I found it to be pretty and well worth the sacrifice on a day like today. Scarlett May had put some eye shadow on me that I wasn't quite used to, but it looked good enough to get my approval.

I wore a more feminine tank than I was used to wearing at the lake. I hadn't packed nice things for our summer trip. There wasn't usually an opportunity to wear them. The silky tops stained with sunscreen, and the beautiful whites that I'd worn in years past always came home with a barbecue stain of some type. But when Scarlett May had insisted I wear her white tank top, I readily agreed. I loved the petite buttons that ran from top to bottom. She insisted I unbutton the first couple to show off a V neckline, rather than the boring straight cut. It didn't really matter to me, but I liked the way her hot pink bikini peeked out from underneath the thin straps.

"Thank you," I mumbled.

"Wow, what have you got there?"

"Paddleboards. Have you ever tried it before?" I asked, kicking them off to the side so I could help tie the canoe to the dock cleat.

"I have not," he said, somewhat unsure of himself. I laughed, but I was worried that I had set us up for disaster.

"We don't need to take them," I shrugged, suddenly deciding against the entire plan. Had I really thought a picnic on paddleboards was a good idea?

"No. It will be fun. I'm looking forward to it." He smiled encouragingly. "Honestly."

The canoe scraped against the dock as it came to a full stop. I held it as Walker hopped out, and we tied it up together. He gave me a brief side hug before awkwardly looking away. Was it awkward for him, too? Or was I the only one who felt the pressure of a day like today?

I didn't doubt my insecurities would play tricks on me, in Baylor of all places. Still, it seemed odd that he hadn't kissed me. Wasn't that something couples did after admitting their feelings for one another? When was that going to start? I hung my head slightly, thinking that sometimes, our relationship felt like the beginning of an endless road, while other times, like now, it felt like it was the end. A dead end.

"Shall we then?" I asked, motioning to the paddleboards.

"After you . . ." Walker eyed me warily.

I smirked as I tossed my backpack over my shoulder. I sat down on the dock and pulled the boards over, one by one, using my tiptoes. After trying rather unsuccessfully to get on the boards from the dock, we finally pushed them to shore in hopes that getting on in shallow water would be easier. It was.

I kneeled on the board carefully and dug my paddle into the silt to push off. Walker followed my lead. "See? That wasn't so bad," I said, feeling quite proud of myself. I'd been worried over nothing.

"Oh yeah? That's the easy part. Why don't you actually stand up, and then tell me how easy it is." Walker glided next to me, his legs dragging in the water and brushed against pads of water lilies. He looked like a natural. I bet he was good at everything he tried. I felt the heat creep into my cheeks. He stared at me with one brow raised, daring me to stand on the board.

"Okay." Of course, I was going to stand up. That's what you did on a paddleboard. I took the backpack off and placed it on the back of the long board, then carefully got a foot beneath me. I crouched, the board wobbling beneath my feet as Walker laughed. "Stop it! I'm . . . I'm focusing."

And I needed it. I needed all the focus in the world to keep me upright.

"Oh! Oh! Oh!" He willed me to fall, but I did no such thing.

"See? It's really not that bad!" I said, nearly erect and trembling like the last leaf on a tree at the end of fall.

Walker wouldn't stop laughing, but I didn't dare take my eyes off my feet. Somehow, staring at my ten little toes gave me the confidence to push through and stand upright. I took one tiny step forward, positioning my foot in a more comfortable spot as I windmilled my arms, the paddle waving in the air. Walker's laugh grew into hysterics. "What? Let's see you do it." I finally looked at him, surprised to see that he wasn't laughing at me. He wasn't even looking at me.

I followed his gaze behind me until I couldn't turn my head any further. I whipped my head in the opposite direction, nearly losing my balance. Gunner was paddling as fast as he could to keep up. He was headed directly for my board. "No. No. No! Gunner, no!" I shouted, crouching down.

Gunner slapped one heavy paw onto the back of my board, and then two. "No!" I screamed as the board slipped from beneath my feet. The paddleboard went one way, and I went the other. I splashed into the lake, cursing myself for such a stupid idea for a first date. The water was cool, but not refreshing. It could never be refreshing after the things I'd seen in its depths. I wanted out as soon as my skin touched the mirrored lake.

I took in a gulp of air as my head breached the surface. Gunner had just tipped my paddleboard, and the backpack slid into the water. Walker tried to grab it, but it was too far.

"No!" I yelled before diving under the water. I opened my eyes, searching for the backpack before it disappeared. I kicked down, barely able to reach it, but managed to grab hold of a single sinking strap.

"Here, boy. Here." Walker patted his board, and Gunner's head bobbed just above the water as he made his way around the mess he'd created. Walker grabbed hold of Gunner's collar and pulled him onto his board, somehow managing to stay upright. I frowned.

I side-stroked to my board and struggled to tip it over. Once it was upright, I threw the wet backpack on top and began the long process of heaving myself up. I was only slightly relieved that I managed it in one try, because just about the only thing I could feel now was sheer embarrassment. I must have looked like a seal trying to board a channel marker. As ungraceful as it felt, it must have appeared ten times worse to my date. By the time I was upright, soaking wet and most likely with makeup marred cheeks, Walker was no longer laughing.

"Did you like that?" I asked, eyeing a very dry Walker and a soaked but happy Gunner. "You know he's going to do that to you too, right?" I willed it to happen. Magic don't fail me now!

"He won't do that to me. He loves me."

"Uh-huh." Walker passed me the paddle that he rescued, and I took it from him with a sharp jerk. "So much for our towels," I grumbled.

"Is this what you imagined when you rented the paddleboards?" Walker asked with a hint of sarcasm.

"Yup," I lied, trying not to let the rocky start ruin the rest of the date, but I worried it was the first domino to fall. It took a little effort, but finally I was able to look past the humiliation. I had a water show to perform, and I would need all my focus.

We paddled around Rock Creek Cove into a smaller deserted area. Boats almost never came here because the fishing was bad and the strip was too short for any water sports. It was the perfect spot for our first official date. We pulled our boards close together and held onto one another's paddles while we ate lunch. Thankfully, I'd shoved the sandwiches inside of a large Ziploc bag, and most of our lunch remained dry.

"Tell me more about Layla," I said, surprising myself. The question passed through my lips before I registered it as a thought in my mind. I'd always wanted to know more about the girl, but I'd intentionally avoided asking Walker. I knew it hurt him too much. But the words were out there now, and it was too late to take them back. He seemed to ponder the question, his hand twirling in the water lazily. I zipped up my backpack, heaved it behind me, and then, ever so carefully, I used the wet bag as a pillow.

"What do you want to know?"

"Honestly? Everything." I knew so little about the girl, other than she was important and beautiful. But at large, she was a mystery to me.

"She was everything to me. I was ready to build my life around her. I wanted to . . ." Walker followed my lead and lay down on his paddleboard, placing his hands behind his head, and his feet before Gunner. I remained quiet, giving him ample time to remember his past love.

"She wasn't perfect by a long shot. She was stubborn and insecure, and sometimes I feared I loved her far more than she did me. Who knows, maybe I was the insecure one?"

"Maybe," I echoed his thoughts, as I twirled my fingers in the cool water like he did.

"She was a lot of fun to be around. She was really creative and always coming up with these crazy ideas. Often, we would talk about the most hypothetical situation she could imagine, and we would laugh about how ridiculous it all was."

I wanted to know everything about Layla, yet I didn't want to listen. It was difficult to hear Walker gush over somebody else. I let my mind drift to the water show I'd wanted to give him. Anything to take my mind off how much he loved her and the brewing fear that I'd always be second best.

"She had the biggest heart. And I had no doubt that one day we would find ourselves old and gray, side by side."

I squinted into the sunlight, trying to get a glimpse of Walker's eyebrow. I couldn't see it very clearly, but I knew that at least the pain wasn't too bad. His cheek was clear of blood, and I'd seen worse before.

Quickly, I lifted my fingers from the lake. A stream of water shot into the air and curled around Walker and me. Walker flinched as the water came pouring down on the other side of him. He looked at me in surprise and then slowly relaxed.

The water had moved somewhat like I had imagined, but smaller. I pushed it higher into the sky and added a second stream, and then a third. We watched the water move across the sky like a running rainbow in a moment of silence. Soon, Walker continued speaking, and I wondered if it felt therapeutic to him. He'd probably never talked about her before. All these years . . .

"She was the best person I'd ever known, and I dedicated my life to her when I made the decision to propose. And just because I never got the chance to ask doesn't mean I feel any different."

I squinted at Walker, afraid of what I was hearing, but the sun reflecting off the water was too bright, and I could barely see him. I needed to see his eyes and, most important, the depths of his wound. I needed to see what this meant for me and my future. The sun grew dark with my needs, and the cloudless sky cast a mysterious shade upon us. That's when I saw it. His gash was opening, and the skin surrounding it was turning purple like a fresh bruise.

"Do you feel guilty for having feelings for me?" I asked, no longer squinting under the sun. It was another question that flew from my lips before I had time to really consider it. Walker didn't immediately answer, so I rotated the streams of water to keep my mind busy. The lake water encapsulated us in a perfect cave, reminding me of a private grotto. Private enough for this conversation.

"No," he said eventually. "That's not where the guilt comes from."

The shock of his answer rippled through me. I thought I knew. If he didn't feel guilty about loving two girls at once, then what was it? I'd always imagined that he felt like his love for me took away from Layla, as if there was some finite amount to be given away.

I waited for him to continue, but he didn't volunteer. "Then where does it stem from?" I prodded.

"I feel remarkably terrible for bringing you here." It was difficult to hear inside the cave of rippling water.

"Bringing me here?"

"Allowing you to stay!" Walker shook his head, riddled

with pain and what looked to be distress. I sighed heavily and rolled my head across the makeshift pillow to look away. I'd heard this before. "No. Listen to me. You shouldn't be here."

"I know that! Everybody keeps telling me!"

"Because it's true, Wilde! Your fate is written, just like all of ours. And you're meddling with it!" I sat up, my jaw dropping. Who was he to tell me what I was meddling with?

"How do you know what my fate is?" I accused. The sky darkened outside our fortress of water.

"I mean, isn't it obvious? You're healed. You should go home now. I can't keep you here for myself. What do you think that would make me?" Walker held his arms wide in question, and Gunner inched toward him offering comfort.

"What do you mean? It wouldn't make you anything, because it's not your choice. I *want* to stay here with you. Are you saying that you've tried to hide your feelings toward me because you're afraid they would persuade me to stay in the afterlife?" Wouldn't that be a shame? If he'd had feelings for me all along, but hid them, making me feel like I wasn't worthy enough to penetrate his heart?

"I'm incapable of love, Wilde. What's the point of all this? As far as I can remember, my family has never had a love that lasted. I don't want to be the reason your heart breaks. We're not even the same kind of entity. It could never work beyond this *twisted* dream of yours."

"I don't believe that," I mumbled, taken aback by his confession. The vulnerability that washed over me was suffocating. We'd been living inside my dreams and haunted by my fears all summer long. I hoped he could feel the depth of my love for him, but all he saw was a twisted dream. That my love was wrong. I didn't know how to make it right.

He gave a resigned sigh. "My father disappeared when I was little," he began. I twisted his father's ring on my thumb, remembering when he'd given it to me.

"I know."

"I wasn't honest with you. While it's true he disappeared, it wasn't in the sense that I led you to believe. He was in an accident." He paused, pinching his bottom lip between his finger and thumb. "He was drunk and got behind the wheel. Nobody in the accident went home that night, or ever again."

"Oh. I see." It was starting to make sense. It must have made him wonder if his father had the chance to return to his family and decided not to. I could see why he encouraged me to go home.

"My mother, sister, and I had to survive without him. I was much too young to remember the immediate fallout, but I grew up in my father's shadow. I grew up watching my mother, a widow, and my little sister, fatherless. I could only imagine what happened to the other family who lost their other half. They didn't deserve it. *We* didn't deserve it."

"I'm so sorry. I didn't know." The walls of our water cave thickened, pumping copious amounts of fluid above our heads. What had started as streams of shooting water was now like being under a raging waterfall. It was thunderous and difficult to hear Walker's words of sorrow. Gunner tucked his tail, and I pulled the paddleboard closer to mine.

"I never drank much because of it, and when I bartended, I often hated the customers that frequented. I wondered how they were affecting their families and if they would ever leave them like my father had us. Of course, the apple never falls far from the tree. I thought by not drinking I could spare the life I was destined to repeat, but I didn't have to drink to destroy the lives around me. Falling asleep was just as dangerous."

"Is that what happened, you fell asleep?"

"Yes. I think so."

"It was an accident. You can't blame yourself for that." I was adamant that he understood that.

"I killed her. And I won't rest until I make it right."

I sucked in a sharp, painful breath. I now understood the depths of Walker's wounds. I knew why his brow would reopen and heal, only to split again. It was because his heart was broken, and it couldn't even begin to heal until Layla safely crossed over into the afterlife. It would never right his wrong, but it was a step in the right direction. Both of them remained in purgatory, waiting on the other's safe return.

I didn't suppose he had much room in his broken heart for me, I thought selfishly. But I couldn't think of myself right now. "How can I help?" I asked, fearful of what he would say next.

Walker sat up, suddenly alive with determination. "We have to get her through that door. It's the only way!"

I nodded eagerly. I was on board with this. I wanted to get her moving along just as much as he did, if not more. "We can do that. I'll get Emma, Scarlett May, and Noah to help us too. We already have a plan in the making."

"That's good. That's a start." Walker ran his hands through his hair, and I could tell he felt slightly better. I did too.

"Hey, Walker?" I asked after a moment of silence. "What would happen if I stayed? Would you feel the guilt like you felt for Layla all these years? I mean, could you ever be happy?" The mist peppered my face, and even though Walker had never fallen in the water, he was beginning to look damp, like he had taken a dip too. The water rumbled, and the cave-like structure continued to close in on us. I was eager to paddle out of my failed attempt at impressing Walker.

"I wasn't lying when I said I came from a long line of cursed love. If you stay, I will love you . . ." I tried to hide the smile budding on my face. "But I'll hate myself for what I've done to you."

I lurched forward. It was no way to live. The water turned dark and the tiny bits of sky that peeked through the fortress of water were nothing but shadows. "And if I go home?" I held my breath, awaiting his answer. The cave began to break apart and rain down on us.

"If you go, I will love you just the same. But every day will be gray, as I wander through eternity."

The water cave collapsed, as I could no longer think of anything other than my two dismal options. Like a tidal wave, the water crashed down upon us, tossing us from our boards and leaving us bobbing in its wake. In the haunted lake, as turbulent as the deep blue sea, we were no more than two lost souls.

CHAPTER 5

"Are you sure this is going to work?" I asked, setting a candle down on the first step.

"Trust me," Scarlett May said confidently. Too confidently, if you ask me.

After my disastrous date last night, I'd spent a good hour crying on Emma's bed. Scarlett May had comforted me in a way she'd never done before. It reminded me of the time we had spent in the guest bathroom downstairs. The night Walker told me about Layla. She was comforting then, sympathetic even, but she still had her edge. I recalled her shoving me away from the door so she could escape when she so pleased. It was a brutal end to the endearing moment we had shared just moments before. But last night was different. She'd genuinely cared that my date had gone sideways, and she wanted desperately to help make it better.

If I was going to take advice from anybody on dating, it might as well be Scarlett May. With her short, wavy blonde hair, her killer legs, and her wicked sense of confidence in a pair of cowgirl boots, she was the queen of attraction. I had always thought that Trinity was more alluring, but that was in a mysterious, almost dangerous way. Scarlett May was the girl all the guys wanted to be with, and all the girls wished they had on speed dial. But her shell was too hard to crack for most. It had taken me months, and even then, I think the only real reason she opened up to me was because she had nobody else. Because Trinity and Kimber had found a way out of Baylor, leaving the rest of us behind.

Scarlett May had a reputation for being fun, and at times crazy. She was a lot closer to Trinity than Kimber. I think that may have been because they used to egg each other on. It was a sort of competition between the two that they liked to feed on. But even though Scarlett May had countless boyfriends before, she was far pickier than anybody realized. Even me.

I hadn't known the depths of Scarlett May's desire until we'd spent a night under the make-believe galaxy in Kimber and Asher's room. She had told me about Sampson, and I never would have guessed. She held him up on a pedestal, and even though she could have him as her boyfriend right now, she was waiting until she knew she could treat him the way he deserved. How a long-term relationship, or perhaps even marriage, deserved. I never expected that from her. She knew I thought the same of Walker, and that's why I put my trust in her tonight.

"But what about Noah? He can't be here. He'll ruin everything," I said, pulling another tea light from a cardboard box and placing it on the top step.

"Emma has Noah covered. She cut a wire in the golf cart and told him it wasn't running any longer."

"What!" I gasped.

"Yeah. They're off to the auto shop. It will take them forever to get there and back. Apparently, that kind of thing is an emergency," Scarlett May said, a proud smile stretching across her face.

"Well, yeah! What did she cut?" For a split second, I feared my parents would kill me. But then I realized they weren't a part of this world, and perhaps I would be dead in twenty-four hours anyway. I took a breath. Why was it Emma couldn't lie dormant when I wanted? How were any of them walking around when I wasn't dreaming them up? I winced. I didn't like the way it made me feel to think of such things. Like simply thinking about the dream state might pull me out of it. Take me somewhere closer to home, to the living. It made my head feel fuzzy and my fingers less dexterous. Maybe I was going dormant myself. *What a terrible thought . . .*

"How am I supposed to know? She just snipped

something and then scratched the hell out of it to make it look like a rat gnawed it."

I rolled my eyes, thinking of the dozens of things she could have done to steal Noah away that had nothing to do with the golf cart. "Does Noah even know how to fix it? I thought he flunked auto shop?"

"Who cares? Get the rose petals."

I groaned but did as she said. Seeing the dozens of candles we had placed from the end of the dock to my bedroom, I suddenly grew nervous. Scarlett May began tossing flower petals on her way out of the cabin and onto the back patio. I went to the window and watched her lightly dust the dock in a covering of romantic red petals. Is this too much? It almost looked like a proposal of sorts. *Oh god, I hope I don't scare him off.* A wave of heat crept down my neck and spread across my back. I clasped the neck of the brown bag while I paced back and forth, fanning myself.

Several minutes later, Scarlett May walked in. "What are you doing? You haven't even done the stairs yet. I'm all out of petals." She raised her hands in frustration when she saw me just standing there.

"Is this a little overboard?" I asked warily.

"What? No!"

"I think I'm going to scare him off." In fact, I knew I would.

"Absolutely not. Don't be ridiculous. Give me your bag." She held her hand out.

Reluctantly, I passed her the bag of petals and followed her up the stairs. "He gave me this weird side hug yesterday. It was really awkward. And I think he hinted that expressing his emotions to me was a mistake. This whole thing might be a mistake. He's not going to like it. And if anything, it might push him away. It's all too much . . ."

"Hey. Stop that. That's just your insecurity talking. Remember what I said before? Just fake the confidence?"

I sat on the bed and nodded, trying desperately not to hyperventilate. The last thing I needed was a new nightmare to take hold.

"Most likely, if you're confident, he will follow your lead. So just fake it. Can you do that?"

I nodded once more, and Scarlett May continued to toss flower petals on the bed. *Oh god, not the bed.* What was he going to think?

She put a firm hand on my shoulder and looked me in the eye. "You've got this. You're going to snag his heart. And then tomorrow, he's going to follow you through that red door like a lost puppy." She smiled and then trailed off to dust the stairs with the last of the petals.

I slumped over, resting my chin on the palm of my hand. I had been manipulating the time in Baylor. Pushing the final showdown out by one day at a time. I needed more days. I wasn't nearly ready to face whatever waited for me at the state fair. If anybody found out that I was intentionally prolonging their time here, they would kill me themselves.

Walker wasn't going to follow me through the red door. But what if he did? Had it really been Walker's cursed heart that kept us apart? Because I was starting to believe it was *me* who was cursed. I had spent the last couple years pining after Noah, and he'd gone after a girl he could never truly have instead of me. Then, I fell for a ghost. What could be more unforgiving than that?

My life hung in the balance between life and death, and the only thing holding me on that balance beam was a phantom. Walker was more real to me than anyone else had ever been, and I was willing to put my life on the line for him, but he was still a ghost. He wasn't real in the world I came from. And most likely, he couldn't survive there. The only way to keep him alive was to join him.

I anxiously played with my fingers as I stared out the window, watching the bend around the cove. I watched as the sun glowed a bright fiery orange and then disappeared behind the forest. Walker would be here soon, and either the awkwardness we shared on our first date would grow into something insurmountable, or it would be squashed and . . .

I peeked at the bed covered in rose petals. My stomach turned at the very thought of us spending the night in that bed together. I knew I loved him, but I wasn't sure we were ready for this. For all of this, I thought, looking at the trail of petals and tea lights. This wasn't me.

Something was off between Walker and me. It had been that way since the night of the balloon festival when he saw me cloaked in the wolf's guise. I imagined it was quite the turnoff to see me as an ugly beast, but I feared it was much deeper than that. The thing that stood between us was a matter of fate. Something he saw and I didn't.

Something he told me I was meddling with. Surely, if I believed in fate, I wouldn't run up against it. But it was not something tangible to me. If it had been, I would bow at its feet and surrender. But fate was something that Walker had only spoken of in riddles, like a secret he kept locked in a box. Was there something he had been hiding from me? Did he know more than he let on? I would ask him tonight. If I was going to make a decision that affected the rest of my life, and possibly beyond, I needed to know what was in that box of his. I needed him to be as transparent as possible, even if it hurt.

My ears perked. I homed in on a melody far, far away, stealing my focus from the window. The sound wasn't just in my head, it was everywhere. It surrounded me from all directions. And it was just faint enough to take all my attention to listen. I turned my head slowly, trying to hear the melody better, but every direction was the same. It was on the tip of my tongue, a melody I recognized from my former life. But just as before, I couldn't pinpoint the origin. I closed my eyes and gently lifted my hand in the air, tracing the rhythm with my fingertips.

"We're all set. He should be here any minute!" I startled as Scarlett May clapped her hands behind me. I spun around to a room full of romantic ambiance and dancing shadows cast on the walls. I turned to peer out the window. She had lit the dock candles, too. A trail of warm glowing lights led down the grassy knoll toward the dock. I must admit, it was beautiful. Breathtaking even. I bit my lip, wondering what Walker would think. How he would feel.

"Thank you."

"I'm just going to wrap a few things up, and then I'll get out of here. I promise he won't even see me. I'll keep an eye out for him, and if I see him coming, I'll sneak out the front." Scarlett May waved her lighter at me and then disappeared. It was time. Ready or not, Walker would soon be paddling around the cove. I wondered if I would see his reaction from this distance. Would I be able to tell if he hesitated? Hesitating would be bad, I decided.

I pumped my hands open and closed, narrowing my eyes toward the bend of Rock Creek Cove. I could hear Scarlett May banging around in the kitchen as the haunting melody grew louder.

I tried not to get drawn in like before, but the more I pushed it away, the louder it sounded. My mind scraped at the edge of my callused memory. My past life seemed so far away, making it difficult to recall the nuances of my earlier years. But the memory was there, hidden in a dark forgotten corner, just waiting to be uncovered. As I tried to recall the distinct song and its origin, the words slowly came to me.

"My heart blooms. Blooms for you. Wildflowers because of you," I muttered with my eyes closed. The song grew louder, enveloping me in its lullaby.

It was a song my mother used to sing to me as a young child. It was a song she favored and played in the car during times when she felt melancholy. No matter how sad the song, singing it always seemed to make her feel better.

I breathed it in, each piano stroke moving me in a way that felt almost euphoric. The song surged as if I were standing in the middle of a symphony being performed in a grand opera house. The music echoing off the tall arching ceiling that I knew was not actually over my head as I stood in the cabin. Then, as clear as day, as clear as an unveiled realm, I heard my mom's voice. She serenaded me with the sweet chords of her favorite song. "My heart blooms. Blooms for you. Wildflowers because of you."

I brought my hand to my heart.

"Come back to me, baby," she whispered. My eyes flew open as my spirit dropped. I grabbed at my ear, still feeling the tickle in my hair where her whisper lingered. My heart pounded in my chest. I heard my mother's voice.

Somehow, I knew it was happening at that exact moment, worlds apart.

"Mom?" I looked around the room frantically. Smoke billowed from under the bedroom door. "Mom!?" I called out, my voice now trembling with fear. *What was happening?*

I had not wanted to go home. Not until the connection with my mother was made. Now, I was torn. I wanted nothing more than to run into her arms. She called me to come home, and I wanted to answer that call.

"Mom, I'm here! I'm here!" I called out.

I closed my eyes and dug my fingernails into the meat of my palms. I tried desperately to connect with her again. But I could no longer hear her singing. And I could no longer feel her whisper upon my ear. "Mom . . . Don't go . . ." I murmured.

My panic grew as I smelled the smoke. This couldn't be happening. Everything I touched turned to dust. And everything I dreamed turned to nightmares.

I sprang into action, alarm growing as I grabbed the doorknob and felt the heat transmit through the metal. I opened the door to find flames blazing throughout the hall. Smoke filled my lungs, and I immediately started coughing. No. This couldn't be happening.

I covered my mouth with my hand and took one step into the hall before realizing I couldn't bear it. I jumped back, coughing and shielding my face. My eyes burned. I ran back to the window, hoping that Scarlett May had made her way out. I needed to get out too. I would have to jump. I grabbed the windowsill and tried to slide the window open, but it was locked. My fingers fumbled over the latch, but it wouldn't budge. How dare it slide open effortlessly when killer bees swarmed the eaves, yet stuck when I would surely burn alive.

"No!" I yelled.

The fire roared, and my heart drummed. I had to make it stop. But how? I ran my hands through my hair, grabbing my head and squeezing my eyes shut, and wished it all away. I wished everything to go back to normal. But this time, when I opened my eyes, nothing had changed. Despite the emergency, I couldn't push the connection I'd made with my mother away.

I hadn't felt her that close for so long. I had talked to her on the phone. I had even seen her in the hospital. I sat next to her as she wept for the health of her child. But I'd never *felt* her love. Not until now. I knew she was sitting there holding my hand as I lay unconscious in that hospital bed. I searched my hands, looking for hers in mine, but I couldn't see them.

"You should get some rest," I heard my dad say in that faraway land.

"Dad!" I called out, hysterical now. They were here. They were here with me, and I was closer to them than I had been this entire summer. I wanted to scrape through the veil that kept us apart and hug them. But . . . I remembered my promise to Walker—I wouldn't leave without saying goodbye.

My mouth grew dry, and the room grew dark with smoke. I coughed, lurching forward and grabbing at the window again. For a moment, time stood still. Walker paddled the canoe around the cove. And just as I imagined, he hesitated. But I couldn't think of that now. I pounded on the glass. "Walker! Walker! Help! Help!" I cried.

Slowly, he evaluated the glowing path of candles and flower petals, contemplating something that no longer mattered. Then he heard me.

"Help!" I yelled, pounding on the window, begging it to break and let fresh air in. Walker spotted me and immediately raced the rest of the way to the dock. He jumped out of the canoe and took off running toward the cabin. I spun around, hoping for help but expecting the worst.

Flames lurched from the walls and crept up to the ceiling. The heat was unbearable, but the smoke was the worst. I dropped to my knees, unable to breathe. I took quick but shallow breaths filled with soot. I felt it coat my lungs in black, suffocating death. My head grew light and my body weak.

"Mom . . ." I called out with what I was sure was my last breath.

"Wilde!" Walker yelled, running into the room. I

whipped my head up to find the fire dissipating from raging flames to a soft yellow hue with the magic I knew Walker had secretly possessed.

My next breath was clean and oxygen rich. I sucked it in, panting frantically. The temperature dropped with every step Walker took toward me. He helped me to my feet, and I collapsed in his arms, crying.

"Shh. It's okay. I'm here."

"I miss my family," I cried. He squeezed me tighter, and I held on for dear life. Feeling torn in two. Is this what he felt like? Did he feel like his heart was torn between Layla and me? Just like mine had been torn between two worlds? It wasn't fair to either of us. Neither one of us could win.

"I know you do. I'm just glad you can see it now."

I buried my face in his shoulder until the tears ran dry and the depression sank in. When I finally opened my eyes, it was clear that even though the fire had cleared, the destruction remained. The walls were stained black, and I could see into the hall where everything appeared decimated. The more I tried in this world, the worse things became. And for the first time, I thought maybe I wasn't meant for this life after all. Maybe Walker was right. Maybe they all were.

Still weak in the legs, I let go of Walker and moved to assess the damage. With every step I took, I kicked ash into the air. Everything was crusted in black and burned to char. The staircase railing was gone, cannibalized by the hungry flames. I stepped slowly down the staircase, unsure if they could support my weight. They creaked and groaned, bowing under my feet. My foot broke through one step, but I managed to stay upright. I stepped gingerly down the last of the stairs.

Thick ash fluttered all around us like a snow globe, lightly dusting Walker's hair and smudging across his chin. I surveyed the den, which looked like the remains of the fireplace after a cold front. This was my home. Where was I supposed to live now?

My heart stopped as I spotted the toes of a beautiful pair of cowgirl boots peeking through the sea of ash.

I paused, feeling for Walker's hand. I grabbed hold of him and held him close as I kicked through the remains of the cabin to get to her. Scarlett May's body lay perfectly covered in soot and ash. Black from head to toe, still as a statue. I leaned closer, supporting myself with Walker's strength. I reached out with trembling hands to feel for a pulse on her neck. Just as my fingertips grazed her burnt skin, her eyes sprung wide open, stark white and beaming with fear. My heart seized.

"Ahh!" I screamed, springing backward and falling onto my butt.

"What? What is it?" Walker asked, kicking up a fine dusting of ash.

"Sss—shh—" I stammered, looking at Walker briefly,

and then back to Scarlett May. My lips parted, but no words came out. Walker looked behind him to where Scarlett May's body had lain just seconds before. Of course, she was gone now. Nothing but a memory to haunt me. The ash lay flat; not even her boots remained.

"What is it, Wilde? What did you see?" Walker looked back and forth between me and the spot on the floor.

My mother sang. Her beautiful soft tone floated in the air, swirling, and mixing with the hideous, black death all around us. Creating something of a paradox, both hopeful and heartbreakingly tragic. The end, and yet still, a new beginning. "My heart blooms. Blooms for you. Wildflowers because of you."

Walker looked all around him now, even more confused than before. Could he hear it too? His lackluster golden eyes settled on me.

"Do you hear it?" I asked.

"She's calling you…" he said, as he lifted a soot-stained hand and cupped my cheek. "She's calling you home." His brows furrowed, creating a deep line of pain. I rested my heavy head in the palm of his hand and found my tears once more.

A new day is a symbol of new beginnings. With the rising sun comes hope, change, and opportunity. But there was something off about the sun in Baylor. As if it were hidden behind a silkscreen, the sun's optimism never struck Rock Creek Cove. It never bestowed its magical powers of renewal upon me and my friends. And with each rising sun came not only a new day, but a new challenge. A new struggle. A new nightmare.

As I walked through the cabin, the morning light filtering through broken glass windows and I saw not an opportunity to seize the day, but the ruin that I had caused from my own self-interest.

I eased my way down the stairs, testing my weight on each decrepit board. The ash still floated in tiny particles, like a snow globe of horror, and there was a chill in the cabin that seeped deep into my bones. I had the distinct feeling that I would not be warm in Baylor again. The state fair was tomorrow, yet again. And for the first time, I wanted no more delay. I wasn't ready for what was to come, but I could no longer stay here. I finally saw what everybody else had been telling me; Baylor was a dreadful place.

The cabin walls looked as if they were painted black, and the ceilings were peppered with swatches—lashings from the flames. The air was desperate and cold, even in the peak of summer. I felt an ache in my heart that I could only describe as being lonely. Not the typical loneliness one would reflect upon in a time of solitude, but the god-awful kind that is sometimes felt in a room full of people.

For the first time this summer, I realized that I wasn't here with my group of friends—my family of misfits. I was here by myself. There was truly nobody here except me and my own rambling thoughts.

And what a scary thought, to be in a remote cabin for an entire summer with nothing but ghost stories to fill your mind. Haunting you with illusions from your subconscious, twisting and contorting in ways they were never meant to be. What had I done to myself? Why did I have to dream at all? And how could I make it stop?

I snuck behind Emma as she kneeled over a small black puddle in the kitchen. She knelt in a mound of ash that covered the balls of her bare feet. The back of her head bobbed up and down mechanically. There was a wash bucket to her side and a stained rag in her hands. She scrubbed the floor in tiny circles as she wept.

The cabin was charred black, and piles of ash littered the floor. The sofa was mostly disintegrated, with a small piece of armrest sitting on the ruined floor. The pool table was gone, the windows were broken, and the doorframe to the back patio was hanging at a slant with no door to help support it. The fog wafted in the house having no protection from the outside elements.

I didn't know how long I watched Emma scrub the floor, wring the rag out in the bucket, and begin again. There was something about the sight of a broken soul, endlessly working toward something that could never be fixed that captured me. Hadn't she seen the destruction? Couldn't she tell it wasn't worth the effort? That it was impossible to do so? Or was she simply the small part of me that wanted to salvage this place? A tiny piece of me that clung to the idea of living in a fantasy.

I approached her slowly as she hunched over the never-ending task. By the time I was in front of her, my shoes nearly in her path, it was clear that she was refusing to acknowledge me. She sobbed gently as she scrubbed the same square foot back and forth.

I opened my mouth to say her name, but my breath hitched in my throat. What could I say? Nothing could fix this. Maybe that was the reason she wouldn't look at me. Because she knew I'd gotten her into this mess, and I was more caught up in my love affair than getting her out of this place.

After a long moment, I left for the fair. I had to do everything in my power to get Emma and Noah out of here. Even if they were just pieces of me, just figments of my imagination, I still owed it to them. To me. I deserved better than this. And they certainly did. I couldn't stand around and watch them deconstruct into apathetic robots. I had to help them, and Gunner too.

There was just one thing I had to do first. I had to find my gran. Maybe there was a deal I could strike with her. Maybe she would help release Noah and Emma and open the door for Walker and Layla in exchange for my coming home. Could she do that? It was my selfishness that continued to make a bad place worse. I'd been so caught up in where I belonged, I'd lost sight of everybody else. I made my decision; I would get everybody home, regardless of which realm I ended up in.

I stepped to the doorway and stood within the collapsing frame, surveying the view. The deck was gone, and the drop was some five to six feet to the ground. Noah threw a handful of two-by-fours onto the grass and sighed heavily. He scratched his head, staring at the empty space where the deck had once been. Defeat was etched in the lines of his forehead as he dragged his hand down the side of his face. He wasn't handling this well.

Noah was great at football, even better at swimming.

He was a decent fisherman, I thought. But he was *not* capable with mechanics and construction. Yet there he stood, just like Emma, trying to fix what I had broken. I cleared my throat, but he didn't look up. A recurring theme this morning.

Rose petals were scattered across the yard, pinched between wet blades of grass. Metal tins from the tea lights were scattered in a trail that led to the dock. And a blanket of fog covered the lake as a pair of loons swam near shore. I had an odd sense that somebody was watching me. And since Noah and Emma had yet to acknowledge me, I searched the surrounding area.

I wasn't surprised to find Layla standing just at the edge of the forest. Without thought, I jumped, landing next to a pile of charred patio furniture. Though I was right in front of Noah now, he seemingly never saw me. I plodded past him, watching for signs of life, but his eyes never lifted, and his demeanor never changed. I didn't think it was possible to feel lonelier than I did last night, but I was wrong.

As I crossed the yard to Layla, I passed Gunner ferociously digging a hole, pausing only to shove his nose deep inside. I patted my leg inconspicuously, fearing he would reject me, too. For a second I thought his ears perked when I beckoned him, but it was something in the hole that piqued his attention. Was I the ghost now? Was that my punishment for not returning home when I was called to do so?

Layla turned and disappeared into the gloom of the forest. There was no reason for me to stay here any longer. Nobody even knew I was there. I took off at a jog to catch her. Somehow, she had always been the answer to all of this. Yet for most of the summer I avoided her. I saw her, and I ran the other way. I had even admonished her with lightning.

And now, just like in the beginning of summer, I chased her. I needed her more now than ever before. *I* needed *her*. Not because my gran told me so, but because Walker needed it as a condition to move on. She was the key to unlocking him from his prison. Plus, if I was honest with myself, the girl didn't deserve to live in a realm where nobody acknowledged her. I'd just had a small taste of that myself, and it was far more miserable than any wolf or ghoul of the lake. Being invisible was the worst kind of torment.

I ran straight into the disorienting fog, chasing hints of long brown locks as they whisked through the trees. I couldn't tell which direction I had been running, but it felt like I was going in circles. I was briefly aware of the apple tree that we'd planted for Lainey. Its red, luscious apples were more than alluring in the sea of gray fog. But I knew one bite would be the end of me here.

My legs never slowed as I kept my eyes on the flashes

of Layla's back. If I could just get Layla through the portal, I was sure all the other pieces would fall into place.

The stone tower appeared down the same trail as the poisonous apple tree. Two things I knew were not near each other. I ran by the massive tower, noting the side was still blown out from where Big Jimmy had crashed through and fallen to his death. Would his body lie at the base now? A disturbing image to throw me off my hunt? No. There was nothing there except the rapunzel flowers.

Layla stopped behind a large tree, and her pale face peeked from behind the trunk. *I'm coming.* No matter how many times she stopped to check if I was following, the distance between us remained the same. She never ventured too far from the trail, and I could keep up a steady jog without having to tramp through the bushes.

Small dome-shaped figures appeared between the trees, and I recognized them as headstones of the hidden cemetery. Of all the things I had seen on this run, the cemetery was by far the most distracting. My pace slowed.

I wanted to see if Scarlett May's name was etched on one of the markers. Layla's sinister laugh echoed through the forest. I looked up into the trees. The cemetery, the tower, the apple tree. I wasn't running through the forest; I was running through my memory. No matter how fast my legs carried me, I would not catch up to Layla until she was ready. Until *I* was ready.

What seemed to be an endless task, Layla playing hide-

and-seek and me chasing a girl who didn't want to be caught, finally came to an end. I found her in a clearing, waiting for me. I slowed my jog to a walk and approached her carefully. I didn't want to spook her.

She looked around warily, as if she was frightened. But I knew that couldn't be true. She possessed just as much power as I did, if not more. She did not need to be afraid of me. And it worried me she might be afraid of something else. Something bigger than either of us.

Layla sized me up, as I did her. My heart hammered in my chest. She was only a few strides away, but I knew if I tried to grab her, I could not hold her long.

"I don't want to play anymore," she said through gritted teeth. "I'm done!" Her intense glower had me turning away and cowering, but she materialized in front of me, closing the small gap between us.

She was done? That was good news. I didn't want to play her games either. I searched her eyes, hoping to talk to the girl, but she looked . . . hostile. It put me on edge. She loathed me. But it didn't have to be this way. If only she knew I wanted to help her find peace. That I realized perhaps she'd been right all along, and I didn't belong in her world. I wanted to say something to make her understand, but she was such a flight risk, I didn't know how to start.

Her weight shifted back and forth as if she was getting ready to run. In the distance, a branch snapped, stealing my attention away. Walker's silhouette spun around on a ridge. He was looking for something. The fog surrounded him with somewhat of an ethereal glow. What was he doing out here? He cupped his hands around his mouth and called out, but I couldn't hear a single word.

"What have you done?" Layla demanded of me. She took a deranged swipe at me. Her hand passed through me like thin air. Her ghostly claws couldn't scathe me, and for that, I was grateful. She eyed Walker nervously and swiped at me again. She was almost helpless. I could see it in her eyes. For the first time, it seemed that I held the power between us. There was no reason for me to fear her. Not today, at least. Still, I didn't know what to do. Should I grab her? What would I do then? Clamp my hand around her tiny wrist and drag her to the state fair, searching for the red door?

"Please . . .," I muttered. *Come on . . . Do better than that.* I had to fake the confidence if it wasn't there naturally.

"Walker!" she yelled, trying to grab his attention. He ran his hands through his hair and called out in silence again.

What was happening? Why did she want Walker to see us? She never wanted him to see her. And why couldn't he hear us? And then I thought of the most important question—why was *she* afraid of *me*? Something was terribly off and yet familiar all the same. It was almost as if I had been here before.

Walker wandered aimlessly, weaving in and out of the trees, yelling my name silently. Layla and I watched as he came close enough that either of us could reach out and touch him. But his eyes were frightened as he passed by, and I didn't dare grab his arm. A chill ran down my spine. Had Layla and I become two of the same kind? Invisible? Forgotten? Undeserving, perhaps? Were we now both under Walker's curse?

I looked at Layla, and her brown eyes appeared to soften. She was hurting, just as I was. We seemed to recognize that pain in one another. I watched her face as the demarcations of her brows lightened and her eyes drooped with sadness. For the first time, Layla and I were in the same boat. We were both invisible to the outside world, both hurting, both trapped, and neither of us wanted it any longer.

My eyes watered with sympathy for this lonesome girl and all the pain she must have lived through. Walker passed by again, leaving nothing but a chill in his wake. I lifted a hand ever so slightly, touching the slight breeze as he passed by.

"You don't belong here," I said, my voice small and empathetic. She looked at me as if she could not hear me either. As if my lips moved in opposition to my words. The fog had blanketed more than just the forest. It muffled our hearing and drowned out our voices.

I searched for other ways to communicate. I patted my jacket, feeling for a pen or notepad. Could I manifest them?

Walker stiffened, and I could tell something had alarmed him, but I didn't know what. He took off running in the direction he'd come from, causing Layla to look more worried than before. I could tell she was about to run. I found what I was looking for just in time.

In my hands was the old worn book, *Waking Dreams*. The familiar sharp, penetrating pain of an oncoming headache pierced my head, and I winced. I had no time to wonder how I'd gotten the book. I scribbled down the message on a random page. *You don't belong here.*

I hoped it would be enough for her to realize that I wanted to help. She needed to know she could trust me. I tore the page from the weathered book, and several more pages came out with it. They swept into the air with a gust of wind and fluttered down to the ground.

"No!" I reached out.

Layla dropped to her knees, grasping at all the pages, desperately seeking a way to communicate.

"I can help you. I know how to get you home . . . if you let me," I said.

She never looked up. More like she couldn't see me

anymore. She had the same distant gaze in her eyes that I'd seen in Noah, and eventually Walker.

Her brown eyes saw through me effortlessly. I watched as her trembling hands grasped at the pages, flipping them over and looking for anything that could help her communicate. I stepped closer, peering over her shoulder as the published print disappeared, leaving only my handwritten note.

"You don't belong here," she whispered.

"You don't!" I murmured over her shoulder. She paused for a moment, and I thought maybe she had heard me. Then she swiftly jumped to her feet and took off running in the direction that Walker had last been seen. In her absence, I found a mound of soil, sticks, and dried pine needles covering the extra pages that had fallen from the book. She'd buried them? Why?

As I stood alone, bewildered by her actions, I turned to the book that I had once coveted. But it was not the mysterious book that took my breath away; it was the crimson velvet of my sleeves. I shuddered as I looked down to find myself draped in a red cloak.

My hair lifted in curled locks, and a weird energy buzzed around me. The locks of hair danced above my shoulders like the snakes on Medusa's head. I *had* been here before, just not in this body.

Power surged through me. My skin buzzed with pure energy. I felt oddly unstable. Fluid-like. As if I could be swept away in a gust of wind. I felt strong, yet incapable. I couldn't make myself be seen or heard, but I was still mighty. Almost too big for my body. *Her* body.

I followed Layla through the forest, more determined than ever. This time, she didn't run, and she didn't look back to see if I was following her. Was *I* Layla now? Had I somehow changed spirits with Walker's past love? Was that the only way to set her free? To take her place in the invisible and forgotten realm in which she lived?

My insides fell hollow at the very thought. I asked for this, hadn't I? I asked for Walker to be happy. It was my one wish upon a shooting star. Of course, I wanted it to be with me. But I would sacrifice myself to give him Layla back—if that was truly what he wanted.

I watched Layla from behind, dusting her palms on the back of her jeans as she hesitated before joining Walker by the shore. I crested the ridge just in time to see them reunite, and it hurt more deeply than I could've ever imagined.

"Are you all right?" Walker ran up to her. I had no difficulty hearing him, now that I was out of the clearing with the weird energy buzzing in the air. He looked concerned for her well-being, rightly so, as she had been missing for decades. "What happened?" he asked, taking her hands in his. He examined the dirt that dusted her pale skin. I leaned against a tree and sucked in a quivering breath. I wiped away a fallen tear with the soft velvet of my sleeve. *So this was sacrifice . . .*

Broken clay pigeons were scattered across the tiny cove, and Walker's canoe was pulled on shore. I remembered this very well now. This was the day he'd taught me how to hone my magic.

Walker picked up a clay pigeon and tossed it into the air. Layla fired at it with a flick of her wrist, a natural at magic. Could he not see that he was with Layla? Did he think she was me? And was she going to pretend she was?

I had half a mind to step out from the elusive forest and unveil myself as the true Kinsley Wilde. I took a small step forward, but something stopped me. Walker laughed. He was happy.

"I don't deserve you," he said to her. I crouched forward, hanging on each spoken word.

"That's not true! Don't talk like that," Layla snapped. Walker's shoulders drooped.

"Did you see her?" He threw another chip of a clay.

"Yes." Layla broke the disk into tiny shards, and they rained down on the lake like hail.

"Did *she* see *you?*" he asked.

"Yes."

What was this? I inched forward.

"And?"

"Nothing. She doesn't get it."

Walker's shoulders slumped, and he seemed to curl in

on himself. He was more defeated now than I had seen him in the past. "She doesn't know me like she thinks she does."

"Then show her!" Layla said, visibly stressed.

"I'm trying! She only sees what she wants to see. Nothing more!" Walker pressed the heels of his palms against his eyes.

"And what is that?" Layla checked behind her shoulder nervously, and I darted behind a tree, pulling the hood of the red cloak over my head. I felt every bit like a dirty secret hiding within the haunted forest.

"She wants me to be her protector. She wants me to be the good guy. But I'm not. And honestly, a part of me is afraid she'll find out. I don't know what to do anymore."

Walker threw a piece of clay angrily, and it exploded into tiny bits all on its own. I couldn't believe my eyes. He had his own magic! He *had* been holding out on me. But why?

"She wants the man of her dreams. Can you blame her?" Layla asked, her tone warm with compassion to counteract Walker's rising frustration.

"No. I guess not. It's her dream after all. She controls what she sees and what she doesn't." Layla nodded and placed a hand on his shoulder. "She just wants a hero. She wants to be loved for all that she is, but more importantly, all that she's not."

I grabbed my chest, right where my heart would be if I

had one. This hurt more than a thousand knives in the back.

"Yeah. I think you're right."

Layla rubbed Walker's shoulder, and then her hand trailed down his back. My chest cinched tighter.

Why were they talking about me like this? How come he never told me he had been in contact with Layla all this time? Had I truly only seen the things I wanted? Surely, I never wanted a fire to rip through the cabin and scorch Scarlett May, turning her to ash in a pair of cowgirl boots.

If I could see all the horror in Baylor, then why couldn't I see the truth? It couldn't have been as scary as everything else I'd witnessed this summer. I watched intently, as if seeing for the first time the other side of the coin. A part of my world that I had unknowingly hidden from myself.

"Do you *truly* love me, Walker?" Layla asked, looking deep into his eyes. My mouth fell open.

"I have loved you for more lifetimes than you can remember . . ." Walker said in a husky voice. He melted at her side.

I definitely did not belong here!

"Then how do we get home? Because I'm losing hope."

"I know. I know."

"I'm scheduled to be home tomorrow," Layla shook her head, as if it were an impossible feat.

"I promise. I'll get you there." Walker bowed his head until his forehead met hers.

I had to get away. I didn't even know what I was fighting for anymore. I would find that door tomorrow, and I would run straight for it. Any world would be better than this. And nothing else mattered.

"And you won't be far behind me?" she asked.

"I promise. If you go, so will I," he said.

I took a step backward and tripped over the tail of the crimson cloak. It ripped off my back, and I took off running through the mysterious forest of memory, fearful that they had heard me stumble.

CHAPTER 7

I ran through the forest as fast as my legs could take me. I ran through the rapunzel bushes and over the fallen trees. I ran aimlessly. Baylor was like a web spun just for me. Ensnaring me deep within its deadly trap. And I was stuck there now, not knowing which turn would set me free and which would entangle me more. I feared I'd never get out alive.

The part I couldn't bring myself to understand was that, in this scenario, I wasn't just a moth fighting for my life. I was also the spider, trying to end it. My wings were bound, and I was trapped in what could very well be a deadly nightmare. But wings aside, I also had short poisonous fangs, and I was eager to live a life full of magic, both dark and light. If I died now, it would be by the bite of my own dark side. My fault, and nobody else's.

The fog was so dense in the forest that all I could make

out was white mist and varying shadows of gray and dark green. The moist air felt as if my lungs were coating with water, slowly dry drowning as I ran.

Which way? Did it even matter? I had followed Layla out to the ridge in what seemed to be a giant circle that was even more disorienting now as I ran away. I had fallen asleep in one place and woken up countless times in another place altogether. Sometimes even an entirely separate realm. The land of the living, the land of my past. I supposed it didn't matter which way I ran. I would wind up wherever my mind took me, regardless.

I recognized the tall stone tower just breaching my vision. I ran straight for it, hoping for answers. What would I find inside? What could I see from the window? And most importantly, would I find a red door? I was certainly ready for my escape. Would it be as simple as my willingness to depart? I doubted it.

I stopped several feet away, checking over my shoulder to make sure I hadn't been followed. When I confirmed the coast was clear, I approached the tower and placed my hand on the stone, feeling its warmth where cool had been expected. These were no normal stones that made up the disappearing tower.

I circled the base, looking for the hidden door. The door that hadn't been available the first time I'd seen the tower. I reached out to grab the corroded doorknob, my hand hesitating just above the metal. Though I felt ready to find the portal home, I was still afraid. In a split second of courage, I grasped the doorknob, ready to meet my fate.

The knob shook with anger. I couldn't pull my hand away. The whole door trembled, and the force exploded up the tower. Dust plumed at the base of the structure as it shook wildly out of control. I tried to pull back but couldn't free myself. My hand was locked in place, cemented by the choice I'd made to enter.

The tower began to crumble, top to bottom. The stones fell to the ground, and the door splintered into shards. I coughed as the dust enveloped me. I was finally able to pull my hand back to hide my face in the crook of my elbow, but the rusted doorknob came with me, still secured within my grasp.

My feet were covered in heavy stone, and it took several tries to pull them free. This wasn't my portal after all. This wasn't my chance to get back home. When the dust settled, there was no pile of collapsed rocks left behind. There was no evidence of the fairytale tower, but for a corroded door handle held tightly in my hand. I threw the old piece of metal as hard as I could and wiped orange rust off my skin. Was nothing safe from my destruction?

I walked down the trail, my head hanging. I was no longer in a hurry. I wasn't sure anything mattered anymore. No amount of effort ever seemed to be enough.

I kicked a pine cone as I walked down a winding trail. Why would Walker hide his magic from me? It could have been fun to learn together. I should have questioned how he knew how to teach me. I should have questioned a lot of things. But I was terribly naïve.

Layla had magic in her, too. That I knew from the shapeshifting, the disappearing acts, and our showdown at the balloon festival when she'd said I was going to ruin everything. *What did that even mean? What was I going to ruin?*

What did Walker mean when he said, *she only sees what she wants to see?*

So much of my reality was false. Make-believe. Was it even possible to see the truth under such circumstances as these?

I didn't know what to believe anymore. The brief conversation that I'd spied on had me spinning. Everything I thought I'd known this entire summer was flipped upside down and turned inside out in the few minutes I watched Layla and Walker. I wanted so desperately to speak with Walker, but the *old* Walker. The Walker that I knew to be true. Not the stranger I had seen on the ridge who spoke of me like a blind idiot.

Did I still love him? I rubbed my forehead, kneading the tension that was building into a headache. My shoulders slumped in defeat. I wasn't sure the man of my dreams existed anymore. Maybe that's why they called him the Phantom of Baylor Lake; because he was delusion in disguise.

It was then that I noticed a gigantic red, glistening apple hanging just within my reach. There were a dozen of them. Twelve of the most sinfully alluring pieces of fruit I had ever seen. My mouth watered at the very sight. Was this it? Was this the way home? A bite of a poisonous apple? Sure, it would end my life here in Baylor. But would I go home, or would I be doomed to stay here and be on the invisible side of Walker's curse?

I reached up and touched the apple gently. It dropped almost willingly into my hand. The skin was bright red with small veins of burgundy. A sheen covered the apple like a coating of clear resin, and the most perfect stem sprouted from the small dip at the top. It seemed ironic that, though I held the most beautiful poisonous apple in my hand, it was my mouth that flooded with venom.

I wasn't sure what would happen to me if I took a deadly bite, but things couldn't keep going the way they had been. And I couldn't stop my mouth from opening.

An unknown force pulled at my hand, drawing the apple toward my mouth. I closed my eyes and felt the apple bump against my teeth. But as I bit down, expecting the sweetness to dance across my tongue and course through my veins, all I got was a mouthful of smoke. A hot, vile vapor filled my mouth. I shook my head, trying to escape the taste of rot and sulfur.

"No!" I shouted to the sky. This couldn't be happening!

I jumped to grab the next hanging apple. I bit into it, hungry, desperate. But just as my teeth touched the apple skin, the entire fruit bled into black vapor, and a putrid, rotten taste coated my mouth and tongue.

I spun around, spitting into the dirt. My stomach wrenching as I dry-heaved. With tears in my eyes, I watched the apple tree vanish.

"No!" I yelled again, but there was no one to hear.

I picked up a rock and threw it angrily. A blue vein of electricity ignited, lighting the base of the now invisible tree and branching out to the tips of each leaf. My tears stopped immediately; my anger replaced by curiosity. I wiped the wetness from my cheeks as I walked toward the tree, still invisible to the naked eye.

Slowly I reached my hands out, taking tiny blind steps until I found the tree trunk. As soon as my hands touched the bark, the same veins of electricity ignited, lighting up the tree once again. But this time, the energy seemed to eat away at the memory. My hands sank through the trunk, and there was no longer any evidence of the memorial we'd planted for Lainey.

How I missed Lainey now. I wished she was back at the cabin so I could talk to her. Pour my heart out. Even though she'd be afraid, I knew she would be there for me. But then I thought of Emma as I left her, scrubbing the floors of the cabin. She hadn't even looked at me. Had she been angry with me for getting her stuck in Baylor? Or had

I been a ghost that she could no longer recognize? I wondered if that would have happened to Lainey, too.

I continued walking, the fog parting with my steps. I didn't stop for the cemetery when I saw the headstones, I just sighed and looked away. I could barely see them from the corner of my eye as they shook and crumbled to the ground. The world I created and lived in was evaporating. And pretty soon, so would I.

When I finally looked toward the graveyard, there was nothing there. There would be no more headstones marked with a terrible fate, and I would never get to see how I died. Though if I was taken right now, I guessed my headstone would read, *Taken an Outcast*. Because that's all I was anymore. I hung my head, kicking up dust as I moseyed down the trail until I finally stumbled home. I was somewhat surprised to see Noah still scratching his head, staring at the same pile of two-by-fours he'd dropped on the ground. Gunner barked at the same hole he had been digging in when I left. He shoved his nose inside, sniffing eagerly. Had time passed at all, or was that broken too?

The hole didn't appear to have deepened since I left. I patted my leg, but Gunner's eyes never so much as shifted from the hole. "Hey, buddy," I said. When nothing changed, I pet his wiry head. I stroked him gently until his head fell from beneath my hand and his nose pushed deep into the hole. I used to think being invisible would suit me, but now I knew it didn't. Everybody wanted to be seen to some extent.

Without the back deck, I had no way of getting to the collapsed patio door. I walked past Noah and headed to the front of the cabin. It appeared the cabin was frozen—not in time, but in a moment. A moment of desperation and destruction. The ash had not settled to the floor but still floated, as if it were never-ending. The air was still thick with smoke, and the same chill wafted in through the broken windows. It did not surprise me to see Emma where I had last seen her, her back hunched over a wash bucket as she scrubbed the same square foot of floor.

"Emma?" She sobbed quietly as she wrung out the black-stained towel. Her hands were red and raw. "Emma, can you hear me?"

I kneeled to see her eyes, and for just a moment she paused. My breath caught. *Please hear me.* My chest tightened with smoke. I reached my hand out, grabbed her shoulder, and squeezed. Emma let out a hoarse sob, as if she had been crying for hours, and her voice was wearing thin.

"Emma! Emma, wake up! It's me!" I shook her violently, but she just stared blankly. I knew she was in there. I knew it.

"Emma?" I watched intently as she continued to scrub the floor without so much as a look of confusion. Wherever Emma was now, it was far away from here.

I was trying to devise a plan to drag Emma out of the cabin when I heard voices outside. I peered out the misshapen door that overlooked the lake and saw Walker and Layla paddling to the dock. My heart thumped in my chest. Layla looked just like me. She was going to fool everyone.

Noah's head lifted, and he turned to watch the canoe approach as if he was waking from a stupor. Frightened, I spun to see Emma toss the rag into the bucket of water and wipe her hands across her jeans. They were waking up! I had to get out of here before they saw me!

I heard the bustling sound of laughter and something in the distance that reminded me of a video game I'd once played with my little brother. As I ran to the front door, I could hear the drone of the bees. The faintest, ghostly outline of Asher walked up the stairs, holding onto an invisible banister. My heartbeat floundered and tried desperately to find its rhythm.

I got the front door open and ran up the driveway, batting my hands at the rogue bees swooping down at me. Looking back at the cabin, I caught a glimpse of the pale outlines of Noah and Kai, dressed in layered clothing and throwing rocks at the hive nestled in the eaves. I ran for the woods, where I knew the shadows would hide me.

Of course, Asher and Kai had died long ago. I was no longer living a linear dream. My timelines were bending like origami creatures, and the entire summer's manifestations were folding in on themselves. The old was mixing with the new in impossible ways, and the dead were walking with the living. If I knew one thing, it was that I didn't want to stick around to see how it ended.

"Mom? Dad?" I yelled into the labyrinth of forest. My voice echoed, bouncing off the trees.

"Get me out of here! I want to go home! I want to go home!" I screamed.

I stopped to bellow out my last plea. "Please! Take me home!" My voice splintered into a million cries, and I prayed they were strong enough to be heard in the realms beyond this one.

CHAPTER 8

My fists were balled as I screamed into the night, demanding that I be freed. The dense fog gave way to the dark of night, and a stillness came over the wilderness. The critters hid, and the leaves stilled. I thought of giving up. If I lay at the base of a boulder, nestled in brush and pine cones, would anybody ever find me? Or would I be lost forever?

I wondered if I would ever talk to Walker again, and guilt washed over me for trying to leave without saying goodbye. I rarely made promises, and I had no intention of breaking this one. There was still a part of me that needed him and hated the thought of running away. I had done it once before, and to my regret, I caused an entire plane to crash to smithereens. I killed people. A lot of them.

I knew I was capable of great things, but it seemed to

only be for the dark. Not once had I made something so beautiful and life-changing here that I could say I was proud of myself. I thought that maybe falling in love would be the beautiful thing that made it all worth it. And it certainly would have been life-changing, had it not been fake.

But I'd been so gaslit by the Baylor phenomenon that I'd fallen in love with an idea, not a guy. I reminded myself that the entire manifestation of Walker St. James was fake, because believing that he was both real and lying to me was far too hurtful. I thought of all the warnings that Walker had given me. He tried to warn me, but it was no good. I ignored them all. And yet, there was still a small voice in my head that said to ignore them now, despite what I had seen. To love him fiercely for the person I knew him to be. The person he *could* be.

I sat down, leaning back against a fallen tree trunk, my head in my hands. It was one thing to be living in a nightmare, but an entirely different thing to fall in love with somebody who didn't exist. To be so willing to open up to a person you could only see half of. I only saw half of Walker. The other half had been with Layla.

I drew in the dirt with a twig, making small broken hearts and zigzags, just to wipe them clean. I willed my gran to visit. I tried to manifest a red door. The hospital. And eventually, after nothing worked, I settled for listening for my mother's distant song. When not even her melody would come to comfort me, hollowness spread throughout my chest, and my body numbed.

I waited on the forest floor for what felt like hours until something finally changed. A clatter sounded in the distance. Clanking and clatter of mass commotion. My back straightened as I turned my head like radar, trying to locate the direction of the living. A small light emanated from between the trees and flickered with shades of blue and green. Like a moth to the light, it drew me through the forest.

As I stepped out of the hidden woods into a secret clearing, carnival music sprang to life. The smell of buttered popcorn and livestock hung in the air. The loud drone of generators hummed near and far. I'd finally made it to the Summerfield State Fair. Or rather, the fair had finally made its way to me.

I lingered in the shadows, tucked between the forest and portable restrooms that skirted the fairground. I surveyed my surroundings, immediately searching for some type of portal to get me home. The only one I knew of came in the shape of a red door. But were there others? Perhaps a picture booth? Or a fortune teller?

Lights percolated on a massive Ferris wheel that seemed to arch over the entire fairgrounds like a radiant rainbow. I stared in awe as my stomach turned in on itself. It was difficult to see all the fair had to offer, but the Ferris wheel couldn't be missed. It stood four times taller than anything else in the clearing, and it matched the vision that had been burned into my memory from the first night I drowned. It was hard to pull my eyes away, as the ride both terrified and excited me. The sheer height of the wheel was enough to make me tremble. Adding my fear of heights to the terror of meeting my unknown fate, it would be next to impossible to take a seat on the ride.

I took a deep breath and stepped out of the shadows. A father walked by with a young boy sitting on his shoulders, and I stepped back to let them pass. A mixed group of pre-teens approached, and I lurched forward, zigzagging in and around the traffic. A girl passed on the arm of her boyfriend as she ate a cloud of pink cotton candy. And for just a moment, it made me miss Walker.

I ran my hands through my hair, determined to stay strong. I was looking for a red door, and I needed to focus. It was proving more difficult than I thought. I spun when I heard the screams. A group was riding the swings, there screams whirring by. A wave of terror washed over me, and I felt my heartbeat quicken at the perceived threat. This didn't feel like fun.

I hated these rides. There were so many people and so many lights. The quick pace of the music and the tinny high notes made me anxious. I felt the familiar crawl of a dull ache spread across the back of my head, and I knew I would be riddled with a migraine soon. I used the pain to propel me forward.

I walked quickly, surveying the crowds. My eyes bounced from face to face, hardly seeing the people passing by. There must've been thousands of them. I didn't recognize a single one until my sight fell upon Mr. Vandal. Our eyes met and locked. He'd been watching me. He averted his gaze and then checked back to see if I was still watching him. My step faltered at the sight of him, but I continued searching; he wasn't the one I was after.

I passed a petting zoo, weaving in and out of the small children lined up to get their hands on a dusty goat. I scanned the shadows behind the pen and peered through the lines of people. I searched the hidden corners of the grounds and searched in plain sight, but I could not find a way home. I finally made my way to the Ferris wheel, following the lights like the North Star.

I wished my gran were here to guide me—if only to tell me I was on the right track. To hold my hand in a moment of uncertainty. Just then, I remembered how Gran had told me to lean into my weakness. It wasn't something I was comfortable with, and I eyed the Ferris wheel with trepidation. Even though Gran wasn't with me now, the memory of her wisdom was almost as good as her presence. Screams, followed by laughter, erupted from the building next to me. It was a funhouse of mirrors. I winced. *Who liked these things?*

I saw the back of a guy who seemed familiar to me; tall, broad shoulders, and black hair. He reminded me of

Kai. Before I knew it, I was in line, pushing through people and trying to catch up to the stranger. The guy disappeared into the funhouse as I got stuck in the crowd. A girl shoved me with her elbow and gave me a dirty scowl. It reminded me I was in a line full of people who had been waiting their turn. I shrank back and waited like everyone else while I drummed my hands against my thighs. Manners seemed so insignificant at a time like this, still I complied.

When it was finally my turn to enter the dark, strobed building, I parted from the crowd at the first available turn. "Kai!?" I called, but the carnival music was too loud and drowned out my voice.

I saw the crowd in front of me disappear around a dark corner, and I turned away, finding myself boxed into a small room of mirrors. I had never wanted to see so many versions of myself, but there I was, extrapolated by the dozens. I tried not to look too closely, for fear my subconscious would take over. The best thing for me now would be to have no reflection at all. I never imagined I would long for the days when I thought I was soulless, but here I was, having the opposite problem.

I convinced myself the girl in the mirror was not me. For she was too plain. Her skin was ashen and her hair frazzled. Her lips were oddly pale, and if I had to guess, I would say she looked cold, as if there were no warmth in her veins. I didn't want to know what it meant. I stumbled around in the dark, patting the mirrors and looking for an exit.

"Kai?" I called out again. It was silly of me to think he was here now, but I couldn't shake how familiar the stranger's stride was. The way his shirt clung to his shoulders, the way his hair lay.

"Kins?" a reply sounded through the walls. What was that? Could it really be him?

"Kai is that you?"

"It's me Kins! It's me!" he yelled. I was so excited, I nearly tripped over my own two feet. I fell through a doorway that opened up into a larger room.

"Where are you!?" I flinched at the sight of the reflections.

I'd thought the cold-blooded Kinsley was bad, but these reflections were far worse. Distorted. Elongated. My face could have been a match for a ghostly Halloween mask. My chin drooped to my knees, and my eyes looked as if they were melting from their sockets like molten lava. Beyond turning my stomach sour, the sight of my reflection did one other thing—it made me fear death.

How could I possibly have wanted to begin my afterlife? How could I have *wanted* to be a ghost? As I looked at my peculiar face in the fun-house mirror, I wanted nothing more than to live. To live a full and robust life. One with pink cheeks and pouty lips, a warm touch, and a beating heart. I yearned to be the flawed human girl who'd once mistakenly felt uncomfortable in her skin. Never again.

"I'm right here!" Kai yelled, pounding on the wall in the room next to mine. I saw the mirror shake, and I placed my hands on top of the warped reflection.

"Just stay there! I'll find you!"

The lights flickered and beamed an electric blue, making everything white appear to be glowing. A group of kids stumbled through the door, laughing and banging into the walls and mirrors. The black lights flickered on and off, and the music drowned out the surrounding screams. I hurried toward the direction the kids had funneled in from, and I found an exit that led to a narrow hall. My fingertips grazed the walls as I felt for the next opening into a room.

When I was sure I found the door that would lead to Kai, I opened it to face my reflections in three warped mirrors in a tiny room. Kai was nowhere to be found. "Kai?" I pounded on the mirrors, thinking maybe he was stuck somewhere in the walls. I had once been stuck inside the walls, too. I caught sight of my body scrunched like an accordion and my legs long and spindly. I frowned, slapping on the mirror. Where was he? Why couldn't I find him?

The glow of white pearly teeth appeared in the last mirror. A smile floated just behind my head. It stretched wide—far beyond what any natural mouth could do. It reminded me of the Cheshire Cat. It's just the effect of the funhouse mirror, I told myself. Nothing more. But I wasn't smiling.

Was there some other entity in the tiny room with me? I reached my arms out, touching two mirrors at once, and then the third. There was nobody in the room but me. I stepped closer to the mischievous smile and peered deeply into the reflection. My eyes morphed into the glowing eyes of a predator.

The big toothy grin elongated into fangs and dripped with sparkling venom. I gasped and stumbled back, slamming into the mirror behind me. A cackle boomed over the high-pitched trickle of music, and I tripped once again, falling into the narrow hallway.

I checked my hands in the flash of the strobing light and was relieved when I saw fingers instead of paws, nails instead of claws. I ran down the darkened hallway, much too fast for the low visibility, and I slammed into Noah's chest. "Kins?" he asked, seeming surprised to see me.

"Noah?" I was even more surprised to see him. And so . . . *alert.*

The last time I'd seen Noah, he'd been like a zombie waking from a century of sleep. And the ghost of his past had been gallivanting with Kai in the yard. If there were two of him, like there were seemingly two of me—no thanks to Layla—then which one was he? I wished I wasn't leery, but I didn't know who I could trust anymore. I took a step back and watched as his brows furrowed with confusion.

"What's wrong, Kins? Are you okay? Do you want to get out of here?" Noah placed his hands on either side of my arms, trying to comfort me, but I stiffened under his touch.

"Did you see Kai in here?" I asked, wanting desperately to get away from the distortion of the mirrors, yet not wanting to leave Kai behind. Again.

Noah's jaw hardened, causing the blue light to flex across his cheeks. I immediately regretted my words. Noah looked at me like I had said something incriminating. Was this a test? Had I failed?

"Kai? You saw Kai?"

A couple squeezed by, the guy's hand trailing behind to hold his date's hand. The girl's bright white shirt cast a glow on Noah's face, and I could see concern in his eyes. For a moment, I wanted to run, but Noah was all I had left. "No. But I thought I heard him."

"That's right." Noah nodded. "He *is* here. This way." He took my hand in his.

Something didn't seem right. His words were saying one thing, but his face was saying something entirely different. He led me against the flow of the crowd through the narrow hall. I pushed up against the wall to let people pass by. I didn't want to go deeper into the funhouse. I wanted to get out into the fresh air. It was my guilt that kept me searching for Kai.

Noah pulled me into a room that I had not seen before, though I was positive I had been in every room thus far. It was a small rectangular room with four mirrors surrounded by brightly colored chalk paintings that glowed in the black lights. Neon orange, yellow, green, and pink. I pulled my hand out of Noah's and rubbed my temple. My head was pounding.

"Well, where is he?" I asked, taking a step back from Noah.

Noah said nothing, but pointed to the first mirror. Hesitantly, I peered within. Just like Noah had said, there he was. It wasn't like seeing Kai behind a glass windowpane; it was more like looking into a magic mirror and barely making out a faint memory. But this wasn't a memory of something I had seen before. Kai hit the walls, calling my name.

"Kai!" I yelled. My hot breath clouded the center of the mirror. Kai spun around, seeing me for the first time. He ran up to me and placed his hands against mine. I desperately tried to feel for warmth, but there was nothing there. Nothing but the sadness and fear in his eyes.

"Get me out of here!"

My heart lurched. "What should we do?" I asked Noah in a panic. The way he stood there perplexed me.

He seemed to be unaffected by Kai's plea. He motioned to the next mirror.

There was more? I bit my lip and looked at Kai, but couldn't bring my eyes to meet his. Slowly, following Noah's gesture, I stepped to the next mirror. My heart broke further when I saw my parents huddled together in a dark corner, crying.

I gasped. "No!" I pounded on the glass, trying to find a way in. "Why are you doing this?" I asked Noah.

He took a step back, beckoning me to follow. I shook my head. I couldn't bear to witness what was trapped in the next two mirrors. I couldn't handle what I had already seen. As it turned out, it didn't matter. It wasn't my choice. The mirrors rotated clockwise so that the third mirror was directly in front of me. This time, it was Layla.

At first, seeing the girl who had betrayed me was far easier than seeing my parents or Kai. I quite enjoyed seeing her in a box. My empathy for her had been squashed, and now there was an anger boiling inside. Oh, how I wished I had the wolf's reflection now. I wanted to let loose on her. But this was a funhouse mirror, and my retribution would have to wait.

I frowned at the girl and stepped forward to give her a mouthful of my most venomous words. She played me, and I would not take it. As soon as my shoes bumped the base of the mirror, our features aligned. Something odd happened. I jumped back, startled by what I'd seen. She and I looked eerily similar. How had I not noticed this before? I looked at Noah, shocked, and he crossed his arms over his chest and waited.

I took a deep breath and really took in Layla's appearance. She was every bit the gorgeous girl I had envied all summer long. Her hair was luscious and long, her lips were a beautiful red stain. Her skin was like porcelain, and it warmed her gorgeous brown eyes. I was drawn in, once again, and watched as our features aligned, not just similarly . . . but perfectly.

I had no way of telling if I was seeing my reflection or hers. "What is this? What kind of trick is this?" I asked.

"You only see what you want to see," she said, repeating Walker's words from the ridge.

"I want to see the truth!" I growled.

She smiled softly. My anger did nothing to her calm demeanor. But that only made me more furious. It was then that I noticed a green fleck in the bottom of her right eye.

"It's about time," she said, as if congratulating me on some unknown success.

Anger seized me. That was *my* green fleck! It was the only thing I had left of my late gran. How dare she steal it from me! I reached back and punched Layla square in the nose.

The mirror shattered, and my knuckles burst open and bled. "Ahh," I cried, cradling my hand to my chest.

"Wait!" Noah said, as I darted out of the room. "Wait, you haven't seen the last mirror!" I barreled through the crowd and slammed into the walls. Eventually, I found my way out of the funhouse.

What Noah didn't realize was that I had seen the fourth mirror. The red had been blinding. I knew it was the door I'd been searching for. But I also knew it was a trap. Layla wanted me to take her place, and I knew she'd convinced everybody else to help her. Perhaps, she'd even risen an army of my dead friends to do it. But I'd had a tiny taste of being invisible, and I didn't want to live like a joker in the shadows. A moth caught in a web.

CHAPTER 9

The fairgrounds were crawling with people. The crowd had thickened, and the lines had tripled. I scurried through the crowd in a hurry. I pushed through a group of young teenage boys and skirted around a family, checking over my shoulder regularly. Not just for Layla, who was out to get me, but for my friends, too. Somehow, Layla had turned them against me. I imagined her coming back from the shooting lesson with Walker and talking to all of my friends, both dead and alive. Convincing them she was me, and that *I* was a traitor.

Well, I'd be the traitor then. I'd get home and leave them all here with her. Could I do that? I felt a sudden weight on my shoulders. I couldn't do that. No matter how betrayed I felt. At this point, I didn't have a plan. No way home, and nobody to trust. It was hard to follow my heart when the pieces lay scattered as so.

What could Layla have told my friends to make them turn on me? That I killed Trinity with my jealousy? That I killed Levi in a fit of rage? Drowned Ethan in my worry? Or perhaps she'd told them I'd been keeping them caged in Baylor for my benefit. Because I needed more time to fall in love with a stranger. And because I wasn't ready to go home, so neither could they.

Would she remind them I'd turned my back on them once? That I tried to catch a plane home and leave them all behind with a killer lurking in the woods? Or that I never trusted them and set up surveillance cameras to keep a watchful eye? The list went on and on. I couldn't blame her for thinking I was a monster that needed to be eradicated. Because all of those things were true. I'd been not just a terrible friend this summer, but a god-awful person. And now, my best of friends were out to capture me.

A warm hand grabbed my arm and yanked me into a tiny booth draped in a heavy curtain. I was staring straight into the eyes of a frantic old lady. Her hair was gray and frazzled, nearly a foot above her head in winding curls. She smelled like sage and wore a loose-fitting satin shift. There was a hunger behind her eyes as she pushed me down into a seat.

"Who are you?"

"My spirits have a message for you."

A small table rested between us, draped in velvet and covered in cards and flickering candles. "I think you have the wrong person," I said, standing in protest.

The fortune teller jumped to her feet and blocked the hidden exit. I eyed her suspiciously, then assessingly. I would not find Layla inside this tiny booth, but maybe I could find some answers.

"Be quick," was all I said. I sat back down, determined to be on my way soon enough.

The lady sat down, closed her eyes, and spread her arms. She tilted her head back and breathed deeply. Her hands trembled before she brought them together, rubbing them as if igniting a power within.

"I feel you're at a crossroads. You're up against a problem, and you need answers." She opened her eyes and peered at me for confirmation.

"Isn't everybody?"

She dropped her hands to the table, ignoring my snide comment, and started shuffling the cards. "So you're having a problem and you need my help? That's what I hear."

I rolled my eyes and sat back in my chair. My leg bounced as I eyed the surrounding curtain, trying to find the slit that I'd come in through.

"I'm hearing there is a love interest. But there's been some deceit. You want to know if you can trust him." My leg stilled as she shuffled her cards and the candles flickered.

Admittedly, this caught my attention, but I gave the same response out loud. "Doesn't everybody?"

The fortune teller appeared to be in some kind of trance. I didn't know if I could ask questions, because she certainly wasn't answering them. She shuffled the cards until one fell out of the deck. Face up. "What is that?" I blurted, more invested than I wanted to appear. These weren't normal playing cards. A wilted rose with a sword piercing the bud couldn't be good.

The fortune teller peeked at me briefly and then shuffled her cards again. "The deceit runs deep and true."

My breath quickened. I already knew this. "Tell me something I don't know."

A new card fell out, as if jumping from the deck to answer me.

"The Emperor!" I arched to see the card, but it meant little to me. A figure sitting in a chair. "Power, authority, and protection. You are being protected. It might not feel like it, but it's in your best interests."

"What's in my best interests?"

"There's more to it than meets the eye. Soon, the truth will reveal itself."

I huffed and sat back in my seat. This wasn't helping me at all.

"I'm hearing things are changing for you. Your path will soon be chosen, and those who have deceived you will stay behind. But not all deceit is evil. Some hide as protection. They will need your forgiveness."

"That sounds oddly generic," I said, with my arms folded across my chest.

Another card fell out of her deck, and I stretched my neck to see. She slapped the card down on the table, revealing a village littered with gold stars. "Wealth. Your hard work *will* pay off. There is great fortune coming your way."

"Okay. I'm done." I popped to my feet and pawed at the curtain surrounding her booth.

"You've chosen your path. It's a hard path, and few take it for this reason. The gold is at the end of the rainbow. But it's not wealth you seek, it's love."

The curtain parted, and a waft of popcorn air whooshed in. The fortune teller grabbed my hand on my way out, sending a shock straight up my arm. I tried to free myself, but her wild eyes caught me by surprise. They were unlike anything I'd seen before. One a deep brown, maybe black. And the other light. Like a wagon wheel, it had dark spokes spearing the center pupil.

"You don't belong here," she whispered. Entranced in

her eyes, it was the first thing she'd said that really meant something to me. I yanked my arm away and stumbled through the curtain. The dim glow of the candles snuffed as the curtain fluttered into place. I disappeared into the bustling crowd.

I tried to convince myself she didn't know what she was talking about. She could have said those things to a hundred people, and they would all make sense in a hundred different ways. Everybody feels like they've been deceived to some extent. Everybody wants protection and love. Everybody hopes there will be a pot of gold at the end of their long, grueling journey. I wanted to believe it for myself, but I couldn't shake the eerie feeling I'd gotten when I stared into her wagon-wheel eye. She certainly had a message for me, and she wasn't the only one.

At first it was subtle, a mother staring at me as I wandered through the crowd. But the more I thought of the difficult path ahead, the more I feared I had chosen wrong, and the more I began to notice strangers with watchful eyes. I told myself that I was paranoid, but when I passed a set of triplets with ice cream dripping down their chins and six piercing eyes following my every move, I stopped to survey the grounds.

I turned slowly in a circle and looked at every single face around me. The background seemed to swirl as I turned, disorienting me. But the faces I saw were rock solid. Most of the strangers looked away as our eyes met, but a few glared back at me with vengeance. I didn't know what they had heard about me, but it was clear that word had spread in this tiny town.

My eyes rested on a man who was familiar to me, but I couldn't place. He was leaning against the back side of a booth. His face cast in the shadows with a single eye visible, trained on me. *Who was he?* Someone bumped me from behind. A large man passed by unapologetically. I whipped my head around just in time to see him checking over his shoulder. But this was no random behemoth of a man. This was Big Jimmy.

I took off running, but he was quick to turn on me. I glimpsed the man in the shadows as he lurched out and followed suit. As the full light cascaded down on the man, I immediately recognized him as the anesthesiologist from my surgery. He was the one who'd been able to see me when nobody else could, and he was after me now. It was a good old game of capture the flag. Only I was playing against a village, and they weren't playing at all. I feared my capture would mean sudden death.

I jumped and pushed through the crowd, accidentally knocking down a young boy. The few people who had been oblivious to me before were now watching. I felt eyes by the hundreds, and I swore they made me feel heavier, like I was carrying their judgment on my back. The more eyes that turned, the more I recognized, and the thicker the air became, making it hard to breathe.

The doctor caught my shoulder, causing my nails to sharpen in defense. I swiped a hand down his arm, leaving deep, open claw marks. He groaned and fell back, causing Big Jimmy to trip over him and creating a slight distraction.

My heart floundered when I saw Kimber in the crowd. Her eyes, like all the others, were set on me. Was she a friend or foe? I didn't know who I could trust, and I was just about done giving chances. I felt the crowd move in on me, and I continued to run, passing by my old friend.

As soon as I made the decision not to trust her, she turned and darted after me. It was three against one, but I knew this was just the beginning. Everybody was after me. The dead and the living. What did they want from me? My need for survival was stronger than ever, and I could feel the wolf's blood waking from its dormant state. It wouldn't be long before I turned bloodthirsty and decimated the crowd of thousands that had come to the Summerfield State Fair.

Kimber was incredibly fast. She whisked through the crowd nearly at the speed of light. My mouth turned dry and my lungs burned as I ran from her. I was giving it everything I had, and it still wasn't enough. She clobbered me from behind. Though she did not weigh enough to take me down, I still struggled to stay on my feet.

She wrapped her spindly arms around my neck, and I

clawed at her to set me free. I knew the beast was rising inside me, but how shameful it would be to let it loose on somebody as frail as Kimber. She was no match for me as I was, let alone my grotesque wolf, who towered over every human here.

I threw her off me with ease, and she slid out into the dirt before me, causing a small brown cloud of dirt to mushroom around her. She wasn't so easily dissuaded, though, and she grappled to her feet with vengeance. Why was she so angry with me? What had she heard? Whatever had turned my friends against me was unjust. A downright lie.

We squared off. My heart pounded as if pumping three times the normal amount of blood. Or was it poison that coursed through me now? All I knew was that my hands were still covered in flesh and that my emotions were the most dangerous threat to cross in Baylor right now. Wolf or not, Kimber was putting herself in the crosshairs.

My anger raged. How dare she attack me like this. Had she expected I wouldn't fight back? Isn't that what anybody in their right mind would do?

"Get back to that door!" Kimber growled. She ran at me, a scream ripping from her lungs.

It took everything in my power not to turn her to dust. The fight was so unfair I tried to keep my emotions back; I knew they would end her life and I didn't want that. She grabbed me, then suddenly froze. A cold, pale blue crept up her fingers and spread up her arms.

"Go! H—" The pale blue covered her mouth, stealing her last words. I watched as her sky-blue eyes turned icy and opaque. Then she was a statue. An ice sculpture. Kimber stood strong, yet incredibly breakable. I breathed out in relief. It was better than death.

CHAPTER 10

It was the first time I noticed the crowd had parted, leaving a wide berth around Kimber and me. Little kids pointed to the ice figurine, and mothers tried to hide their shock with hands cupped over their mouths. The entire crowd, as far as my eyes could see, was still as they watched me and my attacker. My heart continued to drum as I took in the stares of a thousand glimmering eyes.

The doctor and Big Jimmy barreled through the sea of stillness. I took off at once, my shoulder bumping into Kimber's statue. "No!"

I tried to catch her, but there was no time. She toppled over, and as if bursting from the inside out, ice spikes shot out like daggers. There was no sign of Kimber when I looked over my shoulder. I had thought that maybe when the statue broke, she'd be set free; but that wasn't the case. The crowd gasped and shielded their faces from the shards of ice raining down. The same thing had happened to Layla when I'd gotten mad, and she still came back to haunt me. I didn't kill Kimber . . . *I didn't.*

I fought through the crowd, the adrenaline coursing through my veins and turning the wolf's blood into a potent poison. These men were twice my size, and I needed all the help I could get. I didn't mind borrowing a little evil from my nightmares.

On instinct, I cast the same spell on the two full-grown men. Suddenly I was no longer being chased. I watched the color leach from the men as the frost crawled up their bodies, turning them to pale, delicate figurines, suspended in mid-chase.

What was happening? The anger rose inside me. The instinct to fight grew stronger than any other power I possessed. Even my compassion. I had once hated myself for overtly harming Big Jimmy. And now, I'd decimated three people in only minutes. I knew it was only the beginning, but nothing could stop me now.

I vaguely took in the innocent eyes around me, and I knew they would not last through the night. I both needed the beast inside to keep me alive and hated everything it symbolized. But there was no backing down, and there was no shutting it off. Not while I was being threatened.

More doctors emerged from the crowd, stepping forward to capture their flag. It was the very dream I'd had about a war, only in this version, I fought alone. "Kinsley!"

I heard a familiar voice drown out the whispers. Innocent bystanders parted, making way for my new opponent. I stopped dead in my tracks. Because how could I run from my best friend? Lainey stood amid the parting crowd with Gunner by her side.

Lainey could almost pass for normal, apart from the pale green tint of her skin. It wasn't the same paleness that took over my arctic figurines, but more like a bruise that was still healing. Or rather, like she had been living underwater for far too long.

Gunner's mouth gaped open in a wide crocodile smile. Being reunited with his owner made him the happiest dog alive. And for a moment, I felt it too. As if everything was going to be all right. As if I could get through this difficult time if only I had somebody by my side. Lainey could be that person. She had always been my person.

In that moment of stillness, a group of men snatched me from behind. My arm tugged in one direction, and my waist was pulled to the next. I had never played football before, but my little brother had tackled me once, and I imagined this felt similar to being incapacitated by four or five muscular men on the field. I was being pulled in two.

I screamed, slashing at them with my claws, but to only minimal effect. My hand was still made of human flesh and my fingernails were barely sharpened. They were not the small daggers I had hoped for. Even though I slashed through their skin, I made only surface-level wounds. The men were unstoppable. They hoisted me up on their shoulders.

"Let me go!" I screamed.

The men marched on. *Where were they bringing me?* I wrestled as best I could, trying to get a look in the direction we were headed. All I could see was that we were heading toward the funhouse of mirrors. That's when it clicked for me; they were going to throw me through the portal since I wasn't going willingly.

I so wanted to go through that door, but I needed to do it on my own terms. With all the trickery at the state fair, I was paranoid it was a trap. That door probably led to a different realm. One I wouldn't be waking from. And it was so painfully obvious that Layla would take my place here in Baylor. She'd have no problem taking Walker from me, too. She'd already stolen my friends. Resurrected them and turn them against me. No, I couldn't allow them to force me through that portal.

Half dozen men easily moved through the parting crowd with me on their shoulders. The mob turned angry, yelling.

"Get her out of here!"

"She doesn't belong with us!"

"She's a devil in disguise!"

"That selfish wench! Shove her through the door, or she'll kill us all!"

The crowd rushed forward, pushing me off the men's

shoulders and down a long line of angry hands. This differed greatly from crowd surfing at a concert, but only because this wasn't entertainment. Not for me, at least. Everybody else, though, seemed to be enjoying themselves.

"Red door! Red door! Red door!" the masses unified their chants.

I looked up, trying to find a moment of clarity and calmness in this dire moment of life and death. But the beautiful night sky I expected to see held something else. Something dark swirled above my head, reminding me of a baby's mobile tethered above their crib. The darkness whirled round and round. I stretched my eyes, trying to make sense of it. Abruptly, I understood.

"Levi..." I gasped. All the deaths that fell by my hands, or rather my thoughts, were back. Back with a vengeance.

Levi led a flock in a wide vortex above my head. He was the biggest crow of all, his wingspan twice that of the other birds. I grabbed at the hands of strangers and pushed them off me but fighting on my back left me at a disadvantage. I watched the birds funnel downward like a tornado. I was the eye of the storm.

"Red door! Red door! Red door!" a familiar voice chanted.

I craned my head, searching for a voice I had not heard for some time, but did now, clear as day. I looked over the many faces I recognized and the ones that seemed like generic filler. Somebody grabbed my cheek and bumped my head. A finger found its way into my mouth, and I bit down. Hard. All I wanted now was to go home.

A sense of homesickness spread throughout me. The feeling was far greater than any anger I felt toward the crowd or the situation. It was worse than the pain of deceit coming from the familiar voice, though I felt that too.

When I found the face that matched the voice I so wished wasn't here, it was the pinnacle of all my terrible feelings. A culmination, as everything rushed together and exploded. A volcano of horror, suffering, guilt, and regret burst out of me as my little brother stood with the angry mob, chanting for my demise.

The moment I saw his face, I finally unleashed the monster that lay caged inside.

"No!"

The hands that were passing me from one to the next immediately froze and dug into my backside unforgivingly. The vortex of angry crows froze in the sky, just before the first talons reached me. Everything was still. And everything was cold.

I fumbled around, knocking over several icy figurines as I fell to the ground. On my hands and knees, I stared up at the many pale faces around me. My brother's cheeks were dusted baby pink with anger. *How did he get here?*

Gunner's ears were pinned back in a way I'd never seen before. It took a special person to make a good dog turn vicious. *What was wrong with me?* I so wanted Lainey to be the one I could turn to, but even my best friend had turned on me. Gunner and my own brother too.

The crows now truly hung like a dark mobile, as if pinned to the sky with invisible strings. Cool gray wings scarcely contrasted the black night sky, with tiny pinholes of twinkling stars. It was an eerie place, and the shrill carnival music only made it worse. It gave me the horrifying feeling of being trapped inside a music box. A new fear added to an ever-growing list.

I weaved through the crowd, trying hard not to knock over the statues. Had the entire crowd turned to mannequins? Petrified icebergs? Breakable to the touch? A figurine fell as I tried to slide by, causing a domino effect and shattering several people in its wake. I gasped and stumbled back, stepping on the toe of another figure. I was able to catch this one; a young girl, frozen with her cotton candy.

Once out of the thick crowd, I weaved in and out of the stragglers that remained behind the angry mob. It looked as though they were still rushing toward the commotion, trying to see all that had happened while they were stuck in lines. These faces seemed calmer, though, and most of them had a bag of popcorn or a lollipop, some with giant stuffed bears on their backs. The farther I moved from the center of the mob, the less angry the faces appeared.

At the entry of the funhouse of mirrors, I looked again at the immobilized fairgoers. It was safer to enter now that it was entirely my decision. That door was the only way I knew how to get home. If I opened the door and saw myself lying on the hospital bed, it would be safe for me to walk through. On the other hand, if I opened the door and a nefarious black void wafted beyond, I would run. I simplified the decision in my mind.

I took a deep breath, reminding myself to be brave. To lean into my weakness. I entered the funhouse of flickering black lights and weaved through the narrow halls, retracing my steps. It was even scarier now that the funhouse was empty, and I was alone. I caught my reflection in a distorted mirror, and my heart nearly leapt into my throat. I reflexively jumped back and slammed against a wall, and then closed my eyes briefly to catch my breath. *You can do this...*

I found the room that Noah had brought me into. I stepped into the rectangular room with four mirrors surrounded by neon glowing colors. I could see the red glow emanating from the last mirror's reflection, and my hands tensed by my sides.

I took one single stride forward, aiming for the portal, but stopped dead in my tracks when I saw Kai's ghost. Even his spirit had turned to an ice sculpture. He was frozen in time, his fist coming down on the mirror, ice upon glass.

The second mirror contained my parents, caught in a

moment of despair. My dad was frozen still as he wiped a tear from my mom's cheek.

I trailed my fingertips across the mirrors, and a chill came over me when I reached the third one and realized Layla was no longer trapped within. I stepped closer, expecting to see her. I searched within the reflection, but no matter which way the black light flickered, Layla had evaded the spell.

I gasped, whipping my head around, expecting to find her behind me. Her scrawny hands ready to push me through the door. But even though I felt as if I were being watched, I did not see her.

Unsettled and nervous, I moved to the fourth mirror, checking over my shoulder more often than I'd like to admit. Layla had been invisible to Walker all these years. Of course she was invisible to me now, in the shadows of a funhouse.

I positioned myself in front of the red door, and like the many times before, its gold knob enticed me in a way that I could not turn from. I reached for the doorknob, and my bloody knuckles scraped the mirror's surface, leaving marks of red behind.

What was this? I pawed at the doorknob, frantically searching for something to grab hold of, but it was just a two-dimensional reflection. I stepped closer. The door distorted before my eyes. The bottom half stretched long and thin, while the top scrunched into a stubby, wide version of itself.

I bit my lip, staring at the hoax and wishing it were my way home. Had I missed my chance? Was this my new life?

With the heels of my hands pressed into my eyes, I saw the pinwheel of electric lights in my thoughts. And just for a moment, I felt like I was drowning again. I sprang to life one last time. This was my last chance. I had come so far, and all I had to do now was check that Ferris wheel.

I made my way through the funhouse, completely riddled with the fear that another failure awaited me. That I would soar to new heights and cry into the night as I waited for change . . . and nothing would come.

Once in the open air, the arctic night delivered an invigorating breath into my lungs. I skirted around the frozen people and ducked underneath the low-flying crows. I saw many faces I recognized, both from this realm and from the other. I saw old classmates, teachers I'd liked, and teachers I hadn't. I even saw my brother's friends with angry scowls and small stones clasped in their hands, wound like pitchers. But as I passed the figurines by the hundreds, there was one face I continued to search for.

I didn't expect to see him here, but when I passed his pale skin, all the fight inside me dropped like a ton of bricks. The wolf turned dormant. Walker stood amid the angry crowd, encased in stillness, just like the rest. But unlike everybody else, he wasn't wearing an angry expression. His face was frozen in a mask of worry and sadness.

What have I done? More importantly, how do I undo it? I thought of him and Layla, and thought maybe it was for the best. He couldn't hurt inside there, could he? I trailed my finger across his battered brow. The ice was jagged and sharp there, and I knew his heart had been breaking as he'd come to the Summerfield State Fair.

I pulled my finger back, studying the water that dripped down my hand. Somehow, the jagged edge of his scar had been dulled by my touch. I stepped toe to toe with him, and I leaned in close. I promised him I wouldn't leave without saying goodbye, and this was me making good on that promise.

I closed my eyes, imagining the warmth of a farewell wish. It seemed I had little magic left after the volcano of emotions had spurted from me like a natural disaster, but I knew I had this one simple manifestation left in me. I opened my eyes to the warm glow of a single floating feather. It was the only thing left that still felt pure. Its heat sent a shiver down my spine, reminding me of just how cold I was. I leaned into Walker and kissed his cheek. It turned a deeper hue of pink beneath the melting ice.

"Goodbye, Walker," I whispered. I never thought I would say the words, and even though I felt unsure of who he was when I wasn't around. I was still very much in love with the Walker I knew.

I went to pull away, continue my mission, but my feet were locked in place. I nearly stumbled backward, grabbing hold of Walker's firm shoulders to keep me upright. My feet were covered in ice. Walker's shoes were less opaque, and beads of water streamed down his pants as he melted. The colors of his clothing were more prominent where the ice had thinned.

I forcefully jerked my foot back, hearing the tether snap between Walker and me. I loved him, but I no longer wanted to live a life in the shadows. And I no longer would settle for *half* of his heart. And while a month ago I may have chosen to be petrified if it meant being by his side, I had a clearer picture of reality now.

I'd heard my mother calling, and I knew the veil between her world and mine was thinning. And the closer I got to my past life, the further I grew from Walker and his. Plus, something was not right here. I didn't always know who I was in Baylor, and that scared me more than the depths of the haunted forest itself.

With nearly crippled feet and frozen shoes, I took off running for the Ferris wheel. A single thought now could change the course of my life forever.

As the Summerfield State Fair was still, its crowds made of etched glaciers, there was one thing that remained in motion. One massive thing that remained alive in a world otherwise dead. The Ferris wheel glowed with its antique lights. Colored bulbs rotated on the wheel high into the sky. It seemed as I hobbled toward my destiny that an invisible threshold had been crossed. There was no turning back now, and I would soon find out what waited for me.

CHAPTER 11

"Ten minutes!"

Who said that? Was it Layla? Everybody else was frozen. Though, by the sight of Walker, I knew the ice was melting. Soon, the angry mob would be alive to hunt again. Ten minutes sounded fairly accurate.

I had an odd sensation of running through a dense patch of air, a barrier set to slow me down just as a timer had begun. I waded through the thickness, keeping my eyes trained on the Ferris wheel. I felt like my spirit had detached from my body and was struggling to stay with me. As if somehow, it was getting caught in the invisible web I worked to get through.

My head scorched with the pain of a migraine, and I worried I might pass out before reaching the finish line. This was one race I couldn't afford not to win. Even though I continued to run, I couldn't feel my feet, as they were bound in icy shoes and frozen solid. The closer I got to the Ferris wheel, the stranger I felt in my skin.

Was I waking up? I hoped this wasn't what being alive felt like.

"Nine minutes. Don't be late," the voice called. I was fairly certain it was Layla. I heard the call both in my head and in the thick air surrounding me. I tried to hobble quicker, causing me to trip over my impairment. My spirit lagged before boomeranging back into my body, and for just a moment, I felt hollow.

Stay with me. We can do this . . .

I scrambled to my feet, powerless against Layla's magic. The more I saw to be true, the less power I had to change the surrounding reality. I pushed myself forward, my heart racing against time.

As I stood at the base of the Ferris wheel, it looked even taller than from afar when it towered over the fairgrounds. Old, rusted metal framework held the massive ride together. It couldn't be safe. But then again, neither was being lost in a coma.

I opened the safety gate and approached the moving cars, only it didn't slow down for me to get in. I grabbed hold of the next car, and it sped up, pulling my arm with it. I let go, my hand burning from trying to stop the momentum of the massive machine. I wiped my hands on the back of my jeans.

The control panel was nothing short of an antique. Sun-bleached buttons dotted the board, and the remnants of labels were barely visible. There was a single lever to the right of the panel that looked like it belonged in an old stick-shift truck. My palms itched as I debated which to try first. Some buttons had a pale pinkness to them, and I assumed that one day, when the ride had been shiny and new, these buttons were once red. Red was universal for stop, right? I pushed the first pink button and watched the Ferris wheel for signs of slowing.

"Eight minutes. You're not going to make it."

In a wave of panic, I pushed all the buttons that appeared to have once been red. I monitored the wheel as it continued making revolutions, hoping it would slow. It was then that I noticed, in the very top car, a single person. Long, dark brown hair cascaded down from the girl's face as she watched me struggle with the control panel.

"Time is ticking," she yelled down.

I knew it was. With every passing minute, it was harder, my task growing insurmountable. "I don't know how to make it stop!" I yelled back.

I looked up, surprised that the girl was still in the very top car, even though the ride had continued to rotate. The ghost of Layla floated between the many cars that passed by, always remaining at the very top of the wheel, as far as possible from the ground.

"What are you going to do? You only have eight minutes…"

"I know! I know! Stop it!" I yelled, grabbing at my head. If she was trying to make me crack, she was succeeding.

I grabbed the lever and tried to pull it with all my weight, but the metal had corroded, and it would not budge. I looked up at Layla one last time, and I knew what I had to do. But a voice inside begged to differ. *I can't climb that! I'll fall!*

"I can't! I can't do it!" I cried out. Half-frozen crows fell from the sky. I was running out of time.

Layla encouraged me in the same way Walker would have. In the same way I imagined Lainey would. Or rather, the way I hoped she would. It could have been the biggest hoax of all, but I couldn't think of it now. I had just shy of eight minutes left, and I needed to climb a monumental wheel of terror.

"Start slow. Climb up the frame in the center," Layla yelled.

I tried one last time to capture a car in desperation, but as it swooshed by, I realized this was about conquering my fear and nothing else. It wasn't about the mechanics of the old antique ride. It wasn't about being smart enough to figure out how to make the wheel stop. It was simpler than all those things put together.

This was my ultimate nightmare, and I had to do it

alone. I'd been petrified of heights my entire life; I couldn't think of a worse scenario than what I was facing now. My stomach swirled as I gripped the first metal bar. My ice shoes clinked as I stepped on the beam, and the lack of traction made my foot slide. I was only one step from the ground, and I clung to the cold metal for dear life. *Impossible . . .*

"One step at a time!" Layla yelled.

I didn't dare look up. My eyes watered as I reached for the next rung. My feet clattered with every step I braved. My hands became sweaty and just as slippery as my foothold. But Layla drove me forward. *"Just don't think about it,"* I breathed to myself.

Instead, I thought of how my greatest insecurity had become a strength. Maybe I wasn't the best student. And maybe I hadn't made this the very best summer, the way I wished I had, but I'd done some remarkable things. I'd frozen time. I'd turned human flesh to ice. And I had survived a lot of dark days and nights. I was more capable than I gave myself credit for. And I could do this. I could do this . . . as long as I didn't look down.

But nothing was easy in Baylor. A simple thought was all it took. It was all it *ever* took. I looked down. I don't know why I did it. It just happened, as if I was trying to torture myself. My breath turned shallow, my head woozy with disorientation. I could feel my spirit trying to leave my body again.

"I can't do this!" I whimpered, teetering between self-encouragement and self-sabotage like a pendulum.

"Seven minutes. Do you want to go home?"

What kind of question was that? "Well, I'm not staying here! Did you think I would take your place? I'm not giving up that easily!" I stepped to the next rung.

"Answer the question!"

"Yes! Of course!"

I made it halfway. All the spokes met in a single disc. The intricate design came together in corrosion and rust. I eyed a bolt that had unscrewed itself and was ready to fall out from its tethered hole. I didn't want to know how high I had climbed, or rather, how far away the ground was. The very thought made me sick. I moved myself to the next beam and watched the bolt fall out and ricochet off a nearby cable.

"Then why can't you see? Why can't you see this is just a dream?"

"I can! I do!" I had known I was dreaming for quite some time now. Of course, it was heartbreaking in the beginning, when I hadn't understood. But I knew it now.

"But you've never turned lucid. You've never gained full control and awareness."

"And why do you think that is? You stole the damn book from me!" I yelled, climbing a little faster now.

Layla laughed, reminiscent of a witch's cackle. "This isn't about the book, and you know it. *Waking Dreams* was just another obstacle you put before yourself. You've known you were dreaming, and yet, you've chosen to spend your time chasing your dreams and running from your nightmares. Why can't you just open your eyes the way I have? Why do *I* have to be the logical one?" Layla argued.

What did she mean, why couldn't I open my eyes? They were open. I saw the sheer height that I had climbed all too well. And I could see all the lives I'd turned to statues below. They were so small from up here, but I could still tell they were mostly done thawing. I closed my eyes and shuddered. If anything, I was seeing too much.

"You're the furthest thing from logic! You are absolutely crazy! All you do is hide in the woods and run from the very few people who have ever tried to help you! Do you want my help to cross over? Because my patience is running thin, and I have half a mind to throw you off this wheel!" I shouted. At least she was distracting me from thinking about how high I'd climbed.

Layla's laughter rumbled in the sky like thunder. Her ghost was everywhere. It was somehow tied to the atmosphere and living in the very molecules that held this realm together. She was a force I could not reckon with.

"You think *I'm* the crazy one?" Another rumble of thunder boomed across the sky, causing the last of the crows to drop, and the metal rod to vibrate within my grasp.

"Nobody in their right mind laughs like that!" It was true. The only characters that cackled like that were villains. The characters that had fallen on poor luck. The ones that had a tango with a dramatic trauma of sorts, and their only way of survival meant leaving their wherewithal behind. And to continue living a life with half a heart and a darkened mind. What was Layla's trauma? Was it that her soon-to-be fiancé accidentally took her life? It would certainly be enough to turn her into a villain.

"Look again Kinsley. Everything you've seen here in Baylor has been a lie. Most of the conversations you've had have been misconstrued, what you believed you *deserved* to hear."

Why would I believe I deserved *this*? To be haunted by Layla and the ghost of my best friend, the dark dimensions of the woods, and water? I *knew* I deserved better than this! But did I deserve Walker's love? Well, I would never be as pretty as Layla. That was just a simple fact. And they'd had a bond, long before I ever entered the picture. She was just trying to confuse me. I began to look down, but caught myself and averted my gaze. *Stay focused . . .*

"Why have you been hiding from Walker? He loves you more than anything in this world, and you've been hiding from him for decades! *You* don't deserve *him!*"

"You're so far off the mark, I pity you . . . Four minutes." Her tone was flat. I had finally struck a chord.

I had four minutes left, and I thought I could make it. I

had already climbed three-quarters of the wheel, and I was gaining momentum. Nothing drove me quite the same as Layla did.

"Let me ask you this," Layla continued. "You know how Gran has been reading us fairy tales?"

Us? I didn't answer. My gran was none of her business. How did she even know that?

"Yeah. You know what I'm talking about. But what I can't understand is, why have you played along? Why did you allow yourself to succumb to the wolf?"

"I didn't! That beast took over—"

"Because you let it!"

"What was I supposed to do?" I argued.

"Tell yourself you're dreaming. And wake up!"

"That's not how it works," I said, shaking my head, refusing to believe I could have woken at any moment. I grabbed the next rung with a sweaty hand.

"Oh my gosh, Kinsley! You're exhausting! You are so stuck in your own head you can't even see what has been so blatantly obvious!" Layla was looking out over the fairgrounds when she paused. "Oh look, they're all melted now. Better hurry. Three minutes," she said.

I launched myself up to the next rung. My arms were shaking, and I was exhausted. I didn't dare look down.

"Let me ask you this; why do you think you're wearing glass slippers right now?" she continued, sounding bored.

I frowned and tried to wiggle my toes, but couldn't. Ice

encased my feet, not glass. But that was only because the spell I cast on Walker had leached from him to me. But could there be another reason? Suddenly my feet weren't so cold. "I—" I began.

"It's just another fairy tale! If you believe it to be true like you had for all the others, then what do you think will happen next?" Layla laughed, and her roar shook the cables. *Don't fall. Don't fall.*

A single slipper loosened and fell from my foot. I was too afraid to look down, but I heard it fall, chiming off the metal rods for what seemed like an eternity. If Layla was telling the truth, and I had just lost a glass slipper, then I supposed my prince would find it next.

I closed my eyes, wanting to see if Walker was my prince, but I was far too afraid. I felt the vibrations in the metalwork and heard the angry mob below. I knew they had found me, and I didn't doubt they were faster climbers than me.

Layla peeked over the edge of the car, gauging my progress. "Don't you see? You've been imagining it all. But instead of controlling it, you let *it* control *you*. It's just a dream, Kinsley. And it's time to wake up."

"You're right! It's just a dream! You're not real!" I climbed quicker, using the better grip from my freed foot and the fear of the mob to propel me upward. Once I climbed to the top, I'd vanquish Layla, and I'd be set free.

A thread of lightning danced across the sky as Layla

laughed out loud. I grabbed the rim of the Ferris wheel. I finally made it. Now, I just had to get into the car.

"One minute…" she breathed.

I pulled myself up with weak, trembling arms, and her brown eyes met mine. I grabbed hold of the car with what little strength I had left. My moist hand slipped on the wide rim of the car. "No—"

My wail was cut off when Layla grabbed my hand. My body went rigid. For a moment, I thought she would peel my fingers back and let me fall. Just as I had threatened her minutes earlier. Instead, she helped pull me up.

I collapsed at the bottom of the car, thankful to be in something more substantial than the outside of the metal framework, where falling would mean certain death. My arms quivered and quaked. For the first time, Layla rotated with the other cars and we started our descent.

I didn't take my eyes off her as I found the seat behind me. As the ride rounded, several wet strangers tried to swipe at the car as it passed by. I held on tight to the edge of the bench and found that sitting across from Layla was even more intimidating than the mob *and* the climb put together.

"You still don't get it?" She peered at me, her head cocked to the side. "I'm just as real as you are."

"You're a ghost!" I snapped, shaking my head.

"I'm *you* . . ."

CHAPTER 12

I stared into Layla's brown eyes, not comprehending her words. *I'm you.* It was a meeting of two single words that combined like oil and water. They never quite mixed to make something new. I waited for it to click, for it to make sense, but it didn't. Looking into her eyes was like looking into the funhouse mirror. Only, this one wasn't distorted. Her face reflected the same impatient stare I knew mine had. We both cocked our heads to the side, waiting for something that did not come.

"We're *all . . .*" Layla lifted her hand to motion to the angry mob that waited at the base of the ride and the handful of people who were crazy enough to start climbing. "You."

The wheel was now mid-rotation, and we were nearly at ground level. I turned to assess the strangers, whom Layla had indicated were different parts of me, but all I could see was Walker. He was as real as anything, and he watched me with sorrow-filled eyes, a glass slipper dangling forlornly from his hand.

"And him? He's just a figment of my imagination?" I asked, not wanting to know the actual answer.

When Layla fell silent, I pulled my eyes from Walker to read her face. She looked like she was being pulled in opposite directions. It's exactly how I felt, and I wondered if that was another mirrored effect. As our car neared the ground, I dodged the angry, open hands. Their hands still pale and icy. Nobody grabbed at Layla, though, and she sat patiently until we climbed out of their reach again. My heartbeat raced as I was on the verge of collapse.

Layla looked at her watch, and a crease deepened between her brows. I recognized that watch; I wore it regularly. Though I hadn't packed it for my trip to Baylor. The wheel continued to ascend, but as we lifted into the sky, I worried my heart was being left behind. Layla checked her watch again, and her face filled with worry as she peered over the car to watch Walker shrink away. I turned to watch him, too.

Walker's face fell as he checked the time on his own wrist. I knew I was seconds away from meeting my fate, whatever it may be. Whatever was supposed to happen on this Ferris wheel, it was bigger than just me. It would most likely affect Layla and Walker too. Possibly the whole crowd.

"Wait. What do you mean, *you're me?*" The uncoupled words finally mixed, making a small sentence that both made sense and didn't. If she was me, then was *I* the crazy one? I tried to wrap my head around the idea.

The Ferris wheel sped up the moment the thought clicked in my mind. I remained focused as best I could, but I was afraid. Layla's eyes grew wide as she flickered in and out of my reality. One moment there, then not. As if she disappeared into thin air, only to reappear as a true translucent ghost. Her image glitched as the fairgrounds turned to a blur.

I could see the back of the bench straight through Layla's chest and the distortion of distant lights behind her eyes. Just as her energy pulsed, so did the feeling of my soul leaving my body. My breath was stolen as she wavered back and forth, somewhere between my body and the seat across from me. I looked at my hands, trying to ground myself and make sense of the quivering sensation of being whole one second and split into pieces the next.

The Ferris wheel accelerated more than I thought possible, and we reached the top just as we were falling to the bottom. It spun so fast that all I could do was grab hold of my seat and pray I didn't get thrown off. We spun round and round, the sky blurring with the ground in a mixture of black and brown.

My soul flickered in and out, and my head pulverized with pain I had never endured before. My heartbeat raced and lifted into my throat. I knew I could not take this torture much longer. My teeth were chattering, and my grip was slipping off the rim of the car.

If this is a dream, all I must do is, *wake up!*

For a fraction of a second, Layla sat across from me. Her body fully fleshed and her eyes piercing. She leapt across the car and into my body. A bolt of electricity hammered into my chest. My heart was ground zero of a massive earthquake that shook me to my core. The voltage branched out into my limbs, like fingers of electricity, and seized me.

The momentum of the impact swept me from my seat. The remaining glass slipper shattered on a nearby beam as I flew from the car. I had an overwhelming feeling of free falling, but I was not afraid. And I was no longer in pain.

The blur of colored light bulbs swirled around me, dancing in kaleidoscopic fractals as I fell. It was beautiful. It was calming. And then it was red.

I had been so worried about doing the right thing, it felt like pure relief to fall. Because I knew I was no longer in control. My part was done now, and it was up to fate to finish, one way or another.

I closed my eyes and spread my arms wide, feeling the wind that did nothing to slow me. I couldn't tell the difference between falling and flying. I felt light as a bird, soaring through the night sky.

I had a vague understanding that Layla was a part of

me now. That she lived somewhere inside of me. Whether it was my head or my heart, I did not know. But I felt more whole falling to my death, than I had living my summer of dreams.

I continued to fall. My hair whipped wildly in my face, my cheeks were flaccid, and my stomach was in a perpetual state of freefall. Yet, somehow, some way, it was euphoric. Was it because I embodied the ghost of Layla? I never truly liked her. And I had only wanted to help her for my gran, and then later, Walker. But from the moment she and I became one, I found the good in her. I found the side of me I had been missing all along.

I felt terrible that she'd been lost in the woods all summer long. Invisible. If I was in the cabin with all of our friends, then had *she* truly been an outcast? Just . . . alone? Had she spent her time with Walker when he and I were apart? Would I have her memory of that now?

I tried to think, but my mind was racing far too fast for me to latch on to one thought alone. At the beginning of summer, I hunted Layla for sport. Was it my manifestation that kept her on the run? It was sad to think that Layla had tried to get my attention, and I'd mostly spent my time hiding from her. I treated her like a dirty little secret and kept her in the shadows. If only I had known then what I did now. But she did. She knew we were one and the same. Why had she disappeared, then? Why didn't she shake me awake? Make me see?

I thought of her worried expression while she looked at her watch. Then, I thought of Walker's same expression, his same concern for the time. Maybe time played more of a barrier than I'd realized. Maybe I couldn't go home until I was ready. Until the very minute when I was healed just enough to return.

Layla said that all I had to do was wake up. Could she wake? Or had she stayed here, not wanting to leave without me? My heart opened for the girl. The part of me that wouldn't give up on myself.

But what if Layla had gone home without me? Would I have woken up in the hospital a completely different person? A version of myself nobody recognized? I could almost hear the chatter now... *"She hasn't been the same since her accident."*

A wash of gratitude came over me as I began to love the girl that I'd spent the summer loathing. She must have sacrificed so much, and I never even realized it. I wondered if I would've been better off if she went home without me. I shook the thought from my head. I had learned to accept my faults and deficits while in Baylor, and I was done wishing them away. I was the whole me now: beautiful, competent, deserving, and insecure. Sometimes, even a little dark and twisted.

If Layla and I had reunited earlier in the summer, I might have been happier. Maybe I would have actually swung from the stars. Or had the tea party underwater with Lainey as a mermaid. And after I'd drowned in the lake, maybe I wouldn't have felt so alone.

My mind raced in a million different directions at once as I continued to fall through the never-ending atmosphere. The red door swirled all around me, trying to catch me. Were Noah and Trinity just manifestations of my insecurity? Would Walker have loved me sooner if I were whole? Would I have come home sooner? Or would I have made Baylor so magnificent that I'd never want to leave?

I was pulled through the mouth of the portal and swallowed whole. There was nothing but black as far as I could see. I knew this place. This was the void where I sometimes saw Gran. *Our* Gran. I was so used to thinking of Layla as a separate entity that it was now difficult to think of myself as singular.

I felt as though I had fallen from a distant star and was drifting through the galaxy. My hair continued to lash at my face as if in a dark vortex or windstorm. I searched for signs of life, holding my hair back from my eyes, but I couldn't see into the darkness. I fought back a feeling of disassociation. It was far too easy to be nobody, and nothing in the void. And I knew if I succumbed to that oblivion, I'd be forgotten; lost forever.

I was weightless. I couldn't see; I couldn't smell. And the silence was somehow deep and remote, like it spanned throughout space and time. Because I had been living for months with only half a spirit, my body felt full in an unfamiliar way.

"There you are, dear. I'm so proud of you." Gran materialized from nowhere. Her green eyes were magnificent, like shards of pale peridot light and dark emerald shadows. Her skin was flawless—nearly pearlescent. And a radiant glow emanated from within her that instantly soothed me. The feeling in my chest slowed, and eventually equalized, like an elevator slowing for its exit. I stepped forward to meet my beloved gran.

"Where am I? What's happening?" I asked, disoriented still. There were a million questions tumbling in my head, but where and what seemed to be the foundation to begin with. Everything else was subjective, maybe even theoretical. I was sure questions would riddle me for the rest of my years, so I'd take what I could now and here.

"You're going home, dear. You're almost there now," Gran said, taking my hand in hers. Her touch soothed me. For a split second, all motion ceased, and it was just us. Her emerald eyes to my small emerald fleck.

But a moment was all I had before the feeling in my chest reversed with a vengeance. Could I fall in reverse? The sensation began rising from my core. A strong lifting of something inside of me. My soul was on the move, and my body struggled to keep up. My mind, body, and spirit were not used to being united. They fought like triplets.

I grasped Gran's feeble hands in mine. "Will I ever see you again?" I suddenly feared this would be the last I would ever see of her. And there was no time for a proper goodbye. How do you even put such a feeling into words? There were none. None that I was aware of.

Gran smiled warmly and shook our hands. "It's time, dear. It's time."

"Gran? Gran!" I called in a moment of panic. My hand slipped from hers. As if my soul were being siphoned into another dimension, somewhere above where I visited now, I felt the sucking and pulling as I journeyed into the unknown.

Everything went dark in the absence of Gran's glow, but there was a new light quickly approaching. The darkness turned to swatches of orange and gray that danced behind my eyelids. My body was heavier than normal. Like my cavities had been filled with cement.

My toe twitched. It reminded me that my feet were free. A thin fabric brushed against my toes. A sheet? Was I in bed? Had this all been a dream, like so many I had before? Would I open my eyes to see the window overlooking Baylor Lake? Would I roll over into my pillow and scream a muffled cry? A call for help that nobody would answer?

My thumb spasmed, and I felt the hints of a sheet beneath it as well. Suddenly, my eyes became restless, and my heavy lids broke apart. I squinted as a bright light assaulted me, and my eyes fell shut instantaneously. It was only a small sliver of vision, not enough to tell which realm I was in.

I tried again. It took an immense amount of energy to open my eyes. There was a splash of white that trailed down the center of my vision. Dots of pink and a faded pale turquoise. I wasn't sure where I was, but it wasn't the cabin. My eyes fluttered as I tried to keep them open long enough to make sense of where I was. But this tiny task was nearly impossible. I had to try something different.

I lifted my hand ever so slightly before it fell heavily upon my chest. *I can do this. I can do this.*

I opened my eyes again, feeling a rush of dizziness. The room was set into motion. I felt sick. The splash of white was a bed with bland white sheets. The twin peaks at the end of the tiny bed were my feet. And the faded pinks and blues turned out to be the wallpaper in the hospital room.

My hand twitched one more time as I took a deep, labored breath. I knew vaguely that something was in my mouth, but I didn't care. I was too tired to care. *I made it. I made it home.* Then, as if the opening of my eyelids for the first time in months had been a marathon, sleep took hold of me, and I could finally rest peacefully.

CHAPTER 13

A gentle voice hummed in the background. "Hey . . ."

My eyelids flickered, but that was about all I could do.

"Hey," somebody else replied quietly.

"Is she going to be waking up soon?" the voice whispered.

"I think so. That's the plan, at least. They're pushing the medicine now. The doctor said it could take quite a while and to just be patient. I don't know."

I recognized one of those voices. At least I thought I did. I thought it was my mom, speaking in a hushed tone. The same tone I'd heard growing up, when she spoke to my dad and didn't want us kids to hear. The same tone she spoke in when she thought I was sleeping and didn't want to wake me. But this time was different. This time I was awake, only I couldn't open my eyes. I couldn't become fully alert no matter how hard I tried. The sleep was still calling.

"It's all going to work out. You know that. You need to trust, Dad." This voice was familiar too, although I couldn't place it. Not yet.

"Brooklyn swears up and down that everything will be okay. But I don't know how much of it I believe. She's always had these premonitions. When is it real, and when is it just fortune telling?" Mom asked.

"Don't give me that! You know it's real. She predicted my success, and you can't deny that, now can you?"

There was a long pause before a small stent of snickering. I thought I could place the voice now, because only siblings would bicker and boast like that. The other voice must be Aunt Nora. She and my mother teased each other often, and it made sense that she would come here today. Had they planned for me to wake up today? Had everybody known I was waking up on this particular day? I thought back to Walker, checking his watch. How did everybody know except me? It seemed unfair. Like they had purposely kept me in the dark.

I tried to show them I was awake now, but all I could do was twitch a knuckle. It felt like a big sign, as if I had been waving a white flag of surrender over my head. But the small tension building in my knuckle was not the grand gesture I had wanted to make, and nobody noticed. I tried to hang on to each word, but sleep was calling me, and it was so tempting. *Just one more nap?*

"You know it's true. Do you know how many millions I just collected for my client? And they were willing to *pay* in settlement, too. I told them, *I don't settle.*"

"I know. You're very good at what you do."

"You can say that again . . ."

The voices quieted, and the darkness felt like a lullaby, rocking me back to sleep. When they finally spoke again, I startled and again tried to open my eyes. I looked to the left and then the right, but it did little while my eyelids were out of commission.

"Did you hear anything about the boy next door?"

"Actually . . ." Nora said, in what I thought might be a mischievous tone. But I couldn't trust myself to pick up on the nuances and reflections of a muffled voice when I had been unconscious for so long. Heck, I was half unconscious now. Who were they talking about?

"What is that? No! You didn't! Nora, tell me you didn't . . ." Aww, there she was. Perhaps it was the tone I knew best from my mom. Somebody was about to get in trouble, though I couldn't imagine why.

There was a long pause in which I tried to speak. Make my presence known. I flexed my jaw and pursed my lips. *What was this?* Rubber? What was in my mouth? I couldn't feel my lips pressed together, but they had pressed against something foreign. I moved my tongue around, trying to identify the object. But even my tongue was lethargic and wouldn't cooperate the way I wanted. *Come on! Just work!*

"It is him!" Nora said.

"It is?" My mom sounded surprised.

Who was what? What was happening?

"Yeah."

"Why would they do that?"

"Oh, they don't care. They're a hospital. They take in the sick and wounded. They don't consider personal preferences for your next-door neighbor . . . Oh! Wow! It says they had to put a metal plate in his head and partially down the side of his face . . . something . . . to reconstruct his cheekbone."

What was that? They put a metal plate in *my face?* I wanted to cry out. Pull all the metal from my body and rip out whatever was stuffed in my mouth. The only problem was, I was far too weak. Even opening my eyes was a challenge now. There was no way I could communicate that I didn't want to be a cyborg for the rest of my life. Half human, half robot . . . I only wanted to be me.

"Yikes," Mom exclaimed.

"Yeah. It sounds like he got the worst of it."

"So, have you found the toxicology report? Is it in there?"

"I'm still looking. Hold on," Nora sounded like she was

on the verge of something big. A dog catching the first scent of its prey.

"Hey. Hey. Hey," my mom hurried a hushed warning.

"Good morning, Nora. How are you?" It probably didn't look like much, as I felt no movement cross my face, but I felt like crying when I heard Dad's voice.

"Good morning. I'm well. Big day, huh?"

"Yeah." A heavy sigh followed, and I imagined my dad's brows momentarily bunching together before releasing. Though I couldn't see anything except the darkness I had grown so accustomed to.

"Hey, what's that?" he asked.

"Oh, it's nothing," Nora said.

"Well, it's not nothing. It turns out the boy next door *is* the one that caused her accident." I was listening, but I couldn't quite focus. Something about the boy who had nearly killed me, recovering in the very next room. It made me uncomfortable. Or was that the catheter? Either way, I was more vulnerable than I could withstand.

"Really? Geez, I don't think he's going to live," Dad said.

"What makes you say that?" my aunt asked.

"Well, I heard them talking in the hall on several occasions. It didn't seem favorable, I'll say that much. How did you find out it was him?"

"Ugh, she stole the dang file!" Mom complained.

I don't know why this made me happy, but it did. I

always knew my aunt to get what she wanted, and often she would cross into what she called *the gray area* to get it. The gray area was her favorite place to operate, and she spent time there frequently. But it always seemed to benefit her. She was a wealthy attorney, and she was thriving in her own right. Nobody had the confidence and air that Aunt Nora had, and sometimes she had to earn that with a little mischievous behavior.

"Well, he can't die! I'll have a hard time suing him if he's dead!" Nora snapped.

"I'm sure everything will work out . . ." my mom said, her voice becoming somewhat distant.

Had she not noticed that I'd been trying to alert them I was awake? That I was sending smoke signals with twitches and lazy tongue movements? I listened to the pause in the conversation and tried my hardest to lift my hand. I was so aggravated with myself for not being able to do the things I deemed simple. I tried to open my eyes, but they would only crease, letting in a small sliver of light. The blurry figures moved around the room every so often. When one approached me, I tried to smile, but I couldn't with the thing shoved in my mouth. I wanted to scream out loud, "I'm here. I'm here," but I could only think about it. And unlike when I was in Baylor, my thoughts wouldn't get me very far.

I felt the warm touch of somebody's hand caress mine. The velvet touch was unlike anything I'd felt all summer long, and it did wonders to soothe me. I tried to squeeze my hand in response. My eyes gave a small flutter, and I attempted to make a sound with no such luck.

"Is she waking up?" Dad asked. This was it. This was my chance. A small stint of silence followed as I tried to make a sound, any sound. But my mouth was as dry as the Sahara Desert and my throat scorched by a thousand suns.

A small whimper came from Mom. I hoped they saw something in me.

"Kins, can you hear me?" Mom murmured.

I pinched my thumb and forefinger together, squeezing her hand. It felt more like a twitch than anything else, but she recognized it as the monumental victory it was, and that was all that mattered.

"Oh my god, Kins! Doctor! Get the doctor!" Mom flew into hysterics. I could hear the commotion spread across the room, and I tried to open my eyes to see what was happening. The excitement felt like a jolt of adrenaline, temporarily helping me fight the drowsiness.

I felt the bed give on either side of me, and another warm pair of hands caressed the side of my face. It took up more real estate than my mother's hands would have, and I melted into my dad's rough hand. "Kinsley, oh god, I love you so much! I love you so much!" Dad sniffled. I might have cried too if I wasn't fighting the sedation.

"She's waking up! We need to get a doctor in here!" Nora yelled distantly.

It all seemed to happen so quickly, and the amount of effort it took from me was astronomical. I felt the sleep pulling me back toward the darkness, as if the void had staked a claim on my soul, and it was time to report back. But I knew I had to make a show of my awareness, if only for a moment. I had to let them know I was in here. That I had made it. And that I was going to live.

"Has she made any signs of waking?" an unfamiliar voice asked. I felt a hand pat around my neck and chest and something cold press against my bare skin. My eyes fluttered open to see a face I'd never seen before. I groaned in a soundless protest.

"Yes. I saw her eyes move," Dad said.

"She opened them!" Nora corrected.

"She grabbed my hand!" Mom insisted.

I wanted to smile, but that would be far too much effort. It was a bit of a stretch; I hadn't reached over and grabbed her hand. I managed a small pinch. But in her defense, that spasm had meant just as much as me reaching out for a hug. And she knew that.

I sensed the doctor moving around the room, pressing and pulling, checking equipment. I tracked the sounds and tried to flutter my eyes as often as possible. But the one sensation I couldn't comprehend was feeling he had wedged my feet back in the glass slippers. Why would he do such a thing? What a terrible thing to do to a girl recovering from an accident. I tried to squirm. I tried to protest. I didn't like how my feet were unable to move.

My lids parted, followed by several faint blinks. I focused on the doctor standing at the foot of my bed, massaging my feet as he spoke medical jargon. Far too complicated for my injured brain to understand. Instead, I narrowed my gaze on my feet. It highly irritated me that my perception didn't match reality. My mind struggled with the view of a gentle massage, as if the doctor had only been trying to increase circulation, and the feeling that he had slipped my feet into quick-drying cement. Why couldn't I understand this? Why couldn't I put my imagination to rest? I feared some delusional part of my dreaming mind was flipped on like a light switch and would never turn off, even in my waking hours.

How long had this been happening? And how long would it continue? My aggravation with the doctor and the stimulation grew into frustration and worry. What if I never changed? What if my mind was messed up from the accident, and I would never be the person I used to be? I would never fully be able to appreciate the Kinsley I once loathed but had fought so hard to become. I felt the anxiety begin in my chest and spread through my limbs.

"She's awake!" Dad rushed to my side.

"My baby!" Mom cried.

The doctor came to my side, shining a flashlight in my eyes. How rude. The assaults continued from this man. I tried to groan. I tried to shake my head loose from his grip, but all I managed was a blink. I had every bit of mind to slap that flashlight out of his hands and yell, *Stop messing with me!* When he peeled my eyelids open and shined his light at me again, I tried to fight back.

Success! Well, almost. I'd lifted my hand off my chest. It wasn't what I imagined, but still, everybody celebrated, including me. *I did it!*

"Hello there, Kinsley. I'm just checking your vitals. How are you feeling, dear?" the doctor asked.

Seriously? Did he think I had enough strength to rip this thing out of my mouth and have a conversation with him? I blinked, because that was about all I could do. He continued to ask me questions, and I finally understood it was with the expectation I wouldn't answer. It must have been a habit in his line of work. He turned to my parents and explained the protocol. I didn't listen.

I was falling back to sleep when I felt somebody reaching into my mouth, grabbing a handful of my lungs, and pulling them up through my trachea and out my mouth. I was sure I had thrown up something vital, something I couldn't live without. But when I opened my eyes in shock, I saw a long clear tube that in no way resembled my organs. My mouth closed, and my teeth rest heavily against each other. I moved my tongue sluggishly in my mouth. I wanted to ask for a glass of water, but that was too advanced. My mouth was so parched, I was sure I hadn't had a drink in years. How long had I been in this coma? Did they not give me water the entire time?

Something stabbed my lips, and this time I felt a frown crease my forehead. That was an improvement, at least. It was good to show my emotions. It meant more communication. But why were they stabbing me, and why were they pulling things out of my body? It was a difficult process to endure, and I wished I had fallen back to sleep when the room was quiet. They certainly wouldn't let me sleep now.

I forced my eyes open and focused on what was right in front of me. A glass of water with a straw bent to my lips. I should have been more grateful, but I didn't have it in me. I puckered my lips and took in the smallest sip of liquid gold. My mouth moistened, but it wasn't enough to undo the months of damage. The trickle went down the side of my throat in a narrow stream, leaving most of it achingly dry. I puckered my lips again, the only way I knew how to ask for another sip, and took in more. Though it was not enough, I was satisfied with the work I'd done.

The small sips of water felt like an awakening. My eyes fully opened and I took in the room for the first time. Several blurry figures stood around my bed, watching and waiting for my response. It sure felt like a lot of pressure for somebody so weak. I didn't want to disappoint them, or myself. And if I was being honest, I was still confused. My mind was still playing tricks on me.

I strained my sight until Mom became a single human being, her two figures merging slowly under my double vision. Dad enveloped her in a hug, and I took in his kind eyes. It appeared Nora had left, and I wondered if I'd fallen asleep during the process at one point or another.

When my eyes landed on somebody I couldn't recognize, I feared that I should have known her. Her presence made me somewhat leery, and I eyed her suspiciously. What if I had lost my memory? What if she was my best friend, and I didn't even know it? But that wasn't even the confusing part. The part that really rattled me was how Gran could be here. I thought she had died *before* my accident.

Now, I wondered if the whole thing had been a premonition. Was she going to die? Was it my job to tell Grandpa Green? To tell Gran? Had I become some guide that helped spirits move on to the afterlife, and the summer in Baylor was the start of my training? I eyed her just as warily as I eyed the stranger, but her green eyes glimmered with warmth, regardless of my conspiracy theory.

"Mphh." An airy sound passed through my lips as I tried to speak. I searched the eyes of my mom and dad for signs that they understood.

"It's okay, baby. You don't need to say anything. We're here." Mom rubbed my hand. I moistened my lips and tried again, but it wasn't easy.

"Mm. Mom," I uttered. It was breathy, but I think she

understood. She leaned down and hugged me tight. I took in her scent. Her normal perfume was just a hint on her skin now. I focused, really taking her in. She looked unkempt. As if she had been sleeping in the same clothes for weeks. As if her hair wasn't washed, just scraped back into the low ponytail that lay flat against her neck. I felt terrible for what I had put her through.

"Dad," I said, a little clearer this time. Dad broke down crying as he grabbed my hand and pressed it against his cheek. I tried to moisten my mouth, which seemed to be the key to speaking coherently.

Gran, who was still smiling brightly at me, patiently waited her turn. She sat down on the edge of my bed. "Gran..." I said, looking into her eyes. I reached out with a weak, trembling hand. She smiled with confidence, unlike my parents, who were an utter mess. It was good. Comforting. I needed somebody to be strong for me.

Uttering those three simple words was as hard as running a marathon, both physically and mentally. It was taxing, and I was exhausted from the effort. Gran rubbed my leg, and I smiled at her to show my gratitude. But when I glanced back to my parents, all I saw was a worried look, shared between them.

Mom's mouth parted as if she contemplated speaking, but she couldn't seem to find the words. Dad gave a small shake of his head. I must have said something wrong.

As I fought back the sleepy hold the drugs had on me, I

spied my bedside table. A book my family had been passing down from generation to generation lay open as if mid read. It was the old book of fairy tales Gran had read to me as a child. She'd memorized many of the stories and recited them to me over the telephone on the occasions when the book had been left at my house by accident. They were fond memories, but they made me feel somewhat anxious now. A bookmark lay across a page with a beautiful watercolor drawing. A princess climbing into a round pumpkin carriage, decorated in colorful sparkling lights. I closed my eyes and let sleep take over me like a thief in the night.

CHAPTER 14

I had a faint memory of reaching up into my hairline and getting scolded like a child near a hot stove. A peek in a hand-held mirror. And a scraggly, gaunt girl looking back at me. She had purple shadows under her gaunt eyes and a shaved section of her head. But I'd grown suspicious when seeing a reflection in the mirror. I didn't know who she was, but I think they said it was me.

I slept a lot. I wasn't sure how many days and nights had lapsed. It was probably a side effect of the medication. Something that dripped through my IV. I did some toe wiggling though, and I was proud of myself when I passed the test. I wasn't so happy about leveling up to leg lifting. Lifting my legs was like lifting a spoon through nearly set Jell-O. My feet seemed to rise, but the flesh and muscle of my leg lay stubbornly on the bed.

Today was the best I'd felt yet. I still woke groggy, but

it took less time to become alert. I recalled waking only once in the night. I longed for Walker to be by my side, but once I gained some consciousness and realized I was in the hospital, I just let the ache in my heart pull me back to sleep. It wasn't the same sleep I'd been in all summer long. I didn't return to an alternate existence when my mind drifted. It was quite the opposite, really. Nothing happened at all.

One of the first faces I woke to this morning was my little brother's. Conrad came to visit, and I was excited to see him in his true form. The last memory I had of him was one I wished would soon be forgotten. The smile that spread across his face reminded me I'd done right by coming home. Now, I couldn't imagine all the pain I would have brought to my family if I had stayed in Baylor. And it was difficult to forgive myself for having that as my plan for so very long.

"You *are* awake!" Con announced.

I smiled lazily and cleared my throat. "Hey there." Con came crashing into me with a big hug, and suddenly words didn't seem to matter anymore. There was nothing I could say that he hadn't already said for both of us with this loving gesture. He trembled as he grabbed me tight. At thirteen years old, he was as tall as I was, but much stronger. "It's okay. I'm okay." I promised. My throat and mouth were properly hydrated, and speaking was easier now.

"I thought you were going to die!" he choked.

"Conrad!" Mom scolded.

"What?"

"It's okay. I did too." I admitted. Of course, I wouldn't admit all of it. Nobody needed to know the extent of my nightmare.

"You did? Do you remember it?" Con asked, as he pulled back and sat with one leg stretched across my bed.

"Do I remember what?"

"Con. Please. She needs to rest," Mom said.

"What? She literally did nothing *but* sleep!" he protested, his voice cracking as he fought to become a man in a boy's body.

Mom sighed, and Dad rubbed her back. "Honey, it's okay. We have all the time in the world to talk about what happened, and you don't need to go over all of it right now."

"It's okay. Really. Do I remember what?" I asked. It was always like Mom to be overprotective, but I couldn't see how burying everything inside was going to help protect me now. I had already gone through months of damage. Months of being caught in a nightmare, ensnared in a web. If anything, not talking about it would probably do worse damage.

"Do you remember the crash?"

I took a deep breath and looked around the room. My eyes settled on Gran as she sat quietly in the corner of the room. So quietly, in fact, I hadn't realized she was there. I would have to ask my mom how she was doing when she wasn't present. Con's eyes followed my gaze before looking back at me impatiently.

I went over all the facts I'd known about the accident in my head. The car flew off an overpass of sorts. I was wearing a yellow blouse. There was another car that remained on top of the overpass. It was nighttime. The windows had shattered.

I thought long and hard about what it all meant. And I soon realized that most, if not all, of these memories were from seeing the accident from an outsider's perspective. My memories solely came as nightmares that had haunted me while I lay helpless in a coma. And because of that, I supposed I had no actual memory of the accident. I wasn't entirely sure where I was headed that night or why. I didn't even know if it had been my birthday, or if that was something I had made up in my head.

"I think I wore my yellow shirt?"

Mom beamed, encouraging me to continue.

"I think it was, maybe, my birthday?" I asked again, uncertain.

"Yes. It was your eighteenth birthday, and you were heading out to meet your friends," Dad said, and then added in a quiet voice, "You never came home . . ." I could see that he was trying to be strong for me, but his entire frame looked like it was ready to crumble. A strong man brought to the verge of breaking.

"I'm . . . I'm sorry. I didn't—"

"No! Don't you do that. This was *not* your fault! Do you understand? This was *not* your fault," Mom enforced.

"You—" Dad paused to take in a long quivering breath. "You were hit. The guy didn't even stop at the red light. We think he was intoxicated. Somebody said they saw that same car at the bar earlier in the night. You did everything right, so please don't blame yourself. We're just happy you're all right."

I looked into Mom's and Dad's eyes and went with it. Maybe the accident wasn't my fault. It's not like I could recall it myself, so I would have to take their word for it.

"What else do you remember?" Con prodded.

"Well, I remember a lot, actually. I dreamed about you," I said in a teasing voice.

"You did!?"

"I sure did. And I turned you to ice!" I said, twirling my finger around like a witch's wand.

"Wow, really?"

"Heck yeah! I had powers. You wouldn't believe the things I did this summer!"

The laughter in the room faded, and their eyes turned wary, flickering in unspoken concern among themselves. I had the sense I'd said something wrong again. It didn't look like anybody wanted to say the words out loud, but I wouldn't let it slide this time. They were all thinking *something*.

"What is it? What did I say?" I asked Con. He turned to my parents, so I too looked at them for answers. They silently debated, and I turned my questioning eyes to Gran. She slowly pointed to a calendar on the wall, indicating I would find my answers if I looked hard enough.

I had seen calendars countless times this summer, but this one was different. It was real. I'd grown accustomed to seeing only thirteen days in the month, but this one had a full month. I counted thirteen days crossed off in red marker. Honestly, I was just happy it wasn't written with blood. I bit my bottom lip and let it roll between my teeth, somewhere on the verge of fidgeting and finding pain to distract me from finding the answer on the wall. There was something about this calendar, something odd that I couldn't quite put my finger on. *May?* Had I been in a coma for nearly a year?

"How long was I in the coma for?" I asked, suddenly fearful.

"Thirteen days. Thirteen long, terrible days."

That made little sense. I looked back at the calendar. May? But that would mean that summer hadn't even begun yet. Had the entire two months I imagined in Baylor happened in just thirteen days in the real world? Had time slowed so much that I had experienced an entire summer before it had ever started?

"Only thirteen days?"

"Did you think it was more or less?" Dad asked.

"I . . . I thought I was gone all summer."

A nurse came to check on me, but she did little to interrupt our conversation. I let her move about as my family and I talked.

"Oh, heavens no! Not that long."

"Wait? Did you really dream?" Con asked.

"Um, yeah. I did. You wouldn't believe the things I saw."

The nurse stiffened by my side. "You remember having dreams while you were in the coma?" she asked.

"I know. It's probably impossible or something," I shrugged.

"Well, yes. That's what they'll tell you. But if I'm being honest," she lowered her voice and checked behind her shoulder for listening ears. "I hear all sorts of stories about dreams and out-of-body experiences while people are on the operating table, under anesthesia, in comas, you name it. I believe it," she said with a wink.

I grinned, feeling validated for the first time since waking. Like maybe I hadn't been as lost as I once believed.

"Are you going to tell us, or what?" Con interrupted my thoughts.

I laughed. His impatience used to drive me up the

wall, but now it seemed endearing. "What do you want to know?"

"Everything, of course. Start from the beginning, and don't leave out a single thing." He settled in, leaning his back against the foot of my bed where a pillow had been stashed. My parents laughed, and the nurse went about her work checking the machines and readjusting sticky things on my chest.

"Well, it's a long story, but here goes. I went to Baylor Lake for the summer with a group of friends."

It was just the beginning and already my mom was interrupting. "Fascinating! You've been planning that trip all year long with Lainey and Emma. You must have dreamed about it because that's what you were looking forward to doing after high school graduation!"

"Graduation?" I looked back at the calendar. The dates were a little foggy, but I knew that May was early for the summer break, and I had been in a coma for far less time than I had imagined. "Has that happened yet?"

"It's next month, dear."

My thoughts raced. How could I have spent my entire summer celebrating my high school graduation when it hadn't even happened yet? I thought back to my memories of graduation, and I couldn't pull up a single detail other than my gown and cap hanging from the windowsill in my bedroom.

"Yeah. I guess I was looking forward to celebrating," I

murmured. Dad squeezed Mom's shoulder as they waited for me to continue. It was hard for them to see my confusion, and I knew they felt sorry for me. I would have to try to hide it better next time. I didn't want them to worry any more than they already had.

"We went to Baylor Lake and stayed at Uncle Tanner's cabin all summer long. It was going to be the best summer I ever had. Until something terrible happened. Trinity died . . ." I lost myself for a moment in the memory of her body washing up on shore.

I really should have spared the details for my little brother's sake, but it was one of the first memories I had, and it just slipped out. I obviously wasn't going to tell them I had drowned right after my car accident. That would only make them feel more helpless. Right then and there, I decided not to tell them I once thought I was dead, either.

Mom's face turned pale, and Dad's forehead creased with worry. I realized I couldn't really tell them much of the story at all. I should keep all the horror locked up in a little box that nobody would ever find. It wasn't going to do anything but worry my parents anyway.

"Who's Trinity?" Con asked. He was eager to find out the rest of the story, as if it were no more than an old ghost story. That's how it was beginning to feel to me too.

I waved my hand toward my parents and then realized they were waiting for the answer, too. It's not like Trinity and

I had been the best of friends. I tried to think if she had ever come to the house. That's when I caught sight of the cards sitting on the bedside table. I became sidetracked and picked up the ones closest to me to read. Mom handed me the rest.

I had a beautiful card from Lainey, talking about how she was so sorry we wouldn't have the summer we planned before she headed off for college. I had another card from Emma, talking about how she would help me through recovery, and how we could watch endless movies together while I lay in bed and rested. I flipped through a few letters and cards from my family; Nora, Grandpa. But that was it. No letter from Trinity, no card from Noah. I thought back to all my friends and how I'd questioned their friendship over the summer. Maybe they weren't as good of friends as I'd thought they were.

"Did Lainey visit?"

"Yes, Lainey and Emma have been by every couple of days." There was no mention of anybody else, and I wondered why. It hurt. It brought me back to the night I'd drowned and nobody cared. Nobody noticed. It was one of the reasons I didn't want to come back to this life. Because I was tired of being invisible.

Con nudged me with his foot. "Oh, sorry. She's nobody. Just a friend from school. Anyway, we had a wonderful summer, really. We entered the bass tournament." I tried to find something positive to say.

"No way!" Dad exclaimed. He loved the tournament and looked forward to it each summer.

"Yeah. And Emma snuck a store-bought salmon onto the boat and pretended she caught it!" I laughed. It was a genuine laugh but clouded with confusion and an anxious energy. I was still a little cautious of how much to say, and I worried I didn't quite have a grasp on reality yet.

"What? There's no salmon in that lake!" Dad chuckled.

"Yeah, I know! It was so funny. I wish you were there. Um, let me think. We went to the Baylor Parade, and one of my friends got into a fight with Snow White's seven dwarves!!"

"Really?" Mom asked, nervously eyeing the book of fairy tales on the bedside table.

"Yeah. And I threw a ton of parties too. Sorry, not sorry." The laughter boomed. And for the first time, I realized there were several nurses and doctors crowded in the tiny room listening to my stories. The entire room was electric with excitement, and for a moment, everything felt right.

"We may have broken a few things," I frowned. She shrugged lightheartedly, and everyone laughed.

"What happened next?"

"Well, I met this boy," I said coyly. My brother was already bored, but the nurses drew closer. "His name was Walker, and he was so handsome! He took me for a ride in his canoe for the Fourth of July, and all the fireworks froze in time, just like streamers glittering down from the sky. It may have been a date." I shrugged.

Mom and Dad stiffened, and I could tell I'd said something wrong again. But with the audience I had in front of me now, I couldn't ask. I made a mental note to circle back when we were alone.

"We could reach out and grab the fireworks, and they fizzled in the palms of our hands. And this one time, I swam to the bottom of the lake where . . . Mermaids lived!"

It wasn't entirely honest, but after talking about how Trinity died, I wasn't going to give them anything else to harp on. And Lainey had looked majestic under the water occasionally. I remembered the way her hair floated in the dark water and danced around her freckled face. She was, at times, beautiful. This was the only side of the story that Con needed to know. That any of them needed to know. And I would take the rest to my grave.

"Could you breathe underwater?"

"No. But only because I didn't *need* to breathe at all."

"Could you fly?"

"No. But I *did* jump off a cliff. And fall off the Summerfield State Fair Ferris wheel!" I said enthusiastically.

"No way! Were you scared?"

I pretended to think it over. "Actually, it was pretty cool."

"What was the coolest thing you did?"

"Hmmm . . ." I tapped my finger on my chin. I looked to Gran to help jog my memory. "That's a hard question. I turned into a wolf at one point, and I think that was the best. I had claws and fangs, and I was gigantic! I stood on two feet and walked like a human. I even had the strength of a dozen men. But I could also control lightning and thunder with my thoughts, and I could manipulate bees and make movies come to life! Oh, and I could stop time, and walk on water, so it's a toss-up, I guess." Everyone erupted in gasps and laughter.

The room was packed with nurses and doctors, and I could barely see Gran sitting in the corner. "But now that I think of it, the best part of all was when Gran read me fairy tales from a rocking chair, by the light of a wood-burning fire," I said, smiling at her warmly. She smiled fondly and put her hand over her heart.

The room parted to follow my gaze, but something wasn't right. Several nurses shuddered. One doctor looked to have caught a chill as he ran his hand up and down his arm. A wary look passed between my family members and the medical personnel as the room fell eerily quiet. Embarrassment washed over me, but I didn't know why.

"Okay. I think that's enough for one day. Kinsley should get her rest," Mom announced. She ushered everyone out.

The nurses parted as my brother blurted out, "Do you

really think she saw Gran's ghost?" Mom sucked in a breath and smacked Con's shoulder.

I watched all the blue scrubs funnel out the door, whispering among themselves. As the room emptied, I stared at the lonesome seat where my gran had sat moments prior.

CHAPTER 15

The next several days I dealt with what my parents quietly described as withdrawal, but I knew more accurately as ignoring. I mentally checked out on things I couldn't care less about, but more importantly, the things I specifically didn't want to know. Like my craniotomy. Like the fun fact that they'd removed a portion of my skull so that my brain could swell outside of my head. What person in their right mind could possibly want to know the details of that? I had already witnessed the operation when I'd been stuck within the walls of the cabin. I didn't need to hear the medical jargon too.

I tried not to touch the shaved part of my head, because I'd rather pretend it never happened. But sometimes, when nobody was looking, I'd reach into my hair and feel the sharp points of the stitches. It made me feel like a modern Frankenstein. A product of science. Like two girls, Kinsley and Layla, had been stitched together to make one whole person. Because I'd never been enough to stand on my own.

I thought of Layla often. How I hadn't truly seen her during my time in Baylor, but seemingly she was actually a very important part of me. A part I hadn't recognized in myself and hadn't come to accept. Now, when I had a positive outlook on something insignificant or produced a wicked laugh at one of my brother's jokes, I would think of her. I hadn't realized how much my laugh sounded like a witch's cackle until now. Or had that been the rasp in my voice from having a breathing tube in my throat for thirteen days?

The week passed in a blur of check-ins with more doctors than I could count and a multitude of tests. Most of the doctors told me the same thing. I barely lived. Apparently, I only had a fifteen percent chance of survival. And even then, I wasn't expected to make a full recovery. Whatever that meant. They told me I was a miracle, but I didn't believe any of it. By and large, I knew it all boiled down to fate. *Something* had brought me back home, and it wasn't a statistic.

I had a lot of work ahead of me. I had a ton of recovery still to face, and it would be anything but easy. I wasn't looking forward to the challenge, and I often wished I were back in Baylor. I wished that my recovery was as simple as a thought that manifested before my eyes. That it was nothing more than something I could conjure in the cool mist. And sometimes Baylor seemed to be the lesser evil of the two realities. Though having a full recovery from a brain injury was going to be an uphill battle, sometimes I felt capable of that challenge. Most times I did not.

The staff was supportive, though, and they reassured my parents and me that my recovery was moving along faster than expected. Time seemed to crawl by, though, and I couldn't imagine taking things any slower. The more I was awake, the more I pretended not to be. And on several occasions, I rested while listening in on conversations I shouldn't have. Talk of my expected recovery. The pursuit of a possible lawsuit. How much money Nora thought she could pull from the kid who hit me, and whether he was drunk.

I heard them talking about what they called my hallucinations. Apparently, that's what Gran was. The doctor said it wasn't uncommon for somebody in my position to have hallucinations after a coma. And if somebody was hallucinating, it would make sense that they would choose to see a loved one who had passed on. The doctor said they see it all the time in the hospital. Gran made fewer and fewer appearances after I heard that conversation, and I figured they were right. Maybe I had only seen her because I wanted her comfort. And maybe she was the last manifestation I would ever have.

But there was one more conversation I heard and knew I shouldn't have. It was very hush-hush about the kid who was fighting for his life on the opposite side of the wall. When I was in the ICU, I thought about him often. I wondered if he was trapped in a nightmare like I was. And some nights, I fought the urge to sneak over and hold his hand. Other nights, I wanted to unplug him for all that he'd done to me.

At some point in my stay, maybe a week after waking, my time in the intensive care unit came to an end. I got moved to the lower level of the hospital for recovery. The nurses made a big show of it, clapping and lining the hall to the elevator. I tried to appear pleased with my progress, but all I really wanted to do was get a better look into the room next to mine. I could barely make out movement through the slats of the blinds. From what I could see, the kid had visitors.

The following week in recovery went by a little slower. Perhaps because I was awake for most of it. I'd taken several assisted walks throughout the days and was allowed outside for some fresh air. Both Lainey and Emma visited me, but one of the best surprises of all was seeing Gunner. Lainey snuck him in, and none were the wiser because Gunner was wearing his special vest that said he was working. When he jumped on my bed and gave me kisses, all my worry melted away.

It was when the kisses stopped that I realized how

uncomfortable Lainey was. She kept looking at the side of my head, and I knew she was afraid that Gunner would hurt me. I reassured her I was all right, but it didn't seem to help. I still had black circles under my eyes, gaunt cheeks, and if my hair was lying just right, you could see where the hair was shaved. It was going to take time for everyone to realize I wasn't as fragile as they thought. Thankfully, I could avoid all the reminders in the mirror. Lainey and Emma weren't so lucky.

Every single night, I went to sleep trying to get back to Baylor. I imagined the fair. The cabin. Sitting in Walker's canoe. But when sleep took over, the lights were out. The curtain had closed, and the magic show was over. The summer I spent in Baylor was gone, and I worried that it might be lost forever.

The night before I was to be discharged, I snuck out of my room. Walking was still difficult, and I felt unstable all by my lonesome. But I knew if I dragged my hand alongside the wall, I'd draw even more attention to myself, and I didn't want that. Luckily, I found an abandoned wheelchair and made a quick escape into the elevator. I pushed the button for the ICU floor and nervously played with my robe until the doors slid open.

I tightened my grip around the thin tires of the wheelchair as I peered around the corner. The hall was dim, but I still recognized a nurse working in the distance. I waited patiently until her desk was clear and then rolled myself as quickly as I could through the corridor of the ICU to the next hallway. I stopped at the room just before the one I'd been in.

Behind that door was the kid who almost took my life. A part of me wondered if it would bring me closure if I just snuck in and laid my eyes on him. If I looked at him and realized that he was only human. That he was hurt, too. Maybe then I wouldn't be so angry. Maybe I wouldn't feel like this terrible thing had happened to me, but rather, it happened to *us*.

I wheeled to a nearby corner and ditched the wheelchair. I stood up slowly and shakily and walked close to the wall. I didn't have long before the nurse came back to her desk, so I hobbled as quickly as my weakened legs could take me. Someone in a pair of scrubs came around the corner, and I turned the doorknob without a second thought and swiftly vanished from the hall.

Once in the dark room, I felt a sense of relief. I could probably stay here for a good amount of time without being caught. I didn't recall getting more than one or two checks in the night when I'd been in the ICU. I briefly wondered what they would do if they caught me here, but I was going home tomorrow, so I didn't care how awkward it might be. This was important, I told myself, as I thought of my empty bed and the possibility of a nurse coming to check on me. Would they sound an alarm? Code something? I hoped not.

In the dark, I grabbed the edge of the boy's bed and patted my way up to him. By the light of the monitors, he wasn't as young as I'd originally thought. From the outline of his body under the sheets, he didn't look like a boy at all. My parents had made him out to be a newly licensed driver. But he was probably older than me. It was hard to tell with how swollen his face was. His entire head was shaved, and a line of puckered stitches was carved down the side of his face. He looked to be in awful shape.

I listened to the rhythmic beat of his monitor, and I felt oddly at peace in his room.

I had anticipated the possibility of wanting to grab the pillow from behind his head and smother him for all he'd done to me. And I was fully prepared to drag myself out of his room, if that were the case. Because I knew that death was permanent in this realm. But I didn't get that urge, and I quietly thanked Layla for that.

A simple thought here wasn't enough to create something on its own, and there would be no conjuring in the hospital tonight. I wouldn't turn into a dark witch here, and the machine keeping him alive wouldn't malfunction, just because I thought about it. Which I did . . . several times.

As I stared at his closed eyelids, I wondered if he was dreaming. Did he remember more of the accident than I did? He obviously had the other half of the memory that I was missing. Would I ever pass him on the street? Would I know who he was? Or would he not be as lucky as to walk out of here?

I gazed oddly at his face. I thought this would be more of a monumental moment for me to sneak into his room and see him lying here, so helpless. But it wasn't all that I hoped it to be. It was just me, staring at another patient in the dark. Just me, watching a stranger sleep. Whoever he was, he wasn't in this room. Just like I had been far, far away, this guy was too.

Was he fighting to get back home like I had? Or had he made his choice to stay like I once wanted? That didn't sit well with me, and I frowned down at him. I didn't like the idea that he might escape this place by choice. If I had to go through recovery, he should, too.

I leaned over him, doing for him what Gran had done for me. "Come back. You must come back," I said, my voice still raspy.

I watched his motionless face, waiting for signs that he heard me. But there was no response. I recalled the book of fairy tales by my bedside and my mom singing to me when I was deep in sleep. I'd heard those things. They'd seeped into my subconscious and fed into my dreams. I hoped my words would do the same for him. I hoped they would be a beacon of light in an otherwise dark and twisted realm.

I didn't like the guy, and I was still angry with him for what he'd done to me—accident or not—but I needed him to pull through. I couldn't be the only survivor of the accident. Not that misery loves company, but rather misery loves hope. He was worse off than I was, and if he lived, then maybe I really had a chance at having a full recovery. Mentally and physically.

I decided my work here was done. There was nothing for me here, beyond satisfying my curiosity. But when my hands caught on his chart in the dark, a rush of mischievous delight coursed through my veins. Maybe there was something here for me? My Aunt Nora would be proud. I picked up the chart and squinted as I tried to read the tiny black print. The room was dark, and there were far too many words on the page for me to know where to begin.

A door closed nearby, and I feared they were doing midnight rounds. I hurried to place the folder back and scurried to the door. I cracked it open just as Cyndi, the nurse who had taken care of me in the ICU, emerged from the neighboring room. I panicked and my limbs froze, rendering me useless. The door opened and pushed me into a small dark corner between the curtain and the door. I held my breath as the nurse flipped on a set of dim lights. The door swung shut, exposing me. It was only a matter of time before she turned and saw me. I didn't move an inch, and I wished now, more than ever, I had the power of manifestation.

"Walker, Walker, Walker. How are you doing this fine

night? Is that pillow bothering you? Let me fix that," the nurse said as she moved about.

I couldn't believe my ears. In fact, I didn't. Did she say *Walker?* I felt faint. My knees grew weak, and my hands felt cold and tingly. The edges of my vision grew dark as I took a step out from behind the curtain.

"Did . . ."

Cyndi threw her hands in the air and yelled, alerting the other staff to my presence. It was the last thing I remembered before dropping to the floor. Unfortunately, I wasn't out long enough to avoid the discomfort of getting caught. I was sprawled on the floor when I regained consciousness. The security guard reached me before any other nurses or doctors. Cyndi calmed everyone down once she recognized me.

"I know her. She was my patient last week. They moved her downstairs. I'm not sure what she's doing up here. Maybe she got lost? Her room used to be next door," Cyndi said.

"Did she show any signs of aggression toward you?" the security guard asked. His boots were so close to my face, I could smell the rubber soles.

"Oh, heavens no. She just scared me, that's all. The poor thing took a step out and went down. I can't imagine how she got up here?"

"Okay. As long as you're all right, I'll get a wheelchair and escort her downstairs."

"Thanks, Charlie. I'll call a nurse to come meet you."

I sprang to life, grabbing Cyndi's arm as she passed by. "Did you say Walker?" Cyndi searched my frantic eyes, trying to make sense of my words. Then she patted my hand and freed her arm.

"It's okay, Kinsley. Mr. Charlie is going to take you back to your room now."

"But—"

"Shhh, you go get some rest."

"But, Cyndi! Cyndi!" my voice cracked.

The door closed behind Cyndi, and Charlie helped me into a wheelchair, adjusting my feet on the footrests. He spun me around so that he could back up through the door. My eyes fixed on the patient lying in the hospital bed. Was it really Walker? It couldn't be. Walker was a ghost. He didn't live in my world. He couldn't . . .

My eyes lingered on the stranger named Walker until the door shut rather too quickly between us. As we passed his window, I tried to look through the slats of the blinds, but I couldn't see past the darkness.

I turned, looking over my shoulder, somewhat panicked, and saw Cyndi on the phone. "Cyndi?" I waved my arm overhead. She barely lifted her gaze.

"Cyndi!" I called louder. She wiggled her fingers in my direction, dismissing me again. My heart pounded in my chest and my thoughts raced.

It took forever to get to my room, but after some initial

misinformation from the staff, Nurse Martina got me settled back in bed. She shook her head, making tsking sounds as she lifted the bed rails. But she knew it wasn't an accident and that I hadn't fallen out of bed.

"What did you do, Miss Wilde? Roll out of bed and sleepwalk back to your old room? Or were you sneaking up to that boy's room on purpose?"

"Do you know whose room I was in? A patient named Walker?" I pled for answers.

"No dear. I don't have patients in the ICU." Martina peered through thick false lashes and thought for a moment. "Do you know the boy? Is that why you were in there? Oh, honey, he'd better be a cute one if you went through all that trouble."

"Well, no, I don't know him. But—" Martina's forehead creased as she turned away. I panicked. I didn't want to be left alone. My thoughts were far too loud for solitude.

"He hit me!" I blurted out. Martina froze, and then reengaged.

"He *hit* you? That boy is in a coma."

"No. I mean yes, but not like that. His car hit my car. That's how we both wound up in the hospital."

"Oh!" Martina waited for me to continue.

"This is going to sound weird . . ." I tangled my fingers together as Martina sat on the edge of my bed. I could tell that she was into weird by the way she leaned in, yearning for more. She reminded me of Emma, and I smiled fondly.

"Oh, honey, there's nothing you can say that I haven't already heard. I've been working in this hospital for thirty-two years now, and I've heard a lot of weird in my day. Let's give it a go," she said, waving a hand as an invitation for me to continue.

"Well, okay. I had dreams when I was in my coma. You might have heard," I said with a shrug. She nodded, and I felt my cheeks heat. I waited for her to tell me it was impossible, but she barely batted an eye. She was used to this kind of thing, and I relaxed for the first time that night. "And in my dreams, there was a boy named Walker."

Martina pondered this.

"Don't you think it's weird that the boy next door, the very one who crashed into me, is also named *Walker*? I swear, I've never met another Walker in my life. It's not a very common name."

I hadn't realized when I'd done it, but at some point, I'd reached out and grabbed Martina's hand, pleading for it to be true. For the love of my life to be real, and not a phantom, trapped in a dream I could never return to.

Martina thought long and hard, and I waited with bated breath, but her words weren't what I hoped to hear. "Ohhh, I see now. While it's true, some people dream in a coma, it's more likely that you heard his name from the paramedics and staff at the hospital, and that's how his name entered your dream."

A blanket of defeat draped over my shoulders, and I

hunched over. I would have given anything for it to be true, for Walker to be real. Now that I knew Layla was a part of me, I understood that Walker hadn't been deceitful like I once thought. He loved me. All of me. No matter where the bits and pieces of my soul scampered off to.

"Have you ever had a dream that it was raining, and when you woke up, the rain was so loud on your roof that it entered your dream?"

I shook my head, unable to look at her without tearing up.

"Hmm. Have you ever had a dream that you had to pee, and when you woke up, you *really* had to pee?"

"Yeah . . ." I admitted.

"It's like that. Only more complicated."

"But I had all sorts of dreams! My friends were there! And this girl named Layla Barns was lost, but then we found her!"

"Layla Barns?" Martina sat back with a gaping smile. I frowned, and she broke into rolling laughter.

"Oh, honey. This is exactly what I'm saying. They've been showing reruns of *Starlet* all month! Layla Barns has been playing nonstop on the television."

"Huh?"

"Yeah! The new season is coming out soon, and they're playing reruns. It's a promotion or something. *Starlet*, seasons one through eight. I've seen it fifty times this month. But we all know and love Layla. And since she's been on TVs throughout the hospital, it only makes sense that you've heard her name several dozen times. I know I have. These things have a way of seeping into your subconscious, honey. Heck, I've probably dreamed of Layla Barns at this point!" Martina rolled her eyes. "Don't think another thing of it. Mystery solved." Martina stood and dusted her hands as if she had a hard day's work, when all she really did was crush my soul.

"The main character in *Starlet* is Layla Barns?" I asked, though I already knew the answer. If you would've asked me when I was ten years old what my favorite show was, I would have said *Starlet*. Layla was so popular that I once had a poster of her on my wall. I even dressed up as her for Halloween that year. No wonder I felt inferior to her. She was my childhood idol.

"Huh. She kind of looks like you, now that I think of it. Get some rest. And stay in bed!" Martina turned out the light, leaving me alone in the dark. My thoughts clamored in my head.

If Layla Barns was just a character on a TV playing in the background, then likely, Walker was just the name of the patient next door. Or perhaps we did share an ambulance ride together. I had plucked his name from someone's mouth and given it to the guy of my dreams. A character I had made up all on my own. And just like Layla had never been a real person, neither had Walker.

CHAPTER 16

After a summer in Baylor and two weeks in the hospital, I thought I would be happier to go home. The thirteen days I'd spent in Baylor had seemed like an eternity, and the two weeks following passed in a blur of confusion, disappointment, and drugs. I got used to sleeping with all the noises throughout the night, and I worried my house would be too quiet.

Martina was one of my favorite nurses, even if she didn't believe in all that I wanted her to. But what I loved most about her was her willingness to keep me company when she should have been working. Most of the other staff avoided talking to me about my experience as if it were taboo. As if they believed in science but witnessed the unexplainable way too often while working in the hospital. But Martina asked questions, and I appreciated that. I tried not to talk about it with my family as openly as

I did my favorite nurse, because I knew it worried them. And my parents had enough on their plates.

Was I excited about going home? Not really. Home was not my little house in Clover anymore. Home was the cabin, and I knew I wouldn't be returning there again. Not in my dreams, at least. I tried to imagine the day I'd go back to the cabin in real life, but I couldn't picture it.

I wasn't exactly excited to leave the hospital, either. While there was a part of me that yearned for normalcy, there was another part that didn't want to leave the stranger named Walker behind. I still had mixed feelings about him, but the part that ate at me the most was, *what if?* What if he *was* my Walker? I thought back to the time he'd said we were more alike than I knew. I wondered if he'd been trying to tell me that he, too, was alive and dreaming. Though every time I thought about it, I'd shake my head. *Impossible.* Even *I* didn't believe it.

With all the headaches, confusion, and muscle atrophy came anger. I didn't like to admit it, but I was growing angry with Walker. Not the one I'd fallen for, but the one who'd hit me. The one who lay unconscious in the hospital. I didn't deserve what happened to me on the night of my birthday, and I knew I'd be dealing with the consequences of the accident for far too long. In all honesty, I wasn't sure I'd ever recover from the psychological damage I'd undergone. If it was just a dream, why hadn't I forgotten it already?

Martina helped Dad load me into the back seat of our car. She gave me a quick hug goodbye. "It was a pleasure taking care of you, honey. Don't come back now, you hear?" she said with a wink.

"I won't. Promise."

Dad shut the door, and my parents spoke to the nurse for a few minutes longer. I ran my hands across the seat and relished the leather smell. It wasn't the best smell in the world, and it was far from new, but it wasn't the hospital, and I loved that. My eyes wandered through the parking lot and settled on a few people coming and going from the hospital. A wave of melancholy crept up on me.

"Ready to go home?" Mom asked, as she got into the car.

I forced a smile and nodded. I only wished I felt whole and happy. But leaving the hospital was like leaving something behind. I knew I was taking Layla with me, but I was leaving Walker there. Or at least, my idea of him. Every time I tried to find the truth somewhere inside of me, all I found were more questions.

A tear pricked the corner of my eye as we pulled out of the parking lot, and a very serious part of me wondered if I would ever be happy again. I knew the road to recovery was going to be a long one, but I hadn't expected it to be mental, too. I was an idiot for thinking I only had to deal with physical pain. What lay ahead now was a whole lot worse than any pain I could ever bear, and it would run deep, scarring me from the inside out.

"What's that, Mom?" I asked, pointing to a bag in her hand. I hadn't noticed it before, and it appeared she was trying to hide it.

"Oh. It's nothing." Dad pulled his eyes from the road to look warily at her. It only stoked my curiosity more.

"Well, it doesn't look like *nothing*." For a moment, I watched the distress pass between them.

"It's just a bag of your clothing, from the accident. Your cell phone, jewelry . . . We're going to dispose of it when we get home. We didn't want to upset you," Dad said, checking my reflection in the rearview mirror. He took my mom's hand across the center console, like they were lending each other strength.

I sighed heavily and looked out the window. My favorite yellow top was in that bag. But they were right to throw it away. I'd never wear it again. In fact, I'd probably never wear yellow again. Was this how superstitions were born?

"I'm getting a new phone, right?"

"Yes. We'll get you a new phone. We just want you to recover first."

Conrad greeted us in the driveway when we got home. He helped me walk inside and supported me when our dog, Roxie, leapt against my leg. She usually had a sweet disposition, but today, I was greeted with a rambunctious jumble of black fur and white paws. She was overly excited to see me, and it brought a smile to my face. "Hi, girl! I missed you too!" I said, scratching the top of her head as she stretched up my leg. It was always nice to be missed.

"She wasn't the only one who missed you," Dad said, as he kissed my forehead. I smiled up at him. Even though it was genuine, it was also a distraction. I caught sight of Mom tossing the bag of my bloodied belongings in the trash beneath the sink.

"Is it okay if I just lie down in my room?" I asked. It seemed like a lot of pressure, just being home. And even though they probably weren't, I felt like my family was watching me. Judging me. Analyzing my behavior and wondering if I would ever be normal again. I wasn't sure I would be.

"Of course. I'll help you upstairs," Mom said.

Once we reached my bedroom, she hovered in the doorway.

"I'm okay, Mom. I just need to rest." I began to close my door, and Roxie ran through the small crack before it shut.

"I love you."

"I love you too, Mom."

I took in my room for a moment and sighed in relief. My graduation gown was no longer hanging in the window. Would I ever be able to wear it? I fought with myself internally, mentally separating the memory that I had already graduated with the fact that I hadn't. Like two sides of the same coin, they both seemed to exist in one reality or another.

My bed was freshly made, and I grappled with the memory of Walker and me clinging to one another the last time I had thought I was in my bedroom. But it was just another fake memory. Another moment that felt as real as this one now, but wasn't. I saw no real distinction to separate fact from fiction, other than the timing. The summer was as fake as a spray tan. Separating these memories were difficult and would be time consuming.

Roxie jumped onto my bed and curled into a little black ball at the foot of the bed. I wanted to join her, but caught myself looking out my window at Noah's house. Just a few doors down was the guy I'd crushed on for the last couple of years. I wondered what he was up to now and what he'd heard about my accident. It made me sick to my stomach thinking about all the kids at school talking about it like some hot gossip. There were probably many rumors floating around. I suddenly understood why my parents weren't eager to replace my broken phone. I guess ignorance was bliss.

I slipped into a light trance as I stared out my window. I was beginning to feel the comfort of being home, and it made me sleepy. I found myself swept into a daydream about returning to school, and it seemed almost natural when I saw Gran's reflection in the window beside my own. My heart warmed under her gentle gaze, and I finally found the peace I'd been looking for since leaving the hospital. It seemed as if I would survive this mess, if only Gran stayed by my side. I begged for it to be true, though somewhere in the back of my mind, I knew it wasn't.

"Welcome home, dear," a faint voice said, somewhere between my ears. My eyes strained as I pulled back from my daydream and fixed them on Gran's reflection. What was this? How was I seeing her? Did I really hear her speak? Would I have to report this hallucination to my parents?

I didn't want to scare Gran away. If it was truly her ghost visiting me from the other side, I knew what I did next would be crucial. If I looked away from her reflection too quickly, she would likely disappear. But if I remained calm, acted as if it was no big deal, and turned my head ever so slowly, she might just stay. I swallowed a rising lump in my throat and slowly moved my gaze from her reflection to the woman standing next to me.

Gran smiled crookedly, just as she'd done before. Only this time she was in my bedroom, and I knew she was dead. My eyes grew dry, but I was afraid to blink her away. "Is that you?" I whispered, barely audible.

"Dear, who else would I be?" She laughed, and this time I swore I heard her distant voice brush against my ear. Was I hearing this outside of my head? Did that make me crazy? I couldn't deal with the dry eyes any longer. I blinked repeatedly. But no matter how many times I closed my eyes, Gran was still standing before me when I opened them again. Her green eyes still shining bright and pure.

"But, Gran, how?"

"Your mind is still somewhat flexible, dear. You haven't fully recovered, and because of that lack of rigidness, you are able to see what most cannot."

"Are you dead? Really, truly, gone?" I asked, unable to tell from looking at her.

"Am I?" Gran looked down at her own body. Her eyes came back to me as she smiled, and I took it as an invitation to look her over. She was a real, live ghost. My eyes trailed from the deep creases around her eyes down to her liver-spotted hands. "How can I be *truly* gone if I'm also here?"

"Are you really here, I mean?" I whispered, suddenly afraid my family might hear me speaking to myself. What would they think?

"I am, if you want me to be. But if I'm scaring you, dear, I'll go," she said, motioning toward the door, although I imagined she meant it figuratively. She wasn't really going to walk out the door. Would she? Would Con see her too?

"No!" I blurted, and then reminded myself to lower my voice. I looked back at Roxie, who had sat up at the edge of my bed. Her head was cocked to the side with one ear perked up and the other folded over. Did she see Gran too? Or was she just perplexed by me talking to myself?

"Don't go. Please. I need you. Will you stay with me?"
I pled quietly.

"Of course, dear. I'll stay as long as you need me to."

I nodded and stepped away cautiously, checking over my shoulder multiple times to make sure she was keeping her promise. I crawled into my bed and pulled the covers up to my chin. Roxie cuddled up next to me, resting her head on my arm.

A lazy yawn escaped me, and my eyes fell to half-mast. It was midafternoon, maybe three or four o'clock, but the time didn't matter much. After spending so long in Baylor, I wondered if time would ever matter again.

Even though I had been haunted by my own insecurities in Baylor, I had glimpses of my strengths. But my true reality was quite sad. I had no genuine pride in myself. Very few friends. And I had often felt like a ghost myself, walking in the halls of my high school. So, if I had to teeter on the edge of psychosis and allow myself to believe my gran was near, then that's what I would do. I saw no other choice. I couldn't do this alone.

"Gran, you're going to be here a very long time. You might as well get settled in."

"All right, dear." Gran snuggled next to me on the bed, and goose bumps covered my arms as I realized the bed hadn't dipped under her weight.

Before, I had struggled to distinguish fact from fiction. I'd been consumed with trying to decipher what was real and what was not. But as Gran lay next to me reciting old fairy tales, I could no longer fight my phantom reality, nor did I *want* to. Because even though I knew she wasn't real, in my heart of hearts, I knew she was the only thing that would keep me going. And if my heart loved her that much, then she was real enough.

CHAPTER 17

It was dark and cold, and something in the air spoke of familiarity. Feelings of déjà vu coursed through my veins. A small light flickered in the distance, and I was under the overpass again. It was the scene of my accident, and it appeared as though I was early. I shivered, looking for Gran.

In slow motion, headlights grew bigger and brighter. There was a screeching that I hadn't heard in times before. Tires? Tires skidding on asphalt? A loud crash shook me to my core. I instinctively shielded my head and cowered.

The four-door sedan soared through the sky as I uncoiled. Parts of the guardrail chased after it, in a race that none wanted to win. I was pretty sure this memory would be etched into my mind forever. A continuous loop to play through my head on nights I felt anxious, tired, or stressed. A feed that would play while I slept for years to come, shaping the very person I would grow to be.

I spotted the yellow top against the window, and I hurt for the girl trapped in the car. Out of all the times I'd seen this crash, I never once felt what it was like to be me, trapped within. I had no memory of being struck, or of the fear I'd felt from the impending crash, though I was positive I'd been terrified. If I didn't have the scars to prove it happened, I might have thought it was another fake memory of the long-lost summer that never was.

But for reasons beyond me, I remembered standing under the overpass. Remembered the way the windows shattered and the glass danced through the starry night sky. How each tiny shard of glass captured the reflection of the headlights and sparkled like diamonds, cutting through the night that almost took my life. And I'll never forget how there was nobody there to save me. How desolate and quiet it had been after the cars had settled.

The sedan scrunched like an accordion and fell onto its roof. I let the debris finish falling before I stepped out of the shadows. Then I walked to the wreckage, singing Mom's lullaby to keep me company. "My heart blooms . . . Blooms for you . . . Wildflowers because of you . . ." My trembling voice filled the silence in the dead of the night, but it brought little to no comfort.

There was a mass of dark hair pressed against the broken window. I was thankful that my face was covered.

Some things didn't need to be seen. The bright yellow fabric faded as I peered curiously into the window. It was the brightest color in this dreadful nightmare, and it was being leeched before my eyes. I watched it turn from a bright poppy yellow to a dreary gray. And just as the last bit of yellow disappeared inside the wreckage, it reappeared on me.

I wore a satin shift dress, as dark as the night sky. But at the very bottom of the hem, a splash of hope ignited. Yellow seeped up the dress like a sponge, and before I knew it, my entire shift was as bright as the sun on a warm, summer day. My hair curled and wound around my shoulders, and my pale, cold skin warmed. A new life breathed inside of me.

I took a step back, trying to examine the changes that had taken place, and I nearly stepped on my broken cell phone. I stared in awe at the single glass slipper on my foot. I wiggled my free toes against the asphalt. Was I dreaming again? Was I finally the princess?

I tried to get a better look at the car perched above the overpass. From what I remembered, it was some time before the ambulance would arrive. It was far in the distance that a shadow figure stood by the other wrecked car. I had seen this before, and I remembered how it frightened me.

If I was dreaming, my fears could very well be conjured at any moment. But unlike before, I knew I wouldn't die, no matter how bad the nightmare got. I owed it to myself to find out what I could about the guy who'd hit me. I placed one foot in front of the other, trembling as I grew closer to the dark shadow. The last thing I wanted to do was walk right into the hands of the Grim Reaper himself. But I had to know who caused this accident, and I had to look for clues as to why. I'd probably never get this chance again.

Although the figure didn't move as I hobbled on one heel and one bare foot up the desolate off-ramp, I still felt as if it were watching me, turning its head ever so slightly. I had an odd sensation in my chest, as if a magnet was pulling me forward, even when I was afraid. As if I was under a spell, drawing near the shadowed figure.

I tiptoed around the back of the vehicle and met the figure in front of the headlights. It was a man. Or perhaps a ghost or dreamer. I could tell that his soul was wounded by the deep sadness I felt as I grew near, and I was no longer afraid he had come to steal my life. But I was worried about the guy inside the car. The one named Walker. Because he was on death row at the hospital, and maybe this man was here for him.

"Excuse me?" I asked softly. What was I doing? Would I protest? Argue for his life? The figure did not move.

"Excuse me, sir?" His back remained still and rigid as he peered down at the wrecked car.

A life for a life? No . . . I couldn't do that to my family. I only just got home.

I took a step back and peered into the driver's seat of the deformed car. My heart stopped as I saw Walker, bloodied and unconscious. This was not *just* the Walker who had hit me, but the guy of my dreams. The guy I had fallen in love with. The one I had spent a summer at Baylor Lake with, paddling across the lake and fighting demons in the haunted forest with. I had dreamed of this guy for two months straight, and he was *real*.

He wasn't a ghost. He never was. I stumbled back, my single glass slipper clattering on the road.

The shadow turned. Walker wore a navy blue, slim fitting suit, and he was holding my glass slipper between his white-gloved hands. His golden eyes pierced the night and emanated a deep sorrow that I would never forget as long as I lived.

Was this another one of Gran's fairy tales? Had she been reading to me before I fell asleep? I took a step back, my bare foot falling over sharp glass.

"Don't hurt yourself," Walker said. He crossed the short distance between us and kneeled down, sliding the glass slipper over my bare foot. I quickly glanced at the car, seeing his body slumped over in the driver's seat. He returned my foot to the ground, his fingers lingering on my ankle. I shifted my weight onto the other heel and stood a little taller.

"I don't understand." I looked into his eyes as he rose to full height. His gloves were soft under my forearms as I rested my hands on his chest. This was no dream. This was just like being in Baylor.

"We are more alike than you think." His brows knitted as he tilted his head to the side. I'd heard that before.

There was something in the way he spoke. Something in the way his voice sounded. It was different. Or maybe I was receiving it differently. Maybe, because I wasn't under the influence of the propofol any longer, everything was clearer. As if an invisible filter had been lifted.

"What do you mean? Is that you over there? Did you hit me?" I asked.

Walker's mouth fell open. He began to look at the car, but stopped. He couldn't bear it. "I tried to tell you."

"When?!" I nearly shouted. I must have been more upset than I realized. But I couldn't think of a single time he'd tried to tell me.

"I tried to tell you everything, Wilde. I tried to *show* you everything. But you only saw what you wanted to see. I'm *not* the man you think I am," he said in a broken voice. I had heard him say that before too, only it wasn't said to me. He'd said it to Layla. It didn't count.

I trembled. The warmth from my transformation was over, and this was no ball. The night was chilly, and the secrets were drifting freely in the air. Walker slipped off his jacket and wrapped it around my shoulders. I eyed the suspenders over his white button-down shirt. At least he was a gentleman. Could I fault him for telling only one of me? Or was it I who hadn't wanted to listen?

"Then who are you?" I had nothing left to lose, and a life without answers felt like the worst torture now.

Walker sighed. "Well, for starters, I'm that guy," he said, pointing to the figure with blood running down his face, unconscious over his steering wheel.

I peered through the windshield, and my heart broke for Walker. It was one thing seeing myself in the wreck, but it was an entirely different thing seeing him. I felt detached from my body as it lay broken in the car. I couldn't feel the pain or remember the fear. It was sad to see, and I wanted to help myself, but it didn't feel . . . *real*. But as I looked at Walker's lifeless body, I felt oddly protective.

"Is that . . . Is that what happened here?" I asked, as I gently ran my fingers across the scar on his eyebrow.

Walker nodded. It was the first time I felt like I truly understood. All this time, I'd imagined his guilt had been for taking Layla's life. And now I knew. I was Layla.

I trailed my hands down his suspenders. How could I have been so blind? How had I lived an entire summer under a sun of lies?

There was really only one question that burned in me now, and it was the question I was most afraid to ask. "Are you going to make it?" I fixed my eyes on a tiny pearl button in the middle of his chest.

Walker took my hand in his and wrapped one arm around my waist, pulling me close. He took a step out to the side, and I followed ungracefully. Before I knew it, we were slow dancing in the glow of his headlights. I rested my head on his chest, and I swore I could smell his cologne. It reminded me of the very first night I met him. When I had feared for my life. Now, I only feared for his.

The silence grew into an answer I didn't want to hear. I'd just found him, and I wasn't able to keep him. This really was a curse.

"What else did you try to tell me?" I was open now. I'd taken off my armor, and I was ready to hear the truth. All the ugly truth, and all the beautiful poison.

"I tried to tell you I fell in love with you. That I loved you from the very start. That you and I were meant to find each other. I tried to tell you I would have married you, if only given a second chance."

I lifted my head from Walker's chest and I tried to read the pain in his eyes. "But you said Layla—"

"You *heard* Layla. You were so afraid of getting hurt, you pretended I was in love with another girl. Hell Wilde, you were so afraid of being somebody wonderful that you cast that girl into the shadows. You have to understand that you are *everything* to me. All the good, and all the bad."

"How? How do you know?" How was he so sure of himself? I'd never been sure of myself.

"My heart knows you. It always has."

Somewhere, far, far in the distance, I heard a siren. My breath quickened, as I knew our time was running out. "And I don't deserve you," Walker whispered, dipping his forehead to mine.

"What do you mean?" I asked, pulling out of his hands. This sounded like a goodbye. A goodbye that I couldn't bear.

Walker winced. His forehead began to bleed profusely. He reached up, staining the tips of his white gloves. I tried to cover it with my hands, but I didn't know how to help. He writhed in pain and dropped to one knee.

"Walker!" I kneeled down next to him, searching for a way to help him.

The ambulance pulled up to Walker's car first. The lights shined brightly upon us, but nobody could see the two star-crossed lovers caught in the rays of light. The paramedics hurried to assess the accident.

"Help!"

A paramedic crouched by the vehicle.

"Help him!" I yelled, trembling in the thin dress and glass slippers. I begged and pleaded as Walker crumbled into my arms. But we were *nothing* in their world. Not sound nor sight. Not even a prayer.

The poppy yellow of my dress faded to white,

camouflaging me even further in the light of the high beams. I shielded my eyes with a bloodstained hand. Walker's full weight collapsed on top of me as I continued to plea, my cries useless. An intense light brightened all around us until I couldn't see anything at all.

Walker wasn't just a manifestation. Nor was he a ghost. He was real, and he was stuck in another world. A world that was quickly coming to an end.

CHAPTER 18

I watched the steering wheel as Mom drove me to physical therapy. I wondered what it would feel like in the palms of my hands, as Mom babbled about my missing homework and other responsibilities I couldn't care less about. Nothing seemed to matter anymore. Deep down, I knew she felt it, too.

"That reminds me. I need to drive you down to pick up your last check from the art gallery. They won't release it to me, and it's only good for six months."

"Really? It's probably only fifty dollars." I shrugged.

"I know. But we should do it soon, if not today. I heard they were going out of business. Tammy said she heard Mr. and Mrs. Vandal have been laundering money through the art gallery, and they're currently being audited. You don't need to be wrapped up in that mess."

Mr. and Mrs. Vandal? Laundering money? They were

always a little weird. I thought little of it. "Yeah. It's probably true," I said absentmindedly.

We arrived at physical therapy, and Mom walked me inside. My eyes wandered over the colorful mats and resistance bands as she checked me in. This was my new reality. Three times a week, I would be lifting medicine balls, stretching hot pink bands around my ankles, and doing anything else my therapist thought would build back the strength I'd lost while in the coma. The regimen started slowly but grew in difficulty. Sometimes, it was downright agonizing. But when I wanted to give up, I'd see Gran's reflection stretched in a full-length mirror, and it gave me the motivation I needed to continue.

IT WAS WITH GREAT APPREHENSION THAT I LOWERED my hands to the steering wheel, determined to drive myself to the art gallery. I wrapped each finger around the leather, and I held on through the emotional roller coaster I was riding.

My breath caught in my throat, and I had to remind myself to breathe. Each breath was more shallow than the next, and the more I tried to calm down, the worse it got. It was the first time I'd sat behind the wheel of a car since my birthday, and it was terrifying.

It was an amazing thing how my body remembered something my mind couldn't. How physically afraid I was, even though I had blocked the accident from my memory. My hands seemed locked around the steering wheel, and my muscles were clenched tightly. It took some time before I could lean back and sink into the seat. I was afraid I would never be comfortable driving again. What if I became so afraid, I hyperventilated and blacked out? What happened when you passed out behind the wheel? I guess I already knew.

Part of a healthy adult life is independence. I thought I'd gotten that when I moved to Baylor, but I was wrong. It appeared my independence had been stripped from me, and I was moving backward in life. In many more ways than driving. I couldn't bear to live my life alone. I wasn't stable enough. I wasn't strong enough. And the pressure to do so made it harder to try. And the longer I waited, the more fear grew.

If I could pick up my check from the art gallery by myself, I'd claim a small piece of my independence back. The only problem was, I was sitting in a parked car inside my garage, and I was fighting a full-blown panic attack. The garage door hadn't even opened yet, and I could almost see the ambulance arrive.

My eyes fixed on the dashboard, but I wasn't really

seeing it. There was an image on the edge of my memory, and it was trying to break through. Something about how the stereo was playing my favorite song and how the night was dark and desolate. I could see it now, just as if I were there.

There were no cars on the road as I turned off the highway. My light was green as I drove up the off-ramp toward the intersection. The headlights came out of nowhere, blinding me. The car headed straight for me. I remembered lifting my hands off the wheel to shield my face, but I had no concept of what the impact and lack of control would do to me.

Suddenly, the back of the garage door came back into my sights. That was it. That was all I could remember. Exiting on the off-ramp and headlights blinding me. Was the rest of the memory also locked somewhere inside? The part where I skidded off the overpass and crashed below?

I didn't want to remember from behind the wheel. What if, when I finally remembered, I was driving? What if my eyes were hijacked, and the memory played while I was driving sixty-five down the highway?

A face appeared at my window, and I nearly jumped out of my seat, my hands unlocking from the steering wheel for the first time. Mom knocked on the window again. Her face hung with concern. I was ashamed, not only for trying to be independent, but for failing at it.

"What are you doing? You can't drive," Mom said.

"Obviously. I wasn't." Because I would if I could. Because I would've been gone if I had the courage. If I wasn't damaged.

Mom's face softened, and she walked around the car and got into the passenger seat. She sat silently with me, waiting for me to crack. It didn't take long.

"Am I ever going to drive again?" My voice was shaky with pent-up emotion.

"Of course you will, in time." In time. In time. Everything took time. What if I didn't want to wait any longer?

"I remembered." I pulled my clammy hands from the leather and wiped them on my jeans. "I remembered the green light, and turning into the intersection. There were no cars on the road that night. It was late. His car came out of nowhere."

Mom sniffled, tapping a tear from the corner of her eye with a trembling hand. "What's wrong?"

"It's nothing," she whispered.

"Mom, it's not nothing. Tell me."

"I always told myself it was better you didn't remember. Because what I went through, watching you struggle to survive, I could never forget. And it haunts me. I'm so worried that your memories will come flooding back and haunt you like mine have haunted me."

I thought about what she'd said. I wasn't worried about

remembering the accident. Only not being able to control when the memory took hold of me.

I had been tortured for an entire summer. I had forged friendships based on life-and-death situations and the need for family in a time of solitude. I had fallen in love and chosen to spend my eternity living a life of make-believe. I'd turned into a monster, and my deepest fears were those that were caused by my hands, my thoughts, and my worry. When I'd woken up, all those relationships I nurtured were fake. They simply never happened. I had thought I felt alone in Baylor, but that was nothing like the loneliness that had followed me into this world.

As I watched my mom wipe the tears from her eyes, it sank in just how depressed I really was. From the look on her face, my biggest fears should have been flashbacks of the accident. From the conversations we'd had, my biggest obstacle should have been physical therapy. But what I was dealing with was so much darker. And I never wanted her to know.

I looked into the rearview mirror when I felt somebody's eyes on me. There sat Gran, quietly watching us. I had been conjuring my dead grandmother because I was too afraid to be alone. It was that bad.

My thoughts were unstable. I couldn't tell the dreams from reality, and I had to constantly remind myself that the time I'd spent in Baylor didn't exist. It felt as though all my friends had turned their backs on me. As if I was going through a dozen breakups all at once. But the truth was, we were never friends at all.

I took my mom's hand in mine. "You don't have to worry about that, Mom." She didn't. But I wasn't being entirely honest, either. I looked back into the rearview mirror and caught Gran's eyes—a disapproving shade of forest green. "Honestly, I haven't been dreaming much at all."

"Really? You had so many dreams while you were in the hospital. Have they stopped?"

"Yeah. Pretty much." I tried to make my tone lighthearted, and it seemed to work. Mom appeared more relaxed. But Gran was frowning.

I'd only had one dream. And it wasn't even a dream, per se. At least, I told myself it was more than that. It felt like more. So much so, I'd tried to get back to the void on several occasions. I tried to see Walker again and again. Night after night. But nothing worked. As soon as I fell asleep, that was it. The darkness took over, and I couldn't remember a single thing come morning.

"What do you think about talking to somebody?" Mom asked.

"What do you mean?"

"Like a therapist."

"I don't need a therapist, Mom," I said, feeling slightly offended.

I knew I was in awful shape. I didn't need anyone else

knowing it. And I was afraid that if I told somebody, out loud, what was actually going on in my head, it would somehow become more real. More dangerous. And I would be labeled for the rest of my life as somebody who'd had an accident and never fully recovered. But if I just kept it to myself, I thought I could hide the severity. And perhaps, one day, have a better chance at a normal life.

"I'm worried about you. I think it would help. You don't have to talk about anything you don't want to. You could just talk about, I don't know, your dreams, if you wanted." Mom's voice hitched, and it caught my attention.

"I could talk about my dreams?"

"Oh yeah. Maybe a therapist could help you figure out why you had the dreams you did. And see if there's any meaning to them. You know, sometimes dreams mean something."

"Yeah. I think you're right. Maybe," I said. I wasn't interested in doing a deep dive into my feelings of inadequacy, but talking about my dreams seemed like it might be nice. I kept it all inside because I didn't want my family to worry. And I knew my friends would never understand.

I suddenly became excited about the thought of offloading all my baggage, and hope grew that maybe a therapist could help me unravel the mystery that was Walker. Who knows, maybe they've seen this before?

Maybe they could hypnotize me and help me get back to him?

"I'll make you an appointment?"

I nodded.

"In the meantime, I can drive you to the art gallery."

"Thanks, Mom, but if you don't mind, I was going to see if Lainey could take me."

An hour later, I got into Lainey's car and smelled the sweet aroma of vanilla. It was the thing I loved most about riding in her car. She always had air fresheners that smelled divine. Especially after the summer sun had baked the scent into the upholstery.

"Thanks for the ride," I said, picking up a soda from the center console. She always brought me a drink when she drove. It was one of the sweet quirks I adored about her. I was really going to miss her when she moved away for college.

"Anytime!"

"Anytime . . . For the next two weeks," I amended.

"For the next two weeks, anytime. After that, you're on your own," Lainey laughed. I did too, but it wouldn't be funny when she left.

Emma was leaving too, but not until the end of summer, and even then, she wouldn't be far. Lainey was moving clear across the country, and I would only see her if she came back to visit her family for the holidays.

"I just have to pick up my check from the art gallery.

My mom said they were under investigation for laundering money." I sipped my soda, and the bubbles tickled my nose.

"Oh, wow. I should've brought Gunner!" Lainey frowned.

"Where is he?" I glanced into the backseat.

"My mom has him."

"Are you going to take him with you when you move?"

"Yeah. My mom jumped through a bunch of hoops so I could have him with me."

"That's good. Maybe I'll have to come visit and take him on walks while you're in class," I laughed. Lainey didn't know the extent of the relationship Gunner and I had built in my head, but I liked to think Gunner remembered.

"You'll be too busy with classes of your own," Lainey said, looking at me sharply from the corner of her eye. Like any best friend would, she knew something had gone unsaid.

"Actually, I've decided to take some time off before going to college. I don't think I want to do art history, anyway."

"Really? What are you going to do then?" This rattled Lainey to her core. She had been so regimented with her credits, aligning classes like they were pieces on the chessboard of life. Each move was a step in climbing the ladder to success. She was calculated and always in control. The thought of me not knowing my future was enough to give her anxiety.

"Honestly, I don't even know. I really want to write movies, but I just worry it would be an uphill battle."

"Maybe taking a little time off won't be so bad. You've certainly been through enough. I'm sure your family would love to take care of you for another year while you get back on your feet."

"I'm sure they would. It's right here on the left," I said, pointing into a parking lot.

"This is where the drug deals go down?" Lainey joked.

"This is it!"

Lainey parked, and we walked quietly into the art gallery. I was surprised to see most of the paintings had been taken down. The walls were stark white, making the hallway appear elongated.

The door closed behind us, the echo reverberating through the empty building. Mr. Vandal came out from the back room dragging a large, heavy box. My stomach grew nervous, and I took a sip of my soda anxiously.

When it was clear that my old boss hadn't seen us, I forced myself to speak up. "Good morning, Mr. Vandal. How are you?"

"Oh! Kinsley, you're back!" he said, as if he hadn't expected me.

"Yeah, my mom said I needed to come and pick up a

check?" I scratched the back of my head. It was so awkward asking for money, even if I earned it.

"Oh! That's right! Mrs. Vandal is in the back room. I believe she has your check. Um, it's good to see you. Glad you're all right," he said curtly. He continued to drag his box across the glossed concrete floor. Lainey followed me into the back room.

"Good morning," I said, knocking on the door as I walked in. Mrs. Vandal flinched and immediately clicked out of several windows on her computer until she came to a blank blue desktop. She hurried to cover up stacks of paper on her desk with manila folders, while Lainey and I stood awkwardly staring at the walls. There was something odd going on here, but I already knew that.

"Good morning! Sorry, it's such a mess. Your mom said you were trying to pick up your check. I have that. One minute. I know I left it here somewhere . . ."

She turned her back to us momentarily while she rifled through a cabinet. Lainey shot me a quick glance that confirmed my suspicions. I pursed my lips and waited for the check to be handed over so we could get out of there.

"Here it is."

The white envelope found my hand.

"Thanks," I said, lingering while Mrs. Vandal continued cleaning her desk.

Her cheeks were flushed, and she barely looked me in the eye. That was it? It seemed like a weird way to part with an employee, but then again, I hadn't worked there very long, and I had no other jobs to compare it to.

Lainey grabbed my arm, beckoning me to leave. I couldn't help but take a deep breath as I left her office. I hadn't realized I'd been holding it in her presence. I felt a weight ease from my shoulders with every step we took closer to the exit.

Mr. Vandal was dragging a new box as we approached the door. Something shifted inside of me. The axis of dream and reality shifted, and for a slight moment in time, Mr. Vandal wasn't dragging a box, but a black body bag. The glossed concrete floor was flourishing with lush flowerbeds and a pair of rose shears hidden in the grass.

"Kinsley!" Lainey hissed.

I snapped out of it. The light came flooding in, and the body bag morphed back into a cardboard box once again. Lainey was staring at me with bright red cheeks that almost camouflaged her freckles. "Are you okay?"

I opened my mouth, but nothing came out. I was still adjusting to the light when two men dressed in black and covered in tattoos entered the gallery. A shiver ran down my back, and I had a deep sense of trouble in the pit of my stomach.

Lainey took hold of my wrist and pulled me past the men. They barely spared us a glance and then locked the door behind us.

We rushed to her car, whispering and peeking over our shoulders. "What was that? You just froze in there!"

"I'm sorry. I don't know what happened," I said, checking over my shoulder again.

"Those guys did not look like they were buying art!"

"No. They didn't."

CHAPTER 19

I sat in the waiting room twiddling my thumbs. Mom was on the other side of the wall giving my new therapist the rundown on all I'd been through and sharing areas of concern with her. I knew it would not be good. I'd heard her speaking earlier to Aunt Nora over the phone. What had started as a conversation about the lawsuit had ended with Mom's worry about my mental health. Apparently, I hadn't been as sneaky as I thought, and Mom heard me talking to Gran in my bedroom. She told my aunt that I must be having hallucinations. I was beyond mortified. If the therapist brought it up, I planned to deny it.

I rifled through countless magazines, flipping the pages so quickly that my eyes never fully landed on the images inside. It felt like an eternity before Mom finally emerged.

"She seems really nice. She's ready for you. I'll be waiting right here."

I stood nervously and scowled at her as I walked by. I placed my hand on the doorknob but didn't turn it. "Mom? Would you mind waiting in the car?" I wasn't planning on saying anything to the therapist, but if I did, the last thing I wanted to worry about was whether she could hear me through the walls.

"Sure. I can do that." Mom smiled softly and then headed down the hall. I watched her disappear before I opened the door and greeted my new therapist.

A woman in her late sixties or so waited patiently for me. She had a short blonde bob cut that was losing its vibrancy. Her natural gray was seeping through the thin golden tone and turning her hair ashy and distinguished. She had angular rimmed glasses and a petite body that appeared even smaller behind her large, ornate desk. She beckoned me forward with a wave, motioning to one of the seats before her.

"Good afternoon, Kinsley. It's nice to meet you. My name is Dr. Shelton."

I took a seat. The chair was stiff, and I could tell this session would drag on forever.

"I'm so sorry to hear about your accident. Your mother tells me you had quite the recovery story. I'm glad to see you're doing well. But just like with any traumatic event, it's nice to talk about these things. Are you open to that?"

I stared at her crisp white collar and the silver cross pendant necklace that lay just below her clavicle. "I'm not really sure I *need* to talk about it. Honestly, I only came to make my mom happy. She seems quite stressed about my recovery, and I want to make it as easy on her as possible."

"That's very thoughtful of you. How do you think your mother is doing with all of this?"

"Oh, not well. She lost her mom recently. My gran. And soon after that, I had my accident. It was just three days later. She's had a really rough couple of months. I think she's trying to be strong for me, but I worry about her. She might need this more than I do." I laughed nervously.

I looked at the framed photos of Dr. Shelton and her family in her bookcase. One black-and-white photo was of a beautiful lady covered in deep-set wrinkles and bearing a wide toothless smile. Something inside of me softened at the idea of talking to the doctor. It looked like she was close to her family as well, and I assumed she could understand my worry.

"I'm sorry to hear you lost your grandmother. I recently lost my mother as well. It sounds like you love your mom very much. And I don't doubt she's trying to be strong for you. Parents often try to hold up that facade. And after a while, it becomes more difficult to manage. But it sounds like you're doing the same thing for her. Which actually is probably causing her to be more worried. Do you think it would help if you two talked about it? Maybe you can lean on each other?"

"I don't know. I don't think she wants to talk about Gran."

"Why is that?"

"She hasn't said anything about her death, really. And I've just . . . been following her lead, I guess."

"Do you want to talk about it now?"

I thought about it. I picked and pulled at a slight snag on my nail, causing my fingernail to splinter into thin layers. I looked around the room for Gran, and I suddenly understood fully that I was using her as a crutch. My heartbeat drummed in my chest. It was too personal. "I don't think so?"

"That's all right. You don't have to talk about anything if you don't want to."

"Okay."

"It takes time. One of the best ways to heal from grief is simply letting time pass by. It's a slow and difficult path, and sometimes it doesn't feel linear. But I promise, one day you'll be able to look back and remember your gran and smile. Maybe you will even want to share some stories about her. But until then, let's talk about something else. I hear you had quite the adventure while in the hospital. Your mother tells me you had dreams while in your coma? And you remember them?"

"I did!" I sat up a little straighter.

"Fascinating. What was that like?" Dr. Shelton scribbled into her notebook.

"Um . . . Is this confidential?"

"It's absolutely confidential, unless I feel that your safety is at risk. At that point, I'd be obligated to advocate for your safety and health."

"But we're just talking about dreams, right? That's safe?" I asked, nodding my head, though I was still uncertain.

"Yes. That seems safe."

"Okay. I did have dreams. They were . . . oddly realistic."

Dr. Shelton adjusted her glasses on the bridge of her nose. "How so?"

"In how I'm still having trouble identifying what's real and what's not."

"Oh dear! That sounds troublesome. Can you tell me more?"

I sighed and looked around the room for something to ground myself with. My eyes fell upon Gran, sitting in the seat next to me. Her hands folded in her lap as she waited patiently to hear my story. I closed my eyes momentarily and told myself it was just that; a story, a fairy tale. Just like Gran had told me time and time again.

"It all started with a summer vacation to a lake house with a group of friends." I remembered Gran standing on the dock in the dim light, watching us play in the water. But I didn't say that.

"It was kind of an odd thing, because I had a mission to find this girl named Layla. She was a character from an old campfire ghost story. Supposedly, she had been a victim of a crime. I had to help her. But finding her was difficult at first."

"A crime? What kind of crime?"

"Well, it was a killer-on-the-loose kind of story. The guy had tried to kill her, but I guess she got away. She needed my help. Everybody told me so, but I didn't know why."

"A killer? Do you like murder mysteries? Are you a horror fan?"

"No. Not particularly."

Dr. Shelton wrote more notes, and I glanced at Gran warily. The silence grew louder until I had the urge to fill it with my voice.

"The girl was weird, though. Layla. It felt like she didn't want to be found. Like she needed help, but wasn't ready to accept it. There were hints of her here and there, but she was quite elusive at first. On the occasions that I found her, she ran from me. One time, I even caught her. I wrapped my arms around her, but before we fell to the ground, she disappeared." I bent some of my fingers backward and examined all the red creases in my palm.

"Why do you think she didn't want to be found?"

"I think she was just a piece of me. A piece of me I didn't recognize as my own. In the end, she told me that she and I were the same person." It sounded awfully weird coming out of my mouth.

"And what did you think of that?"

"I couldn't believe it. I'd looked at her like she was, I don't know, better than me?" I bit my lip, uncertain of how I was coming across to the therapist. "I know it sounds weird, but I kind of admired her. It felt like she was a better version of me and that I could never be like her. She was happy and free-spirited, or at least that's how she appeared in the beginning."

"Are *you* happy?" Dr. Shelton tilted her head to the side, and I felt a strong burn in the back of my throat as if I wanted to cry. Was I happy? I didn't know how to answer that. I still didn't feel whole. I accepted Layla in my dream, but ever since I woke, it was like I'd lost her again.

"I . . . I felt empty in my dream. I felt invisible. Inadequate. It was so bad that sometimes when I looked in the mirror, I had no reflection at all. Like I had no soul." My chest tightened. I glanced over at Gran for comfort. She nodded her head, and I knew I was doing good by her.

"Do you feel inadequate?"

It was hard to admit something like that to a doctor who obviously had her life together. She was smart, driven, and from the pictures on her bookshelves, she was well loved. And me? I didn't know who I was. "I guess so."

"If you had to tell me a reason for your inadequacy, off the top of your head, what could you come up with?"

"For starters . . . I'm dyslexic. I don't read well. It's something everybody can do, and I always felt, I don't know, behind? I mean, I get good grades. B's most of the time. But it's an unbelievable amount of work. It's a struggle every single night. My friend Emma, she reads a couple of books a week. She loves it. I've always wanted to be like that. I've always wanted to escape this world and fall into another, but I can't. I just read the same line over and over again. I stumble on the words and skip lines. My eyes become unfocused, and it's hard to decode the symbols on the page. It's something everybody takes for granted. I think I've used it as a measuring stick of sorts. I never quite add up."

Dr. Shelton took off her glasses and held them in her hand while she spoke. "Well, struggling in school when all of your peers seem to find it easy can take quite a hit on your confidence. It's important that you know it doesn't mean you're inadequate."

"So I've been told." I forced a grin. She cleaned her glasses with a thin cloth she took from her desk and then delicately slipped them back on as she gathered her thoughts.

"Did you know that being dyslexic isn't *all* bad? Neurodivergent minds just work a little differently than neurotypicals. And sometimes there are even perks, like having a greater chance of being gifted in unique areas like engineering, industrial and graphic designs, architecture, and construction. They are also known to be fantastic at 3D spatial reasoning, imagination, art, and creativity," Dr. Shelton said, tapping her pen on the rim of her notepad.

"Really?" It sounded a like what Emma and Walker had tried to tell me in my dream. "Like maybe my disadvantage is also a strength?"

"Yes! Yes! Exactly! If I had to guess, it might have something to do with why your dreams seemed so real. With all of that creativity and imagination, the ability to visualize and conceptualize life in 3D imagery, it's no wonder you're having a difficult time telling the difference between memories and dreams."

I chewed on my lip as I thought about it. Maybe therapy wasn't such a bad idea after all. I scanned the book spines on her bookshelf and sat up a little taller.

"You know, you don't have to read. They're plenty of books on audio that you could listen to. Have you ever tried that?"

I shook my head.

"Your mom tells me you're not excited about art history anymore. What is it you want to do?"

"I never really wanted to sell paintings. I just seemed to be naturally good at it. What I really want to do is screen write. I want to create movies like the ones I see in my head." I felt the heat creep into my cheeks. Admitting a dream of mine was embarrassing. It was nothing more than a pipe dream, and I knew I should try to be more realistic. "But I know that's a lot of writing and reading." I shrugged, feeling defeated at the mere thought of it all.

"They're tons of dyslexic screenwriters out there. Authors too! If you have the gift of creativity, don't waste it in the face of hard work." Dr. Shelton's voice took on a more authoritative tone. Don't waste it in the face of hard work, I thought . . .

"Really?"

"Certainly. I think you should try it. Plus, Kinsley, you've been getting decent grades in school. You've learned to be hardworking and persistent from a young age. Being dyslexic has given you the gift of grit and drive. You've been training for this your whole life!"

"Ha, I guess you're right." I felt somewhat proud of myself. Maybe she was on to something. Maybe, just like in my dreams, all my insecurities started with something that wasn't all *that* bad. Maybe it would take me longer than anybody else to write a movie, and maybe it would be two or three times harder. But the more I thought about it, the more I thought it was worth it. Because I'd rather be bad at something I loved, than good at something I hated.

"Yeah. It's just like my gran told me, lean into the darkness."

"Your gran used to tell you that?" Dr. Shelton asked. I caught my slip, then pursed my lips. This time, I waited out the silence. She would not trick me into talking about Gran. I fought back the need to check on the ghost next to me. I didn't need to give her any reasons to dig deeper.

"Well, it sounds like one of your reasons for inadequacy might come down to perspective. I know it's hard, dear, and I'm not trying to take away any of the hardship that you've dealt with in school, but if you can learn to embrace it, I think it will help build your self-confidence."

"Yeah. Maybe," I agreed.

"So, you said you found this girl. Layla, was it? What happened next?" She flipped to a clean page, ready to make more notes.

"Well . . . She kind of fell into me," I said, uncertain of how else to say it. "It was like her soul adhered to mine, and we became one." The embarrassment climbed to new levels as Dr. Shelton wrote fiercely on her fresh piece of paper. I prayed nobody would ever lay eyes on that notebook of hers.

"And how did you feel about that?"

"At first I didn't like it, because I was jealous of her. But in the end, I felt more whole. Like I was a full person instead of this empty creature. I don't know how else to explain it."

"That sounds . . . wonderful. Maybe you could take her health and happiness and fully embody it?"

"I wish . . ." I said, exhaling a big breath. "It doesn't feel like I will ever become healthy again. I just don't understand it," I ranted.

"I felt lost before. Like I was caught in a web of complex thoughts and feelings inside my dream. But in reality, I was just lying in a tiny hospital bed. I wasn't lost at all. And now that I'm back home—or rather, awake—I feel more lost than ever. My memories are a mixed bag. Some are real and precious. Some are nightmares. Hollow reflections and split personalities. If I'm being honest, I don't fully recognize myself when I look in the mirror. If I'm not the girl that I was this summer, then who am I?"

I guess there was a lot bottled up inside me, because it all came exploding out. And to think, I wasn't even going to talk to her . . .

"Well, I would imagine you are the girl you were *before* your accident. Don't you think?"

"No. I don't. Because that girl was going to college for art history. And I'm not. That girl was content being insecure, and I'm not. I want to be this bigger, brighter, and better version of myself, just like Layla, yet I don't know how to get there." I ran my hands through my hair and closed my eyes.

"I'm physically weak, and I'm mentally drained. I can't even get behind the wheel of a car! I'm a completely different person than I was three months ago." I opened my eyes to see Dr. Shelton looking at her watch, and I had to remind myself that no matter how much I opened up to her, she was still paid by the hour.

"It looks like our time is up for today." She scribbled down a few notes before closing her notebook and folding her hands across her desk.

Time's up? But how was I supposed to feel right again? Did she have the answers or not? I stood up as Gran faded away.

"Kinsley, I think it's possible that you are in a period of growth. You're right. You're *not* the girl you were before the accident. But it sounds like you're stronger already. Remember, healing takes time. I'll see you next week." I nodded and then turned around and walked out of Dr. Shelton's office feeling unsettled.

CHAPTER 20

On the morning of my high school graduation, I lay in bed scratching behind Roxie's ears and staring at my open closet. I was beyond intimidated to return to high school. I didn't know how to face all my peers after an accident that almost took my life and caused so many rumors to spread far and wide. I knew people would be staring and whispering as I walked by, which was terrifying.

I had given up on my independent studies weeks ago. I had two classes that I needed to pass in order to graduate high school in my last semester, but my grades had dropped because I had missed so much work. In one of my classes, the final exam was worth fifty percent of my grade. I had every intention of catching up from the comfort of my bed, but every time I tried to work on my laptop, my brain parted like the Red Sea. My mind would wander, and I would daydream about faraway lands.

Why did homework matter anyway? It seemed like a silly thing when I was fighting for my life not too long ago. When I was trying to decide whether to live, or live beyond. And now, my entire general education hinged on a single test. I couldn't make myself concentrate any more than I could make myself care. I didn't know if it was because of my brain injury or if it was a new perspective I'd been given after the accident. Maybe I was just giving up.

One of my teachers graciously waived everything he'd given in class from the day of my accident. He was willing to give me the B I had earned at the beginning of class. But my other teacher wouldn't bend the rules. She wouldn't bend the rules in the least. And for that reason, and my failures to comply with independent studies, I would not be graduating with my friends. I would never wear the graduation gown that had hung in my window for weeks. I would never hang a picture of my graduation day in my bedroom or throw my cap high in the air. The accident had taken yet another thing from me.

There was a knock on my bedroom door, but I didn't answer. I knew Mom would walk in after a moment anyway. When she did, I didn't bother to look. I didn't want her to see the redness in my eyes.

"Are you okay?" she asked, as she sat down on my bed next to me. My eyes betrayed me by glancing at my graduation gown, which I had pulled out of the closet and hung on the door just to torture myself.

"Oh, honey . . ." Mom caught sight of the gown.

"It's fine," I lied with a shrug.

"You will just have to make up that one credit. You can do it this summer and graduate in time for college. I promise, in the grand scheme of things, this will not matter." Mom reached forward and stroked Roxie.

"I don't want to go to college anymore."

Mom sighed, but she didn't seem overly surprised.

"What? I don't. You know how I feel about art history. And I don't want to spend the rest of my life doing something that I don't love." I folded my arms over my chest.

"But you're so good at it."

"So?"

"You know, it wouldn't hurt to put off college for that year we spoke about and take time to recuperate. Doesn't that sound nice? I'm telling you, I think it would be really beneficial. And if going to a different college is something you want to do, you'll need time to look into it and apply."

"Yeah. Maybe that's what I'll do."

Mom ran her hand down my head. "You should start getting ready. We don't want to be late."

"Do I *have* to go?" I asked, even though I knew the answer.

"You don't have to go, dear. But it would be a nice thing to do, to show Lainey and Emma some support. Plus, you haven't been out of the house except for therapy. And I worry about you. I think it might be good for you to see everybody, even if it's just for a little while. If you're feeling overwhelmed, we'll leave early, okay?" Mom rose to her feet.

"Promise?"

"Just say the word, and we'll go," Mom smiled on her way out.

I eyed my graduation gown with a frown. What was I supposed to wear now? I rummaged through my closet for what seemed like an eternity. I refused to wear anything with a spot of yellow, and given that it had been my favorite color before the accident, I had many sundresses with yellow accents.

I ended up wearing a blue skirt and a mismatched top. I curled my long, dark locks to give body to the shaved portion of my head that often caught my attention in the mirror. Nobody could see the shaved spot unless I ran my hands through my hair, which I never did on that side. I tossed my heels aside and slipped on my sneakers. I was steady on my feet now, but I didn't want to torture myself as I walked on the field.

Walking onto school grounds made my palms sweat. I

swore everybody was looking at me, even though I trained my eyes on the ground. My mom kept a protective hand under my arm, and I pulled away when I heard the first whisper. Mom eyed me suspiciously, so I gave her a quick shake of my head. She knew.

It was hard to sit behind the sea of navy-blue gowns and not join them in celebration. I had worked so incredibly hard, and an accident had stolen my chance to walk in my high school graduation. It was as if some unknown force had doomed me from the very start. If dyslexia didn't hold me back, the car accident certainly would. It wasn't fair, but it was life.

I sat with all the parents and family members who had come to celebrate their graduating student. It wasn't until the ceremony started that I felt the social pressure ease. These parents didn't know me, and they certainly weren't talking about me. Though I instinctively turned around when I heard a whisper. My eyes landed on Gran sitting a row behind us. She smiled and waved her pamphlet at me with a giggle. I turned back around, feeling more confident in myself, and finally engaged in the ceremony.

I shielded my face with the pamphlet containing all the graduating seniors' names, trying to get relief from the blistering sun. I watched student after student who, presumably, had coasted through high school receive their diploma. But with each name called, my open wounds grew deeper. I should be up there, I thought.

"You should be up there," Mom whispered in my ear.

I sighed. Should be, but wasn't. I counted the heads in the upcoming row and waited for Emma and Lainey to be called. When their names were announced, I clapped hysterically, and Mom took several pictures at my request. I spotted Lainey's parents and Gunner several rows ahead, and I wondered if Gunner would feel like we had a connection, or if he would ignore me like he had on my last day at the lake.

When the ceremony was over, I wanted to say the words that would bring me home, but I fought them back. I would not jump on a plane home and run from my friends when times got tough. I'd made that mistake once in Baylor, and I died regretting it. Never again. I would stay, and I was going to be the best friend I could be, no matter how afraid I was to face my classmates. I could do it, as long as Gran was nearby. I checked on her often, and she was always there, somewhere within the crowd.

I trudged through the blue gowns, careful not to step on the hats strewn across the grass field. The excitement was electric, but my jinx cut through it like a hot knife. The misfortune seemed to float around me, guiding students out of my path. Had I been cursed like Walker?

I caught Emma's eye, and she came bounding over to me with open arms and a huge smile. She nearly knocked me over with a monstrous bear hug, and I couldn't help but giggle on the outside. On the inside, I was very aware of just how different we'd become.

"Congratulations, Emma! You did it!"

"Thank you! I wish you were up there with us!"

"Girls! Girls! Squeeze in for a picture," Emma's mom said, waving us together.

"Wait for Lainey!"

"Lainey!"

Lainey found us easily enough. We wrapped our arms around each other, oblivious to the cameras snapping a mile a minute.

"I'm so proud of you guys," I said with tears in my eyes. I *was* happy for them, but I was also feeling left behind. It took little to draw tears from my best friends. We all laughed at each other as we tried to keep the mascara from running down our cheeks.

Gran stood silently by her lonesome, always an arm's length away. No matter how hard I tried to be present, I couldn't fully get there. Gran was a gigantic white elephant that only I could see. She both fulfilled something inside me and stripped it away, all at the same time. Her presence made me feel like Layla was alive in me. And that I was every bit the beautiful, capable girl I'd once thought of as my childhood idol. But she was also a dreadful reminder of how much tragedy had recently occurred. On days like today, I put on a brave face, and none were the wiser.

Emma and Lainey fell silent as they spied the large group of popular kids gather to take epic photos. I, too, got sucked in and watched them longingly. Asher swept Kimber up in his arms, and she thrust her graduation cap high in the air as she hollered. I wished I had a picture of myself like that. Unfortunately, my boyfriend was a phantom, and I didn't graduate.

Trinity looked like a model, with her long black hair and striking hazel eyes. Even from this distance, it seemed like her eyes were a portal to a witch's brew; if you looked for too long, a spell might befall you. Most of the guys in our high school spent too much time looking into her eyes, and they were all under her spell, as were we.

Trinity didn't even have to smile, just a smirk from the corner of her mouth, and she was drop-dead gorgeous. Most of the girls hated her for it, and she only had a couple of real friends. It took a seriously confident girl to be friends with someone so stunning, and most of us weren't up for the challenge.

Scarlett May had white and yellow plumeria flowers pinned to the side of her short, beach-blonde hair. Although she wasn't in cowgirl boots, she wore a pair of sky-high shorts underneath her gown and a pair of stilettos that made her legs look twice as long. Levi grabbed Scarlett May's leg like a guitar in a big show for the camera.

"I bet her stilettos are sinking into the grass. Why would she even wear those?" Lainey asked.

"Because she can," I muttered. Her stilettos were impractical, I'd admit, but she obviously liked them, and they looked amazing on her. I thought back to the night she and I had bonded under shooting stars, and I wondered if she had a real live Sampson of her own. I wanted that for her. A pang of sadness ached in my chest. I missed Scarlett May. I missed the person I thought she might be. But then I had to remind myself, I never really knew her at all. Just like Kimber and Trinity, I only knew the assumptions I'd come up with in my head, and those were based on jealousy and rumors.

Kai wrapped his arms around Ethan and Noah, and the three boys yelled and hollered as their parents clicked dozens of photos. The three of us had been watching the group grow up throughout high school. And instead of moving on with our own lives, we wished we had theirs. The funny part was, we didn't even know them. We'd only seen pictures on our phones every Friday night and heard rumors on Monday morning.

"Oh my god. Is he coming over here?" Lainey whispered, gripping my hand tightly. Noah and his mom were walking toward us. My friends were aware of my long-standing crush on Noah, and it seemed like everyone else knew too. It was all we ever talked about.

A wave of nausea washed over me as I wondered how I felt about Noah now, and if I really wanted to speak to him with part of my head shaved, no matter if he could see it or not. I still knew it was there.

"Clara, it's so good to see you. I'm sorry we missed you when we dropped off the casserole," Noah's mom said as she hugged my mom. Noah stood awkwardly by her side.

"Congratulations," I said meekly.

"Yeah, you too," Noah said, before quickly trying to redirect his comment to Lainey and Emma. Of course, there was nothing to congratulate me about on this hot summer day.

"I mean—"

"It's okay," I said, cutting him off.

"How are you feeling?" he asked.

"I'm doing better. Thanks for asking," I said, trying to clear the tension in my throat. The truth was, Noah and I had spoken little since we were younger. We barely spoke at all, and that was part of the reason I'd watched him and his friends move on while I stayed behind.

As Noah rose to rule our high school, I retreated into the shadows. He became loud and confident, while I became quiet and uncertain. He excelled as a double star athlete while I struggled with my homework at the kitchen table. He had girlfriends, and I watched from my window.

While he partied, Emma, Lainey, and I would wonder what it would be like to be at those parties. Somewhere along the way, I had missed an invisible fork in the road that separated Noah and me. He excelled, and I was too afraid.

Lainey and Emma were the same way, though for different reasons. Emma preferred to live in the world of literature rather than the real world. I understood that more now than ever. Meanwhile, Lainey wanted something that Kimber and Scarlett May had, that intangible thing that we all wanted, but she was too anxious to chance failure. Lainey would rather put her effort into building a career with a predictable outcome than take any kind of risk. As a result, the three of us had huddled together at lunch under the shade of a giant tree telling stories we'd heard whispered around the classroom.

"Are you girls coming to the after-party?" Noah's mom asked us. Noah's cheeks flushed.

"After-party?" Emma asked.

"Yeah, come on over. We're just having some of Noah's friends over before they leave for the lake. Nothing big, just loads of pizza," she smiled.

"If you're around, stop by," Noah shrugged. I froze. Was this a pity invite? Everything inside me stopped. But that wasn't the case for Emma, though I wish it had been.

"We'll be there!" Emma exclaimed, gripping my pinkie finger so tightly I thought it might fall off.

"We will?" Lainey asked.

"We will!" Emma insisted, giving her a stern look.

I couldn't believe what was happening. Graduation

day had just become a nightmare. My stomach churned with anxiety at the thought of walking into the lion's den. I hoped Gran would be there.

"Are you sure that's a good idea?" I asked quietly.

"It'll be fun!" Emma said, choosing to not pick up on my hesitation. I wasn't sure about the *fun*, but it was too late to back out now.

CHAPTER 21

Emma, Lainey, and I exchanged heated glances at one other on the way home. Though Mom seemed pleased I had friends coming over, we hadn't expected to be joining her across the street for Noah's graduation party. Mom would have been devastated if she had the slightest clue what I'd actually dreamed about in my coma and how this was going to mess with my head. It would probably take months to unwind the knot in therapy. And had I known that keeping secrets from my mom was going to leave me so vulnerable, I never would have done that either.

The three of us tromped upstairs to make a plan behind closed doors. Lainey balanced on one foot while unbuckling her heels, and Emma carefully placed her graduation cap on my desk, deep in thought. "What was that all about?" I asked Emma, my pitch much too high to hide my true emotion.

"What? You know you wanted to go! I saw the way you looked at Noah!"

"You mean, *you* wanted to see Levi!" Emma's eyes rolled back in her head, and Lainey sighed. The room fell quiet as we all worried about how we would get through the next couple of hours.

"Guys, we can't go. It's going to be so incredibly awkward. Let's just not show up," Lainey pled. I nodded. It was a solid option. The *only* option, as far as I was concerned.

"No! We're graduates now. All of that awkwardness of who's who is behind us now. Come on. We can do this. It's not a big deal," Emma quipped, though the crease between her eyes told me she was bluffing. She was just as scared as Lainey and I were, if not more. Her eyes turned watery as she waited for our answers.

I looked to Lainey and shrugged. "I guess we can eat some pizza . . ."

"Yes! Oh my god. We're doing this! It literally took until the very last day of school to get invited to one of their parties, but it still counts!" Emma rambled as she fixed a smudge of eyeliner under her eye in the mirror. I caught my reflection looking back at me. My eyes were dull, and I struggled to recognize myself. Who was I among this family of misfits, if we were strangers?

"We got invited by Noah's mom. That doesn't even remotely count," Lainey said. It was true. It didn't count.

I thought back to the time that Noah and I had shared an English class earlier in the year. He and I had been stealing glances at one another, but I always told myself otherwise. I remembered the time his mom was out of town and his dad was on a business trip. He was planning on throwing a big party, and he invited me. It seemed like no big deal as he nodded to a group in English class, myself included, and said to stop by.

But come lunch hour, I knew that if I told Lainey and Emma, there would be no backing out. At the last minute, I chose not to tell them about the invitation. I ended up watching the party from my window that night. Curled on my window seat, underneath a blanket, I fell asleep with my forehead pressed against the windowpane. I'd regretted my decision all night long, and I promised myself if I ever had an opportunity to be bold, I'd take it.

"Girls! Are you ready?" Mom called from downstairs. We hadn't even had time to freshen up.

The girls and I shared a look of panic before I called out, "Coming!"

Mom led our small group with a bowl of hot cheese dip, and I dragged behind with the bag of chips. Several cars were parked along the curb, and a few more were showing up as we approached the house. I'd been inside this house a hundred times before, but not in recent years.

Noah's mom greeted us at the door. She gave me a big hug and whispered in my ear, "I'm so glad you came." It seemed she meant something more than she was letting on, and I wished for just a moment that nothing had gotten in the way of my relationship with her son. She was a sweet woman with a kind disposition.

Asher and Kimber squeezed past us in the entryway. Kimber's eyes trailed behind her, and Asher's brows furrowed at the sight of us. My stomach sank immediately. We didn't belong here. It was a closed party for their group of friends. I saw the same recognition in Emma's eyes as she folded her arms tightly across her waist.

"Come on in, girls. There's plenty of pizza in the kitchen. Help yourself to a drink. I think everybody's outside."

I took the first step. Lainey and Emma were quick to follow. The three of us loaded our plates with pizza, taking as long as we possibly could before joining everybody outside. I picked the pepperoni off my pizza and then pretended to search the kitchen for napkins. As if I didn't know my way around.

Trinity appeared out of thin air. I could feel Emma and Lainey stiffen, though nobody was more uncomfortable than me. I was the only one who was wondering if Trinity and I had actually thrown everybody's clothes off the dock during the naked cheetah races. But that belonged in the summer that never was. It didn't happen, I reminded myself. I used it to my advantage, anyway. Pretend as if it were real. As if I belonged. It was then that I saw Gran wander through the back yard, passing by the kitchen windows. I relaxed immediately.

"Hey, Trinity. Congratulations on graduation. I love your dress. Where did you get it?" I asked.

"Thank you. Um, I didn't see you up there. Did you graduate?" Her hazel eyes burned through me like lasers. My palms turned sweaty, and I quickly remembered that she and I had never been friends for a reason.

"I didn't."

"Mrs. Black wouldn't allow one credit to slide! She *should* have been up there with us," Lainey said in my defense.

"Oh. Well, a credit *is* a credit." *Ouch.*

Trinity reached for a plate beside me. "I didn't realize you were friends of Noah's?" Trinity's voice was like a snake in the grass. I wasn't sure where she was going with her questioning, but I knew the ending would bite.

"Actually, Noah and I have been friends for a long time. We grew up together. And I live down the street." It wasn't exactly a fib, it was true. Though I never would have claimed to be his friend under other circumstances.

"Then why have you never hung out with us?" Her voice was bitter and taunting. It was no wonder she'd been the first to go in my dream.

"I . . . I don't know—"

"Weren't you in a coma or something?"

Emma gasped.

"Didn't you used to lie in elementary school and say you were in a kid's swimsuit commercial?" Lainey snapped. With Trinity momentarily silenced, Lainey grabbed my wrist and yanked me out of the kitchen and into the back yard.

"Why is she *so* mean?" Lainey asked.

"I can't believe you said that!" Emma said. It was unlike Lainey to stand up to anyone. She didn't have a mean bone in her body.

Even with Lainey's comeback, I knew Trinity had gotten to me. Trinity obviously didn't care that I'd recently been fighting for my life. So why did I care what she had to say? It was easy to shrug off in the moment as I looked into the back yard full of living characters from my summer. But I knew when I was alone at night, with nothing to distract me, I would think about what it felt like to be struck by Trinity's venom.

Kai tossed a football at Noah just as he turned to see us, and the football struck his shoulder. Lainey, Emma, and I took a seat far away from the crowd, sitting on a stone wall on the outskirts of the yard. All the patio furniture had been taken, which made us appear to be even more out of place than we already were.

Noah nodded his head, and I gave him a quick smile in

return. He picked up the football and threw it back with no remorse. Nobody else noticed us.

"Why are we even here?" Lainey asked Emma. "Are you planning on talking to Levi? Because we could've just stared at him through Kinsley's window if all you wanted was a view." Lainey was so far out of her comfort zone, she was turning snappy in a way I'd never seen. I understood, though, because I was on edge too. We all were.

"You guys, I just wanted to end high school on a good note. Plus, I finished a series this morning, and I'm not sure what to read next."

I groaned through a mouth full of pizza.

"I didn't want to be afraid of them anymore, because you know what's going to happen? History is going to repeat itself in college, and I don't want that. We could've gone to any of their parties if we wanted to. It's not like they hand delivered invitations with a wax seal or anything. I'm sure half the people showed up without an invitation. That could have been us. But it wasn't," Emma said.

"Because we didn't *want* it to be," Lainey complained.

"That's what we've always said. But is it really true?" Emma tossed the crust down on her plate.

"You're right Emma. We should have gone. But we're here now, thanks to you. And honestly, I think it reconfirms the fact that we never really wanted to be here. These aren't our people. You guys are my people," I said.

"You're my people too."

"I'm going to miss you guys," Lainey said.

"But just for the record, we never would have known that these weren't our people if we hadn't come. And now we can stop guessing, right?" Emma asked.

I nodded. It had been difficult spending all of those semesters in high school just wondering, what if we did this, or what if we'd said that? Emma was right. If we would have just gotten to know these people, we would have stopped wondering. And we probably would have moved on to find better friends.

"Kinsley! Come sit over here!" Ethan gestured to three seats at the table. Trinity, Mason, and Levi had just gotten up, leaving the seats empty. A little taken aback, we left our spots on the ledge for prime seating in Noah's back yard.

"Hey, I heard they didn't let you graduate. That's shitty. Sorry about that," Ethan said as I sat down. Unlike Trinity, I could feel the sincerity in his voice.

"They didn't let you graduate?" Kimber asked.

"Um, no. I had quite a bit of missing work from being out of school the last month."

"That's bullshit!" Scarlett May hissed. I smiled. Once upon a time, she and I were friends. And I thought I might have seen a glimmer of why.

"It is!" Emma agreed.

"So, all of that was true, huh? You were really in a coma?" Scarlett May asked.

"You can't ask that!" Kimber snapped. The table fell quiet, and everybody's eyes landed on me. It appeared they were all curious, and I didn't mind sharing.

"There were that many rumors?" I asked.

"Yeah." Ethan's tone was matter-of-fact.

"I heard you died," Scarlett May said through gritted teeth.

"Scarlett May!" Kimber barked.

"What? It's true! She asked!"

"It's okay. Really," I said. "I don't really remember any of it. The accident, I mean. I have a good idea of what happened, but it doesn't feel like an actual memory, if that makes sense. I was in a coma for a couple of weeks. Thirteen days, to be exact." I lightly traced the rim of my red plastic cup as I spoke.

"Wow. What was that like?" Ethan asked. It was weird to be having a conversation with these people. I wanted to tell him, you would know, because you were there. But I constantly had to retrace my thoughts and remind myself that they didn't know me at all. And what I knew of them most likely wasn't true either. Apart from Trinity, that is. I think I had her spot on.

"What do you think she's going to say, Ethan? She basically slept for two weeks," Scarlett May said.

"Actually, I dreamed. A lot." Out of the corner of my

eye, I saw Lainey look to Emma. I don't know why I said it. I hadn't spoken about it since leaving the hospital. And this certainly wasn't therapy.

"No way! That must have been so trippy!" Kimber said, leaning in. I smiled and nodded. It absolutely captivated them. And at that moment, I couldn't remember why I was so afraid to come here.

"You have *no* idea."

"Do you remember any of your dreams?"

It was the moment of truth. Was I going to tell them? Was I going to say that I had spent two months with them? I couldn't. I would sound like a stalker, or worse. "I remember some of them. They were weird, though." I shrugged.

"How so?" Kimber asked.

"Do you really want to know?"

"Um, yeah!" Scarlett May blurted.

"Yeah, I don't know anybody that's been in a coma before," Ethan said.

"I can see that. It's weird because I can remember the dreams like they were yesterday." I glanced at Emma and made a split-second decision that I hoped I wouldn't regret. "Have you ever heard of a place called Baylor Lake?"

I had known all along that Scarlett May had been planning a big summer trip there after graduation with all of her friends, including Noah. It was a weird coincidence that my uncle had a cabin at the same lake. That's when we'd come up with the idea that the three of us would go to my cabin for the summer. It was the perfect place to make memories. We planned to hit all the local events: the Summerfield State Fair, the Baylor Bass Tournament, the Baylor Parade. And we may or may not have hoped to run into Noah and Levi while visiting.

And somewhere in the back of my mind, I had imagined that our small group of three would join theirs. And the one thing we all had in common—that we were brand new at being adults—would have united us into some type of family. An unruly and most likely dysfunctional family, but a family, nonetheless. We would argue over bonfires, crash the golf cart, and who knows, maybe even fall in love.

It was supposed to be the best summer of our lives, and the memories would be ours to cherish forever. But the whole thing seemed stupid now.

"Are you serious? I have a place in Baylor Lake. We're all going there right now!" Scarlett May checked her watch, and I caught sight of Emma's ruby cheeks.

"No way!" It was my turn to get Emma back for making us come to this party. "Same with us! I have a cabin there too! Well, my uncle does."

"Wait, what?" Lainey coughed. The toe of my sneaker met her shin.

"No way!" Scarlett May echoed.

"We should hang out! We're going up in a couple of

days and staying most of summer. Will you be at the Water's Edge Concert?" I asked.

"Yeah! I already have my cowgirl boots packed. This is going to be so much fun!" To my surprise, she was sincere. It made me wish I was too. But I had absolutely no plans to go to Baylor Lake. I would cancel last minute and say that I couldn't escape because of my physical therapy. Everybody would understand. But most importantly, Lainey and Emma would still go and get a chance at the summer we'd planned all senior year.

"All-night parties, a little fishing, barbecue. Damn, I can't wait!" Ethan's eyes twinkled with hope. Lainey wore a look I hadn't seen on her face for a long time. I recognized it as equally excited and terrified.

The rest of the group gathered around the table. It seemed the party was wrapping up, and they had a flight to catch. "Hey Noah, did you know that Kinsley and her friends were going up to Baylor Lake this summer?" Ethan asked.

"What? I didn't know that!" Noah exclaimed.

My insides screamed. A couple of months ago, it would've been a dream come true to be sitting at this table and be invited to hang out in Baylor. But as I sat here today, I no longer had feelings for Noah. All because he'd done something in a dream that I hadn't forgiven him for. It was ridiculous. I knew that. But it didn't change the way

I felt. Plus, I kept comparing him to somebody else. Or rather, the *idea* of somebody else.

"Yeah! Apparently her uncle has a place on the lake, and the three of them are going in a few days. We're going to hang out at the Water's Edge Concert next weekend! Hey Kinsley, do you have cowgirl boots? Because I have an extra pair, and they're already packed if you need them," Scarlett May offered.

"I'd love that. I actually needed to find some. Thank you," I said. She had no idea how much that really meant to me. I was touched beyond words, because even in my wildest dreams, Scarlett May had barely warmed up to me.

"Well, it's time to hit the road. Our plane leaves in two hours," Kai said. The group started to break apart, just as Trinity opened her mouth for revenge.

"Didn't you have a part of your head removed or something?"

Everybody froze. Trinity's tone had cut through the commotion and rung like a gong. Everyone's eyes flickered between her and me. Not even Lainey could find the right words now.

I'd suppressed a particular side of myself for a very long time, but drew strength upon that side of me now. I slowly ran my hand down the side of my head and lifted my hair to reveal a scar that was puckered and ugly. I said nothing.

Gasps erupted around the table, and my stomach

plummeted. They could accept me or not, but I was done hiding.

"Gross . . ." Trinity murmured.

"No way! That's bad ass!" Kai argued.

"Wow! That's so cool!" Ethan said, leaning over to get a closer look. I dropped my hair and looked around at the crowd as they stared with wide eyes. I didn't know which rumors I'd just confirmed, but they were shocked.

"I wish I had a battle scar!" Kimber said to Asher.

"She's such a tough chick!" Mason said, as he headed for the door.

Out of everybody here, *Mason* was calling *me* tough? *Kimber* was wishing for something *I* had?

Trinity snarled and broke away. The group departed and made their way into the house. As I pushed my chair out, I shared a look of shock with both Emma and Lainey. This was not what we had expected from coming here. It was so much better.

Noah hung back from the group, walking by my side. "Don't mind Trinity. She's just jealous the entire school knows your name. You're kind of famous now, like it or not."

"Leave it to her to be jealous of something so terrible."

"Right. So, are you really going to Baylor this summer?"

"Yeah. We've been planning it all year. Such a coincidence."

"Maybe we'll hang out?"

A bolt of heat trailed down my back as we made our way to the entry. I wasn't sure if my old self was coming alive or if I was just completely uncomfortable with the whole situation. I loathed lying. "Yeah, I'd love that. I'll text you our address so you guys can come by," I said, with no phone and no intentions to actually follow through.

"Promise?"

I smiled as Ethan slapped Noah's back and ushered him out the front door. The cars were already packed and waiting. Noah's mom squeezed by to find her son for a hug before he left for the airport.

"I guess we'll see you girls up there then! Have a safe flight," Kimber said, waving goodbye. The three of us waved as the multiple cars pulled away from the curb. We stood in his driveway until the last of them vanished from sight.

"And they're off," my mom said.

Noah's mom wiped a tear from her eye as we stared down the empty street. "It's okay, Mrs. Hampton. You raised a good son. He's going to be all right."

By the end of the night, with Mom's help, we had not only secured two plane tickets, but a spot for Gunner as well. The girls were excited to have the summer they thought they'd lost out on, but they were ashamed to show it. Luckily, I wasn't ready for Baylor anytime soon.

CHAPTER 22

Gran and I sat side by side, staring at the back of the garage door. Mom's car was parked, my hands were wrapped tightly around the steering wheel, and I was acutely aware of the seconds ticking by. My therapy appointment was starting soon, but I was frozen. I'd convinced my mom that I could drive myself into town. But I may have been exaggerating. I hadn't driven since the accident, and she knew that. We all knew that.

Gran was biting her fingernails in the passenger seat. It wasn't the vote of confidence I was hoping for. Of course, I would drive again. But when would I be brave enough to do it? I told myself I was brave enough now. With Lainey and Emma off to Baylor Lake, the least I could do was drive myself to therapy. It was a few short miles away, and I didn't have to take the highway to get there. It was easy. It was daylight. And I had Gran riding shotgun. What more could I ask for?

"I just need music." I shrugged, turning on the stereo.

"Or will that distract you?" Gran asked.

I turned off the stereo.

"I just need to go. I need to stop overthinking and go." I quickly hit the garage door button and threw the car into drive.

"Not now! Wait for the door to open!" Gran arched her back to see over the dashboard. She braced herself with spread arms, holding onto the door and the back of my seat with white knuckles.

I slowly lowered my forehead to the steering wheel. "I *can't* do it."

"Yes, you *can*."

"I'm never going to drive again." I put the car in park.

"You're going to drive *today*!" Gran said, slapping at the gearshift. It was a sad sight to see Gran try to make use of her hands. It was probably the only thing I felt more deeply about than my failed driving attempt. I wasn't about to let her fumble in such an inadequate way. I placed my hand on the gearshift, and she held her ghostly hand on mine. With her cool touch over my hand, we put the car in drive together.

"I'm going to drive today . . ."

I saw the garage door swing open, and Mom appeared. She leaned against the doorway and folded her arms over her chest as she watched me struggle. She was coming to give me a ride. She had probably been counting down the minutes on the other side of the door, just waiting for me to freeze up. I wouldn't allow it. I opened my window and Gran disappeared into the oblivion.

"I'm going! I'm going! I can be there in seven minutes."

"You don't need to rush, honey. But your appointment is going to be starting soon. How about I drive you there and you drive back?"

"No, Mom, I've got this. I'm going right now!" I took my foot off the brake and eased onto the gas. Mom hid her worry behind a hand that covered half her face. I forced a smile and a small wave before rolling down the driveway. I made a wide turn at the mailbox and drove excruciatingly slow down our street.

"She gone?"

Gran's voice was faint. She was crouching low to hide from the window. I smiled. She didn't need to hide from Mom, of course. Nobody could see her but me. There was nothing better than an invisible grandmother hiding from her own daughter.

"She's gone," I said, laughing.

"Well, don't look at me! Keep your eyes on the road! You're driving!"

"I'm driving! Hey, it's not so bad. I don't know why I waited so long," I said, pulling up to my first stop sign. Gran's eyes were round and full of wonder. She couldn't have been happier to see me break free, and I loved her for it.

But by the time I came to my first light and saw dozens of cars, I knew why I'd waited so long. The cars made me anxious. The intersection was busy, and everybody drove too fast. Somebody honked at me for waiting too long after the light had turned green. But all my anxiety melted when Gran turned around and gave them the finger.

I stand corrected; there's nothing better than a feeble old grandmother with a threatening middle finger and a scowl that nobody could see. Gran knew every bomb in my path and every way to defuse them. She was absolutely my guardian angel, and I didn't know how I could live without her.

I pulled into the parking lot with two minutes to spare. I wasn't even late. I grabbed my bag and opened the door but had the sense that I was leaving something behind. I went to rummage through my bag to see if I had my keys, something I hadn't carried with me in a long time. Instead, I found something I wasn't looking for.

An envelope with "Kinsley" penned across the front was nestled in my bag. How had I not seen this before? Gran's handwriting was elegantly written on the envelope. I looked at Gran in my passenger seat, who appeared dimmer than before.

"What's this?" I asked. I glanced around to make sure nobody had heard my belligerent self-talk.

"I wrote a few letters in the weeks before my departure. Grandpa stopped by the other day to see you, but you were in physical therapy. He'd been holding onto this letter for a special time, but I convinced him there's no better time than now."

"You wrote me a letter?" I looked down at her handwriting. It was so real, so tangible, that it made her ghost less true. This letter I held in my hands was from my *real* Gran. Not the one sitting in my car that I had conjured. And certainly not the one I had dreamed about while being under sedation in the hospital.

I sat back down in my car and closed the door. "You're going to be late, dear . . ."

I shook my head. Nothing mattered but this. Carefully, I opened the letter. It was a beautiful one-page letter. Her handwriting was something I could never get back. I ran my fingers over the indentations of her script on the page. I somehow felt closer to her in that moment than I did with her ghost by my side.

My Dearest Kinsley,

I have had the joy of watching you grow into the young woman you are today. You were my first grandchild, and you brought so much happiness into my life. I am so sorry that I won't be able to be there to see all the special moments in your life, but I hope that, in some small way, you will always carry a piece of me with you.

Just because my time on this earth is coming to an end,

it doesn't mean my love for you will ever fade. I will always cherish the special bond we share, no matter how far apart we may be. You are my granddaughter, and nothing will ever change that.

I know it's hard to say goodbye, but please promise me you will remember all the happy times we had together. It can be difficult to miss someone so much and still be able to hold on to the good memories, but when you think of me, I want you to find happiness. I know you are stronger than you realize.

And one more thing, I want you to take care of your grandpa. I know that seeing him will remind you of how much you miss me, but please try to be there for him. He will be all alone in our house, sitting in the rocking chair on the front porch, staring at the sunset each evening with a cup of tea and a book, but he won't be able to read. Please encourage him to continue to get out of the house and see you, your brother, and your mom and aunt. Play poker with him and cheat wildly—he loves that.

Life can be exciting, and you'll be going off to college soon, but please remember that nothing is more important than the relationships you have with the people you love. Don't leave them behind. And never be afraid of love— regret can be worse than a broken heart.

I love you, my dear. Until we meet again,
Gran

A tear fell onto the page and splattered on her

signature. The blue ink immediately spread. I folded the letter with shaky hands and tucked it back into its envelope before my tears could ruin the keepsake further. I sniffled, running my arm underneath my wet nose. Gran looked up at me with hazy, loving eyes. Her figure was dimmer, even more transparent than before. I gave her a little nod, still unable to speak. My throat was swollen, and I was working overtime to keep the tears back. I had an entire therapy session to get through, and I couldn't come in late *and* sobbing.

Gran and I walked side by side into the building. Her words sank deeply, where they would find a forever home. *You are stronger than you realize.* I thought about all I'd endured. Every struggle. I had been through a lot. But my strength was only a byproduct of my survival. I wasn't sure I could take credit for that.

I sat in Dr. Shelton's office frozen, in a daze. Gran sat in the open seat next to me.

"How are you doing today, Kinsley?"

"Good," I lied.

"Last time we spoke, you were taking on a different persona. I believe you called her Layla. Have you put any thought into that since our last session?"

I stared at the wood grain on the arms of my chair. I didn't answer her. All I could think about was the letter from Gran.

After an uncomfortable amount of time, Dr. Shelton

asked a different question. "Your mother told me your dreams took on the life of fairy tales. Which fairy tale did you resonate with most?"

"The next story in the book was Cinderella. And I'm fairly certain I would have dreamed about that next. However, if I choose a fairy tale that resonated with me, I think it would be Beauty and the Beast."

"What do you mean, you would have dreamed of Cinderella next?"

"I mean, if I stayed in the coma, somebody would have read that fairy tale, and its elements would have created the next several weeks of my summer."

"Interesting. What resonates with you? Why do you think of Beauty and the Beast?" she asked, as she pushed her glasses up the bridge of her nose.

I chewed on my lip, not wanting to say his name aloud. I hated how the fresh wave of pain hit every time I said or thought it. "W . . . Walker said he was cursed. Which would make you think he would be the Beast. But I'm not so sure. I think *I* was the cursed one. Every time I looked in the mirror, I'd see a homely girl, or worse, nothing at all. I had trouble recognizing myself. Hence, I would've been the Beast."

"If you're the Beast, than who's Beauty?" Dr. Shelton scribbled down a note on our hypothetical conversation. I couldn't imagine it was noteworthy.

"Walker." I thought of his deeply etched dimples, his lustrous golden eyes. Of course, he was Beauty.

Dr. Shelton tapped her pen across her lips. "Have you considered that, perhaps, Layla was Beauty? And you were the Beast. Opposite sides of the same coin?"

I ran my hand through my hair and traced the scar along the length of my head. I was definitely the Beast, but could I also be Beauty? "How is that possible?"

"It's possible that Layla, as a part of you, was the person you've always wished to be but never allowed yourself to become. Perhaps your dyslexia hindered your confidence, casting you into a self-fulfilling prophecy. Putting a wedge between your current poor self-image and your future ideal self. A wedge so massive, so incapable of bridging, that you felt as though you could be none other than two entirely different people."

Dr. Shelton paused, and I thought about what she had said. There was a part of me I loathed, but was very comfortable with. And there was also a part of me, very much outside my comfort zone, that I strived to be. And no matter how detrimental, comfort was easy. It was definitely possible that Layla was Beauty.

"And perhaps, when your grandmother died, your two personas grew even further apart. The grief set you back from reaching Layla, that happy, healthy girl. And now, when you feel hurt and lonely, when you don't understand life and why things have happened to you, you look at

Layla, so far in the distance, and think you might never reach her."

How true it was. I hung my head.

"But it doesn't have to be that way. As soon as you see yourself for all that you are, you can bridge that gap. You can be both Beauty and the Beast. You can wear your grief and insecurities, all while living a happy and fulfilling life. There *is* room for both of you."

I shrugged and looked down at the carpet, my eyes catching the faintest outline of Gran. I thought about how I'd been my own worst enemy. How I became my own monster. In a world where I had the power to give myself anything I wanted, I gave myself a broken heart. I could have had a smile, but I chose fangs. Why? Because I wasn't ready to own my shortcomings, and now, my grief?

"I'm stronger than I realize . . ." I repeated the words from Gran's letter as I began to believe them. Maybe struggle had found me, but that didn't mean my strength wasn't earned.

"You're right. Most likely, you'll never know just how capable you are. Most people will never realize their full capability."

I gazed at the ornate detail of her wooden desk, my eyes unfocused, my mind far away. "I've been avoiding my grandpa. I didn't even realize it," I admitted.

"Oh? And why is that?" Pen met paper with quick deliberate strokes.

"Because why would I want to go to his house when all I smell is my gran? Why would I want to visit when all I see are her belongings? What if I see her shoes, and I think she'll never wear them again? What if I see her books and think she'll never read them again? There are too many reminders that she's not here, and I don't know how to deal with it." I closed my eyes for a moment, squelching the burn. "Does that make me a terrible person? A terrible granddaughter?"

"Avoidance can be a common side effect of grieving. But the first step is acknowledging it. Which it seems like you've done here today."

"I don't want to push my mom and grandpa away just because I'm afraid of the pain. They're hurting too. And all I've done is make it worse."

"To be fair, Kinsley, they may be pulling back themselves. It's easy to isolate when we're in pain. What are some ways you think you could help change that?"

"I think I should talk to my mom. I think I should let her know that I'm stronger than I look. That she can talk to me. Lean on me."

"Yes, we talked about this a little last time. About you taking on a better version of yourself. Are you ready for that?"

"I've been through a lot. I can handle this too." It was the first time I truly believed it.

"What about visiting your grandpa? Do you think that

would help?" Dr. Shelton put down her pen and clasped her hands.

I thought about walking into my grandparents' home. It was a custom home Grandpa had built in a beautiful clearing, high on the bluffs of a mountain top. It was the most peaceful, serene home I had ever been to. But somewhere along the way of cars and boys, I'd stopped going. Gran was right; life became too busy with meaningless things, and I would never get that time back. It seemed the longer I waited, the harder it would be to visit.

"I think it's going to be difficult," I said, meeting her gaze for the first time today. I could still see Gran out of the corner of my eye, though barely.

"You're not wrong about that. It absolutely will be difficult. There's nothing about the grieving process that isn't. But remember, time heals everything. And it *will* get easier. Don't rush yourself. It could take years, and that's okay, too."

Slowly, I dropped my gaze from the doctor to my lap. I interlocked my hands and twisted my fingers. I found a smudge of dirt under my pinky nail and worked diligently to clean it out. I was stronger than I knew. And I was going to face the fact that I'd lost my gran. I was going to ask my grandpa for stories about her and play cards with him again. I would find new and creative ways to cheat and win. I smirked.

The first thing I was going to do when I got home was give Mom a hug. I was going to ask her how she was doing, because in all honesty, I hadn't. I hadn't asked her once how she was holding up from the death of her mother.

I had been so wrapped up in my own feelings, and then the accident happened. I hadn't even realized everybody around me was going through tough times of their own. And now that I thought about it, I was the only one who'd had extra time with Gran. I'd spent a full summer with her. I'd been able to call her on the telephone and chat with her in my bedroom months beyond her death. Until this moment, I hadn't realized how *lucky* I was.

I felt that way now. Lucky. Lucky to have had her in my life, even though I felt our time was too short.

It was in that exact moment that the ghost beside me glimmered. Just like a thought taking flight in Baylor, the fresh perspective grew wings of its own and changed reality before my eyes. I turned to meet Gran's disappearing emerald eyes. They sparkled like precious stones and spoke of quiet joys. Before I knew it, the chair beside me was empty, and I knew I wouldn't be seeing my gran again.

I had finally reached the moment where I was strong enough to stand on my own. I'd just never realized what that meant. Gran had to go back to wherever she belonged and leave me behind. Since the accident, her world and mine had collided in a mixture of natural and supernatural, and it was in this exact moment that our two worlds parted. I would be lying if I said the fear hadn't crept back in. But this time, I knew I was strong enough to handle it on my own.

CHAPTER 23

All I saw was the gray sky, full of storm clouds. The air was thicker than normal. My fingertips trailed in the frigid water as my arm hung lazily over the edge of the canoe. I swirled my hand back and forth through the rippling water. Where was I? My back was stiff, as if I'd been lying here a while. I lifted my head from the belly of the boat and peered out.

Sitting in the middle of a lake, in a canoe with no paddles, I recognized the shoreline as Baylor Lake. My heartbeat spiked. Panic took over. I ripped my hand from the evil waters and cradled it against my chest. Why was I back here? I didn't want to be back here.

I thought my dreams had ended. I tried on countless occasions to get back to the void and to find Walker. But ever since he slid the missing glass slipper on my foot, I hadn't been able to get back to him. But this was no false reality. I was back in Baylor, and I didn't know why, or for how long.

I rubbed the goosebumps on my arms, trying to pinpoint which direction the cabin was. I couldn't tell the time of day, as the sun was hidden deep behind the clouds. I only hoped I could get out before nightfall.

It didn't matter that I knew where my monsters had spawned from. They were still just as terrifying. And I didn't want to spend my time fighting between the jaws of a beast when I had a job to do. I needed to find Walker. And I needed him to come home with me.

I took a deep breath and plunged my hand into the cold water. I cupped the water and pushed it behind me. Hard and fast, I dug through the lake. But I tired quickly and found the canoe was moving in circles. It was useless. I was stuck in the middle of the lake, and time was ticking. *Think. Think, Kinsley.*

Would manifestation work? Now that I was completely aware I was lucid dreaming, would any of my old tricks work? I closed my eyes and tried to warm my wet hand between my legs. I thought of the cabin. I imagined the canoe gliding up to the dock and Walker waiting for me on the back porch.

I opened my eyes when I felt the canoe bump against shore. I was surprised to find I wasn't at our dock, but a small cove I didn't recognize. Warily, I stepped out of the canoe and into the shadows of the forest. I tromped through blackberry bushes and scraped my legs on thorns until a small trail appeared, winding through the dense trees. I hurried along in search of help.

"Walker?" I called out.

At first, I thought I saw a person in the woods, but as I looked closer, I could see it was a full-length mirror leaning against a pine tree. A girl I used to know stared back at me. And as I'd been somewhat traumatized from the funhouse and the many hours searching for my soul in empty mirrors, I hurried into a jog down the trail.

Tiny hairs on my arms rose, and I knew the quicker I got out of the forest, the better. Things in Baylor had changed since the last time I was here. Small, decorative mirrors hung like Christmas ornaments from the trees, causing multiple pairs of brown eyes to watch me as I crossed the forest floor. I sucked in a deep breath as one dropped and shattered on the path. Woodland critters scampered into the shrubs. I had to remind myself to be brave, that I was stronger now.

After making eye contact with my reflection a handful of jarring times, I realized the eyes weren't always the same. Sometimes they were bleak, empty eyes, and other times they were mysterious and prevailing. I was certain now that somebody was watching me.

I spun in a slow circle as my eyes studied the depths of the forest. There were clumps of purple rapunzel flowers, a noisy crow jumping from one branch to the next, and a trail of black smoke in the distance.

"Layla?" I called out, hoping the mysterious eyes belonged to her.

A loud crash sent me leaping forward as I covered my head. A large mirror broke just feet behind me. I looked up into the treetops where several giant mirrors perched between branches. How did they get up there? And why?

The crow hopped about, causing branches to bow under its weight. When the next mirror hurtled down, I jumped out of the way with a yelp. The clatter echoed throughout the forest, and the trail was littered with broken glass. I had to be very careful if I didn't want the sky itself to break. I knew it could.

I walked on, trying to remain calm and collected. At first, I thought a reflection from the gray sky had peeked down through the leaves and ricocheted off the fractals of broken glass that lay on the trail. The slight movement of dancing light illuminated the forest floor. But as my eyes found the sharp fragments of glass beneath my feet, I saw something I wasn't expecting.

There, in a triangular piece of broken mirror, I saw Walker pulling me from the lake. I kneeled down, watching the memory play out before me. My shaking wet body fell helplessly into the canoe. Starlight lit my face from a perspective I'd never seen before. And Walker's mysterious and warm eyes shifted from wonder to . . .

"What the hell were you doing all the way out here? We must be miles from the nearest shore." I could barely hear his voice floating somewhere near and yet far at the same time.

I scanned the hundreds of mirrors, all reflecting distinct memories, throughout the forest. And that's when I could hear them. I could hear them all.

"We get to stay here all summer?" Kimber asked in awe.

My head snapped in the opposite direction, and I rose to a crouching position. A TV newscaster spoke, sending chills down my spine. "147 people died Thursday night on flight 351 to Clover. Caught in the storm, the plane came crashing down in the middle of Grand and Fifth, demolishing the historical bank here in Charlee City."

"No!"

I reached out, eager to find the memory and smash it. Stop it from ever happening in the first place. But I froze in my tracks when I heard a small, frightened voice, more familiar than the rest.

"What happens if I don't go home?"

"You mean if you stay here?" Gran asked, her tone worried and faint.

"Yeah, if I stay." I felt the heartbreak and all the uncertainty that had plagued me over the summer. I searched for the memory, but it was lost in a sea of voices. I walked in circles, trying to find it.

"And you won't be far after?" Layla asked. I took a few steps off the path before finding the vision in a massive mirror that was lying on the ground, slightly hidden behind a rock. Layla was speaking with Walker, and I was peeking out from behind the trees. Eavesdropping on a conversation that would change the course of my entire life.

"I promise. If you go, so will I," he said.

I watched myself trip over the crimson cloak. Both Walker and Layla whipped their heads around, peering into the forest. But I was long gone, the cloak left behind in a cloud of dust.

He'd told her he would follow her home. Why didn't he?

My mom's song drifted in the distant air. "My heart blooms. Blooms for you. Wildflowers because of you." Her song clashed with the other voices, pleading for my attention. I closed my eyes.

"I'm not going to spend eternity rotting in my own guilty conscience!"

"Secrets? Secrets are for the living. What do you need to hide in your afterlife?"

"Just read it!" . . . "I can't! I don't want to!"

"Everything you've ever thought or felt has a home. A place to live in a dark, forgotten corner of your mind."

A voice yelled from above. "Wake up!" Lainey hissed. I looked up just in time to see a pair of desperate yellow eyes reaching out from the haunted water. I screamed as the mirror crashed down, breaking on my shoulder and slicing open my arm.

Voices surfaced near and far. A different dimension. A different time. All flooding back into a single moment. I tightened my fists and blocked everything out the best I could. The desperate voices, the regrets, the burn of my open wound. There was only one reflection I needed to see now.

"Layla!" I cried. I waited for her reply, but nothing came. Movement flickered like an ancient TV screen, but I saw stillness in her eyes. An old Victorian mirror swayed gently from a low-hanging branch, and a pair of deep brown eyes met mine with a knowing gaze.

I crossed the path of broken glass, reached out, and took the decorative mirror in my hand. I stared into Layla's eyes as my breathing slowed. "Layla . . ." I whispered. I watched her ruby lips move in unison with my plea for help.

This time, I saw myself in her. Everything I had ever needed to get through this nightmare was hiding in plain sight. I was capable of finding Walker and bringing him home.

I nodded into the mirror and let it go. It spun fiercely on its cord, causing a small glimmer of light to flicker throughout the forest, until it was wound so tightly the light stopped, illuminating a path I hadn't seen before.

I worried there wasn't much time left and took off running toward what I hoped would be Walker. The strung mirror unwound itself, throwing flashes of light wildly throughout the forest. Mirrors dropped near and far, and shattering glass exploded like grenades on a battlefield.

It's only a dream. Lean into the darkness. Gran's words echoed in my mind. I hoped I would make her proud, wherever she was.

I ran until I broke free from the web of memories. The cabin sat peacefully in the clearing. Then, I saw Walker's canoe, floating like a burning barge in the middle of Rock Creek Cove. A trail of black smoke signaled high in the sky eliciting fright and panic.

"Walker!" I screamed, as I barreled down the hill.

He couldn't die. I wouldn't let him.

"Walker!"

I ran straight into the water and dove when the surface met my thighs. The flames were shrinking. The canoe snapped in half, both ends tipping up as the center began to sink. I floundered, searching wildly for a body I couldn't bear to see.

I ducked under the water, kicking hard to catch the sinking wreckage. I knew I could hold an infinite breath when I was in Baylor, but something seemed different. My lungs spasmed, and despite my best efforts, I needed air. I was living now, and the thought of running out of air frightened me. I didn't want to die.

I surfaced and took a gulp of air, then dived deeper, but no matter how many times I tried, I couldn't reach the canoe. Air bubbles nipped at the surface as I cried.

Had he ended his life? Was it so miserable here without companionship? Had I been too late?

I remembered the spontaneous fires in the trees, the campfire chairs, and even the clouds. Had the poison finally rolled through Baylor, sweeping away all the lives left behind?

I swallowed water on my way back to shore, crying and coughing uncontrollably.

"Wilde?"

I climbed out of the lake on hands and knees. Silt covered my legs, and blood ran from the wound on my arm. Standing where the back patio door would have been —if it hadn't caught fire—was a silhouette.

"Walker?" I took a muddy step. He cocked his head and slung a black washcloth over his shoulder. "Walker!" I screamed.

He was alive! He was lonely, and most likely heartbroken, but he was alive!

I couldn't imagine what living in Baylor would be like had I done it alone. My friends were the only things that kept me sane, and I hung on to that sanity by a thread.

I ran up the hill, slipping on wet grass under muddy

shoes. The deck was missing, and the backside of the cabin was a sorry sight. Black char covered the collapsing doorframe and surrounded the broken windows. The cabin appeared not only abandoned, but haunted. And Walker was glum enough to be the ghost that lived there.

Walker jumped to the ground in the staircase's absence. I ran straight into his arms, crashing into him. I cried on his shoulder, unable to get the words out.

"You're shaking like a leaf."

"I thought . . . I thought you were . . ."

"What's going on Wilde? Why are you here?" Walker pulled back. He seemed more confused than anything else.

"I thought you were dead." That single word crushed me, and I crumbled before him.

"What? No! I'm right here. I'm right here." He cradled me in his arms.

I sank back against his chest, trembling involuntarily at the very thought of losing him. "I saw the canoe."

"Everything's burning. It has been for some time now. The canoe and dock went this morning. It looks like I'll be staying here. Let's go inside," he said, shifting his arm around my waist.

"You don't have to stay here. Come home with me." My voice quivered, and I realized I was more afraid now, as I waited for his reply, than I ever would have been fighting my nightmares in the fog-dense forest.

"That world's not meant for me . . ."

"Yes, it is. What are you talking about?"

"Wilde, I don't belong there anymore." He shook his head, and the lights went out in his eyes. "This is my home now."

I followed him through the front door, and it shocked me to see the cabin was exactly how I had left it. Exactly.

It was suffocating. Flakes of black ash were still settling in the air, as if the fire had just happened. The walls were charred black and crusted over. The smell of smoke made it difficult to breathe.

Immediately, I looked to the corner where I had seen Scarlett May's cowgirl boots peeking from within a mountain of embers and ash. The pile remained, but I was relieved to find that her boots were gone. I had to remind myself that she was back home. Or rather, on the other side of the lake now. Yes, she was in Baylor, but she wasn't in this Baylor.

"I've got some cleaning up to do, but hey, I've got time." The look on his face seemed pained. He seemed lonelier than ever before, and that was saying a lot for Walker.

"You can't live here. It's inhabitable. It's . . . a nightmare," I whispered. It was my nightmare.

Walker's eyes flickered with recognition. It almost seemed like he had forgotten he was in a dream. Forgotten that he had a family to get back to. I remembered how easy it was to succumb to the darkness. When the light seemed so far away, so unobtainable, I'd convinced myself I didn't want it any longer. I feared that if I didn't get out in time, I might be swallowed up by the night and lost forever. I had to focus.

"You have a family. You have a life. You're in a hospital, and everybody is rooting for you. You need to come back!"

"You don't know that." Walker hung his head and walked into the kitchen, avoiding eye contact with me. What had happened to him in the time I'd been gone? Time moved slower in dreams. Exactly how long had he felt abandoned? Long enough to lose feelings for me?

"Yes, I do! Because I was in the room next door. I spent a week listening to your monitors through the thin walls of the hospital. Listening to your friends come and go. Listening to your mother cry when visiting hours were over. I had to hear your little sister try to comfort your mother in a way that no child should ever have to do! I know this because I was there!"

Tears clouded my eyes as I pointed an angry finger at his chest. I felt so very alone in the hospital. And even though my family was often present, nobody knew what I was going through. But Walker would have, if only he'd chosen to fight.

Walker pulled the dirty black towel from his shoulder and kneeled in front of a small wet spot on the kitchen floor. He dipped the rag into a bucket of black water, wrung it out, and plopped it onto the floor. And then, mindlessly, he began scrubbing.

It reminded me of Emma when I'd last seen her in Baylor. She had been scrubbing the same soiled spot, trying to clean the soot stain from the floor. It never came clean, and she never gave up. Something inside of her had gone dim. Dormant. The lights had gone out, just like I saw in Walker's eyes now. I'm certain that she would have spent eternity trying to clean the same square foot of the kitchen floor if I hadn't climbed that Ferris wheel.

"Walker?" My voice was but a whisper.

He said nothing.

"What about your family?"

He scrubbed vigorously. His muscles bulged from his arm, and veins popped across the back of his hand. Had he not heard me?

"Is this because of the curse? Because you don't think you can find love? Well, I'm right here! You found it! You just have to come get it!" I spread my arms open, wishing he'd claim his prize.

His back stilled for just a moment, but I could tell he'd given up on that thought long ago.

I did the only thing I could think of. I crossed into the kitchen and pulled a dish towel from a blackened drawer. Then I kneeled beside him and submerged my towel in the dirty water. I wrung it out with two hands as I caught Walker's eyes unwillingly shift back and forth. Fighting between caring just enough and being too numb to care at all.

"What are you doing?" he asked, his voice grave. Somewhere inside, he wanted to come home. I guided him the only way I knew how. And in this twisted realm, dark psychology was my best bet.

"I'm cleaning." I slopped the wet towel down on the black floor and started to scrub.

"Don't bullshit me, Wilde! What are you doing?" I flinched. I'd never seen Walker this angry before, but at least the fire was back in his eyes, and for that, I was thankful.

"If you stay . . . I stay," I said, glaring at him.

"You belong with the living!"

"Don't test me! You know what I'm capable of!" I said through gritted teeth.

"I will not let you ruin your life because of me!"

A minute passed with no words spoken. I briefly wondered how I'd possibly get him home. Even if he agreed. I didn't have a plan beyond this fight, and I didn't know where the next red door would be.

His eyes narrowed. "Don't test me," he countered. "You have no idea what I'm capable of . . ."

"If you had magic, then why didn't you use it?"

"Because! I could have killed you. I did kill you. I made a promise when the paramedics pulled you from the car. I stood on the overpass, and I made a deal with the devil. If we owed a life, it would be mine." Walker beat his chest.

"You what?"

I searched his eyes, looking for the smallest sliver of hope. I saw nothing.

"You cursed yourself?" A tidal wave built inside me. How were we going to fight this? "But you said you were going to come back! You were supposed to follow us . . ."

"I'm a monster. A killer. It's in my blood." Walker shook his head. Though his confession was raw, it couldn't be real. A place like this could take a sound mind and twist it till it broke. And he was very much broken.

"Did any part of you want me to stay?"

Walker threw his rag into the bucket, and water splattered the floor. "Loving you was the hardest fight I ever fought. And I lost. I hated myself for it. I begged Layla to take you home. But you were so stubborn! You sabotaged yourself at every turn!"

He covered his face with his hand. "And the longer I spent with you, the more I wanted to believe that I was the guy you dreamed of."

I took his wrist and pulled his hand from his face. "You are!"

"I killed you!" he yelled.

I dropped his wrist and leapt backward. My heart pounded. "It was an accident," I insisted.

"Don't you see? I'm no good for you." Walker's golden

eyes turned watery and red. "I belong here . . ." He gestured to a fluttering flake of ash.

Walker wasn't a murderer. He wasn't the Baylor Butcher, and he wasn't his father. He was just a guy who'd had an accident. A guy whose life changed forever in a split second.

"Your curse is my curse. If you don't come home, I'm the one who will never love again." I threw my rag on top of his and placed my hands on my hips.

Walker shook his head painfully. It wasn't what he wanted. And I could tell he'd never considered that if he punished himself, he'd punish me as well. If he wanted me to be happy, he'd have to forgive himself first.

"Come home with me."

A single tear spilled from Walker's eye. He quickly averted his gaze and tightened his fists. "I'm sorry, but I can't. Keep your promise, Wilde. Say goodbye."

The ground moved under my feet, and I nearly stumbled backward. Walker and I both slid toward the opening where the patio door used to be. A wide-open red door called to me. I felt my soul flutter as if getting sucked into the vortex just beyond the portal.

Walker was using his magic, and I feared it would be the spell that broke us. "Walker! No! Don't!" I continued to slide backward as if on some invisible conveyor belt. My hair rose from my back as the wind became stronger.

I lunged forward in one last attempt to save Walker

from himself. I grabbed hold of his flannel collar and pulled him to me. I pressed my lips against his in the most passionate kiss I'd ever had. I kissed him like my life depended on it. And this time, I didn't hide behind the guise of a wolf to do it.

I clung to him. My shirt beat against my back. My hair lashed violently. The vortex pulled and pulled. When I tripped backward, we were sucked through the door. The shackles of the curse broke and fell away as we plunged through the clouds. I felt Walker grin into our kiss.

CHAPTER 24

D awn was breaking outside my window, and the night sky lightened to a hazy purple. My chest rose and fell quickly as I brought my fingertips to trace my lips. I could have sworn they were still warm from Walker's kiss. A smile spread under my touch. *I did it.* I brought him home. I leapt out of bed, slipped my feet into my sneakers, and grabbed a hooded sweatshirt to pull over my head as I ran out of my bedroom.

I tried to be quiet, as my parents were still sleeping, but my enthusiasm was thunderous as I ran down the stairs. I grabbed the keys from beneath the never-shrinking pile of unopened mail on the kitchen table, and I ran into the garage. I didn't hesitate to start the ignition or pull out of the driveway. Driving no longer scared me.

My mind raced as I drove to the hospital. Was he already awake? Was he just waking now? Would my face be the first he'd see since the accident? I pulled into the parking lot and scurried into the hospital.

I slipped past the check-in desk and made my way to the elevator. I drummed my hands on my legs until the door glided open. How would he respond? Would he remember me? My pajama pants and messy hair kept the questions at bay in the ICU. I must have fit in with all the other visitors who looked like they hadn't slept in days. Knowing my way around the hospital helped too.

My sweaty hand nearly slipped off the doorknob. But I couldn't take the time to prepare myself or I'd get caught in the hall. I wasn't sure what I'd say, or how I'd say it. I only knew that I had to get to him. I opened the door and hurried inside. My heart sank as my eyes fell upon his empty bed.

What? Was I too late? Had they moved him to a different room? I grabbed his chart but froze when I heard the toilet flush. I pressed the clipboard against my chest and took a deep breath. I turned to face Walker for the first time in real life.

"Well, it isn't much," a grumpy man said as he shuffled toward me. He reached out and handed me a cylinder of warm amber liquid. The stars vanished in my eyes, and the heat from my cheeks turned cold. I realized not only was this man *not* Walker, but that I was holding his chart . . . and urine sample. He turned for bed, his robe parted and exposed a labyrinth of dark curly hair on his upper back.

The toilet seat was still lifted as the restroom door swung shut. "Don't be scared. It isn't gonna bite."

I ran out. I discarded the man's file in a slot by his door, then ran to the nurse's desk, the sample still pinched between my fingers.

"Excuse me?" I asked. "Do you know where Walker went? He was in that room before." I hooked a thumb over my shoulder.

"Are you related to the patient?" the young nurse asked.

"Yes," I lied.

"You mean Lance? He is downstairs in room 24. Is he your father?" The nurse typed on her keyboard, glancing at me only briefly when I faltered.

"Lance?" I stuttered, trying to come up with a believable lie when I saw Martina.

"Martina!" I called out, slamming my free hand down on the counter.

It took a moment for her to recognize me, but when she did, her face lit up. "Hey Kinsley! What are you doing back here? Is everything okay?"

"Yeah. Everything's going well. I was just checking on Walker St. James?" I pointed to his old room. "Do you know where they moved him?"

Martina tilted her head and leaned in close. "Now you know I'm not supposed to tell you other patient's personal information."

"I know. I know," I pled.

"I can't tell you much . . ." she hesitated.

"Anything! Anything you can tell me! I'd be so grateful."

"He's not here. He hasn't been for a long time. His mother took him to a new hospital, and I don't know which one, so don't ask me!" She pointed her finger at me, silencing my next question before it arose. "Now, don't tell anybody I told you that much. You hear?"

"I understand. But—"

"No buts!"

"But why did he get moved?"

Martina's face fell and her shoulders slumped. One corner of her mouth lifted as she said, "I don't know. Something about this hospital not giving him what he needs. Now it's time to go back to wherever you came from." She put her hands on my shoulders and spun me around.

"Thank you," I whispered over my shoulder.

"Don't thank me. I did nothing." She gave me a knowing stare.

"Wait!" I spun around.

"Now, I told you—" I handed Martina the urine sample and left without another word.

After stopping in a restroom and washing my hands under hot, soapy water, I drove home. I couldn't imagine Walker waking up in a hospital without me. I remembered how confused I'd been when I woke up. I knew he needed me. I wasn't sure where I would find the answers. The world suddenly seemed so large, and I was too small. I reminded myself that he'd found me once on the road, and I had found him once in a dream. I hoped that fate would bring us together for a third and final time.

Mom was upset when I got home. Something about me taking the car without asking. But I was eighteen now. Not exactly graduated, but almost. Still, I didn't fight with her. I didn't have the energy. She and I had been talking a lot more recently, opening up about Gran and things. I didn't want to ruin our newfound trust with a battle over independence.

Mom slammed her phone down on the table and rubbed her temples. "I'm sorry. I'll let you know next time. I just, I couldn't sleep, and the sun was almost up. I wanted to go for a drive and listen to music. That's all." Normally I was an honest person, but one small lie led to many.

She waved her hand dismissively. "That was a message from your Uncle Tanner. Apparently, there was a noise complaint last night at the cabin. Do you know anything about that?"

"A noise complaint?"

"They said there was a party, and they had to call the sheriff to shut it down at nearly two in the morning."

Lainey and Emma threw a party? I couldn't imagine such a thing. I mean, I certainly could imagine throwing a party at the cabin; I had done it several times in my dreams. But Lainey and Emma? In real life? Not possible.

I poured Mom a cup of hot coffee after the machine beeped. Her face softened when I put it down in front of her. "I'll call Uncle Tanner today and apologize. And I'm going to call Lainey and Emma right now to get to the bottom of it," I said.

"Thank you." She took a sip of coffee and then stared blankly out the window. I slipped away to call my friends.

It surprised me when Lainey picked up. She was typically an early bird, but if they had a party last night, I would have figured she'd sleep in. I was wrong.

"Hello? Kinsley?" Lainey whispered into the phone.

"Hey, it's me. Why are you up so early?" I asked as I settled in my bed, still in my pajamas from the hospital run.

"Gunner won't stop barking. He doesn't want to be inside, but he can't stop barking outside. Your neighbors are going to be so pissed." I heard the door open and slam shut. Gunner's bark sounded like an alarm in the distance.

"What is he barking at?"

"I don't know. Something in the water. A duck maybe? It's too foggy to tell."

I had the clearest memory of Gunner barking at the end of the dock. It made me uneasy to think anything, anything at all, was similar now. "Where's Emma?"

"Gunner! Gunner!" Lainey hissed.

"Where's Emma?" I repeated sternly.

"Oh my god, Kins. Your parents are going to kill me. He's dug holes all over the lawn!"

"Lainey!" I snapped. "Where. Is. Emma?"

"What!? She's sleeping. What's the big deal? Come on, Gunner. Come on."

"Are you sure?"

"Yeah, I'm sure. Where else would she be?" Lainey's breath was uneven and labored, and I could hear Gunner grunting in the background.

"Go check! Check right now!" I had felt helpless before, but sitting at home in my pajamas was a new low.

"I'm going. God Kinsley, you're scaring me." I listened to the door swing open on a creaky hinge. Gunner's toenails pranced on the kitchen floor and footfalls thumped up the steps. I held my breath, waiting for confirmation that Emma was okay and hadn't sunk to the bottom of Rock Creek Cove. When Lainey sighed in relief, I did too.

"She's sleeping! Like everybody else is doing at six a.m. What was all that about? I just tracked mud through the house. You have no idea how much cleaning I have to do today."

I closed my eyes and tried to relax. I had to remind myself that their trip was not the same one I'd taken. It wasn't the summer from hell. It was their graduation celebration. It was everything it was supposed to be, minus me. Nothing more. Nothing less.

"Well, I have an idea. I heard the neighbors called the sheriff on you guys. Did you throw a party last night?" I asked with a chuckle. The thought was so unlikely, it seemed ridiculous to even ask.

It took too long for Lainey to answer, so I pressed the phone closer to my ear. Did she really throw a party?

"About that—"

"Oh my god! You threw a party!"

My Lainey threw a party. How I wished I were there. I tried to imagine such a thing, but when I did, my smile died. I saw a red door in the hall beckoning me. Luring me. At first, I felt like I'd missed out, but now I felt like I'd dodged a bullet.

"I'm so, so sorry. I didn't plan it. I tried to stop it for like two hours! They just kept coming!"

"It's okay. I'm not mad. I'm a little shocked is all. I can't believe *you* threw a party. Was it fun? Wait, tell me nobody broke my pottery . . ."

Lainey laughed. "I don't think anything was broken. And yes. It was so much fun!" she squealed. I snuggled up in bed, ready to hear all the stories. It was the perfect distraction from losing Walker.

"Tell me everything! Who was there?"

"Okay. So we met up with the group after running into them in town. We didn't even try; it just happened organically. Scarlett May was asking where you were. I mean, they all were. But she, especially, seemed sad that you weren't here. They asked where the house was, and we told them. We thought nothing of it when they said they might stop by. When they showed up, we were mid-movie, and Emma had a face mask on!"

"No!" I gasped.

"Yes! When they knocked on the front door, she bolted upstairs and sent Gunner into a panic!"

I threw myself onto a stack of pillows and covered my face with secondhand embarrassment.

"I opened the door, surprised to see everybody. Noah held up chocolate, marshmallows, and graham crackers, hoping for an invite in. I could tell it crushed him you weren't here. But before I could get any words out, Mason pushed through the crowd with a case of beer on his shoulder, and everybody just followed him inside. At first, I was really stressed, but then the boys made a fire out by the shore. It was actually really fun, Kinsley! I'm so sad you missed it."

"Don't worry about me. I visited my grandpa. He plays a mean game of Go Fish. So, did you toast marshmallows?"

"Yes. We sat around the fire toasting marshmallows and telling scary ghost stories. It was the best. Even Emma told one! But then we heard this creak in the woods. It totally freaked me out. I was actually terrified, but everybody else just laughed. That part was embarrassing," Lainey rambled.

I could hear her voice turn dismissive, but I *knew* that sound in the woods. I knew it was more than a settling branch or a nocturnal critter. There were predators out there, invisible to the naked eye. Invisible to the vulnerable likes of Lainey and Emma. My chest tightened to think the summer was repeating itself.

"You have to trust your instincts, Lainey. Don't go into those woods alone! They're dangerous!" Goosebumps prickled my arms.

Lainey laughed. "No, no, no. It was just Scarlett May's friends. Apparently, she's friends with a couple of the locals, and everybody is super connected here. She invited a couple of people last night, and when they heard us telling ghost stories, they snuck up on us. It broke the ice, and we all laughed pretty hard. We even have an inside joke about it. Can you believe I have an inside joke with Kimber and Asher? Like, what is this world we live in?" I could hear her smile through the phone.

I believed it, and then some. The more she talked, the more my summer came to life. I'd been working diligently to make sure my dreams were contained. Placed in a neat box that I could shut the lid on, and padlock for good measure. I needed my dreams to be silenced, because when they were free, they spread throughout all my memories, making it difficult to tell where the fiction ended and the truth began.

All the work I'd done to tame my nightmares were diminishing now that stories of Baylor were hot off the press. Of course, they weren't having the summer I had, but there were similarities. Something as little as the dog barking, or a blanket of fog over the lake. It all had meaning to me.

Lainey and I talked a little more that morning. But the more details I received, the more I grew anxious. I lost count of the number of times Lainey told me I was scaring her with my *cryptic* warnings. Finally, I had to get off the phone.

The first thing I did after hanging up was grab a notebook off my desk and start jotting down the things she'd told me. I separated them from the similar things I had dreamed. Over the next couple of weeks, that list became pages and pages long.

Lainey and Emma ended up staying three full weeks in Baylor. It wasn't the whole summer, but it was a great start. They had more stories to tell when they got back than they'd had their entire high school career combined. I couldn't have been happier for them. Emma had even spent some time alone with Levi. Enough time in fact that she was no longer attracted to him. I told her it was probably for the better.

Both Emma and Lainey found something in Baylor

that had been lost to them. A sense of belonging, a sense of connection. And as it turns out, Baylor was a magical place after all. Because I had found something in those woods too. I found a girl named Layla. I found not only acceptance there, but pride too. It only took me months of therapy and one special ghost to realize it.

Emma and I saw Lainey off to college that summer, and I was able to concentrate enough to finish my GED. I graduated high school, and when the certificate showed up in the mailbox, I celebrated.

I eventually finished physical therapy and began exercising regularly. I got a job at a small bookstore, a place I never thought I'd enjoy. But I learned a lot about story, and I even began to write my first screenplay. Several pages in, I crumpled it into a ball and threw it in the trash. The only story I wanted to tell was that of a haunted cabin in a remote forest. Once I gave in, the story flowed effortlessly. It changed in new and fascinating ways. It became my new guilty pleasure. And as I wrote my story, I began to silence the summer that never was. I could finally put a lock on that box and throw away the skeleton key.

The only setbacks I had were when Aunt Nora updated me on the pending lawsuit. It was my only real connection to Walker. I knew I'd see him again, and that kept me from fully healing.

Everything inside me screamed to let him go. Open my heart to somebody else. Somebody real. Somebody living outside of a fantasy. Because even though Walker had been real, the time we'd spent together was not. I didn't know him. And he didn't know me. Still, it would take a great deal of time to get over my idea of him.

I couldn't help but compare the few boys I dated to Walker. And soon, that became a recurring conversation with Dr. Shelton. She helped me realize I was afraid of putting myself out there and getting my heart broken. That's the reason I compared my dates to a fictional guy. She reminded me over and over, and the more times I heard it, the more I believed it.

One year later, I'd forgotten what Walker looked like. I tried to picture his face in my mind, but I couldn't quite remember if he had dimples or not. I thought maybe he had. I couldn't remember what shape his lips were, or what shade of pink they were. And I thought his eyes might have been hazel, but I couldn't remember them either. His hair was dark; I was certain of that, and I was pretty sure he had a scar on his forehead. Other than that, Walker became a symbol of perfectionism. An invisible marker that I used to compare and measure against. A shadow of a man that I wanted to love, but was too afraid to.

CHAPTER 25

A little more than a year after the accident, I had grown very comfortable with what I used to call Layla. Now, it was just me. I was attending college locally. I chose the same college Gran and Grandpa Green had attended, and sometimes, when the sky was gray and glum, I'd see her.

Not the Gran I'd known, but a younger version. A student, walking between classes. I'd watch from underneath a large oak tree, my knees bent, and my back curled against the trunk. Gran was beautiful and vibrant, but most of all, she was mysterious. She'd disappear into the crowd, and I'd never be able to hold on to her for very long.

Lainey was thriving, but Emma had moved back home. She didn't like the university and quit after her first year. She enrolled with me, and we moved out together into a small studio apartment. I visited Grandpa often, and I got quite good at playing cards. Sometimes I'd join him and a couple of his retired police academy friends to play poker. And when I did, I cheated.

My Aunt Nora kept me updated on the pending lawsuit. Not long after she officially filed suit, we were shocked to find out that Walker's attorney had filed a cross-complaint, alleging that *I* had caused the accident.

At first, I was outraged, but my aunt described to me how both witnesses had diagnosed brain injuries. My testimony wasn't very credible, and neither was his. To top that off, both our vehicles' black boxes were destroyed, and ironically, the police report had come back with little to no information as to what had happened. All either of us knew for sure was that we'd incurred an astonishing amount of medical debt.

Nora called the lawsuit an outright brawl. She said that if we wound up in trial, it would not only be outrageously expensive, but stressful too. She didn't want that for me or my parents, and neither did I. As a family, we agreed to mediate before incurring more cost, and Nora was confident that she could get a favorable settlement in a single day.

For the better part of the year, my dreams had completely stopped. I thought I'd be sad about that, but as my mind quieted and my life fell into step, I couldn't be more grateful. In the weeks leading up to the mediation, I was happy to be past the idea of Walker. And just like any normal dream, I could no longer remember him or the time we'd spent together. On the day of mediation, the only thing I was certain of was his name.

I knew I'd been in an accident, that I'd spent two weeks in the hospital and months thereafter recovering both mentally and physically. And I remembered having twisted dreams and struggling with them after I woke. It had been a dark time in my life, but one I found necessary to get where I was today. I had a lot of growth come from that accident, and as painful as it was, I wouldn't trade it for the world.

I finally moved past my nightmares. Past the insecurities. I grew to love myself. I even learned to grieve for my gran instead of burying it deep inside. All my relationships had strengthened in one way or another, and I was currently in the process of getting an agent for my screenplay. Which had turned out nothing like what I had truly experienced, though I couldn't fully remember why. I had notes about what was real and what wasn't scribbled down everywhere. But when I read them now, they hardly made sense. The summer that never was had vanished, just as it should. The last piece holding me back was the lawsuit. And soon, that would be over too.

Aunt Nora honked outside in the early morning. I clutched a hot mocha to my chest as I walked to her car. I faked a smile as we pulled out of the driveway and took a deep breath as we began the drive to downtown Decord City.

"Are you okay?" Aunt Nora asked.

"Yeah."

"You don't need to be nervous. This is standard practice."

Maybe for an attorney. But this was a lot more to me than settling my case and putting the accident past me. This was more than money and the opportunity that came with it. Deep down, I knew I'd face my last demon today. I had to confront a man whom I'd never met yet was responsible for shaping the very person I'd become. "I'm not nervous."

Aunt Nora raised a brow.

"Okay. Just a little bit."

"Let's go over what you should expect in there. I don't want you to be intimidated by the process, okay?"

"Okay."

"First, this is *not* a trial. There won't be a judge or jury. We're privately agreeing to see a third party who specializes in trying to reach settlements and get people to agree on terms. He is called a mediator. And actually, I've worked with him many times before. Jon Walon. He's a friend of mine and will give it to us straight."

"That's good."

"Yes. He's very good at what he does."

"So, am I going to tell everyone what I remember?

Because I remember some of the accident, but not all of it. And what if I'm wrong? What if—"

"No. It won't be like that. In fact, it's just going to be us in our own private conference room all day. From sunup to sundown if necessary. Most of our time will be spent waiting. You won't even see, or talk to the other side, if you don't want to."

"Wait, what?" I didn't have to see Walker? All this time I'd been so nervous to look into his eyes, and now I might not even see him?

"The mediation will take place in separate, private rooms. Sometimes we get together, but that's only if everybody wants to. I don't even know if Rushbrooke's client is going to be there. Sometimes, when the insurance company is involved, they just leave it up to their attorney to deal with mediation, and the client doesn't even show."

"Who's Rushbrooke?" I cracked my knuckles, trying to anticipate what lay ahead.

"The boy from the accident, St. James, his auto insurance company is on the hook for this, so they appointed their own attorney. And he's a real ass." Nora pulled onto the highway, and the acceleration threw me back into my seat.

"But, Walker, he might not be there?" I asked, my mouth running dry.

"He might not be."

I sighed. All this stress for nothing? "Wait. Then did I

have to come?" Could I have let my aunt fight my last battle for me?

"Technically . . . no. You are not required to attend."

"Aunt Nora!"

"But how are you supposed to become a lawyer if you don't fall in love with the process?"

"I'm not becoming a lawyer!" my voice climbed. Aunt Nora chuckled, and I groaned.

"I just wanted to spend the day with you, my dear. It's not often I have such a wonderful client."

"And it's not often I have such a *sneaky* attorney. Oh wait, it is."

"Hey, you want a sneaky attorney. Trust me. I will fight dirty. I'll fight tooth and nail for you, and you know it." She pointed her oval red nail at me.

"I know. I'm just anxious."

"You don't have to be. Promise."

I turned on the music and looked out my window. The thought of not seeing Walker eased my mind. Nora promised this would be a painless day. Boring conversations and subpar lunch. She hoped we would walk away with the settlement and the promised cash would be coming my way. I hoped for closure.

When we got to the business park and I climbed out of Aunt Nora's fancy car, I scanned the parking lot for a face I had only seen in my dreams.

I was even more nervous when we entered the

building. I had passed several men in suits, both young and old. I trained my eyes on the floor before me. A tightly woven navy-blue carpet with orange and tan diamonds.

"Ms. Faye, I thought I'd be seeing you today." A middle-aged man in a burgundy sweater smiled fondly at my aunt. My heart thumped in my chest as I looked at the surrounding suits, wondering which one was Walker. Wondering if he was around the corner or if I'd bump into him in the halls.

"Jon Walon! Meet my favorite niece. This is Kinsley Wilde. She's my client today."

"Oh boy! This is going to be some mediation," he said with promise. I hoped it wouldn't be. I wanted to skip the negotiation, sign the papers, and leave. I didn't care what they said. But Aunt Nora wouldn't allow it. She was determined to make me *whole*.

Mr. Walon escorted us to the conference room where one other gentleman waited. "Kinsley, this is Robert Brown. He is your other attorney, appointed by your auto insurance, and he will be helping us today."

"It's nice to meet you, Ms. Wilde." Robert shook my hand and I smiled. I didn't know I would have two attorneys. It all seemed a bit much. I took my place at a large oval table, and my two attorneys sat by my side. Across from us, the mediator placed his belongings.

"Kinsley, is this your first time in mediation?" Mr. Walon asked.

"Yes."

"It's important for you to understand everything that you discuss with me in here is a hundred percent confidential between us. I will share nothing you say with the other side unless you allow me to do that. There is no right or wrong in here, and nobody is judging you. Please speak up and ask questions. It's going to be a long day, okay?" Walon peered at me from behind his glasses.

"Okay."

"Okay, let's start—"

"I have a question," I blurted.

Mr. Walon smiled. "Go on then."

"Is the . . ." I leaned over to Aunt Nora and whispered. *"What do you call him? Defendant?"*

"Correct. St. James is the defendant," she said.

I cleared my throat and tried again. "Is the defendant here today?"

"Yes. St. James is here. His personal attorney, Bradly Barratt, is here. And his insurance attorney, Rushbrooke, is running late." Walon rolled his eyes, and I felt the same annoyance ripple down my side of the table. "But he'll be here too. They're down the hall in their own private conference room. I'll go back and forth between the two rooms for as long as it takes to get this case settled on terms that you are comfortable with."

"What if it doesn't get settled today?" I asked. The last thing I wanted was to drag this out.

"Well, that's up to you guys. You may demand more written discovery, take depositions, request another day in mediation, or decide to go to trial and let a jury decide your fate. But it's in everybody's best interests to settle. So, we're going to work real hard to do that. Okay?"

"Okay. I'm ready to start."

Walon nodded, and the negotiation began. I glanced over my shoulder at the floor-to-ceiling glass wall. It didn't feel very private. I tried my best to engage but was terribly distracted. Over the next several hours, a few things became more apparent than the rest.

Walker and his attorneys were relentless. They didn't come here to defend Walker's case; they came here to fight. Their demands were in excess of all my insurance policies combined. I was terrified, but Aunt Nora rose to the challenge. In fact, she welcomed it. The more allegations they came at us with, the dirtier the fight became, and the more money Nora demanded they pay.

"I'm telling you, Walon, he's got a killer in his blood! His father was a drunk and killed a family in an accident of his own! The apple doesn't fall far from the tree!" Aunt Nora seethed.

"Now, Nora, you know we can't use that."

"Tell him! Tell him she had a craniotomy. *Two weeks* in a coma, *two weeks* in the hospital, *four months* in physical therapy, and a *lifetime* of psychotherapy. You tell him he *stole* her eighteenth birthday, *stole* her graduation, and caused hallucinations for *months; maybe for the rest of her life!*" Aunt Nora leaned over the oval table and prodded her red nail into the open air.

"No! Don't tell him that!"

She whipped her head around and stared at me in surprise. "Why?"

"Because that's embarrassing," I complained.

Nora sat down and called for a break. It was past noon, and it felt like we were in a worse spot than when we started. I excused myself to the restroom, where I planned to hide for the rest of eternity.

CHAPTER 26

Needing a break, I walked down the hall and made my way to the restroom. I peeked through the glass windows at all the meetings going on and wondered if they were having as bad a day as I was. But when I came to the last conference room near the restroom, my steps slowed and time stilled.

An attractive guy in a white collared shirt sat at an oval table. Two men were caught in a quarrel, but he paid them no attention. He sat with fire blazing in his eyes as he spun a gold ring on top of the conference table. I knew without a shadow of a doubt it was Walker.

He had dark hair. A shadow on his unshaven face. And there was a scar running from his eyebrow to the corner of his eye. I knew from reading his chart that there was a metal plate beneath the skin of his cheek.

He looked nothing like what I remembered, yet something about him was oddly familiar. I knew exactly how he felt in that moment. Angry, robbed, frustrated, and utterly exhausted with it all. I felt that way too. And as I watched him through the glass, compassion softened all my rough edges. I didn't want to fight any more.

His eyes ticked upward, locking on mine. I stiffened at once; a deer caught in headlights. I spun around and bumped into a gentleman who was coming out of the restroom. I faltered and then barreled into the women's room. I leaned against the cold tile wall and hid my face in my trembling hands. Seeing Walker brought up a mixture of emotions that I couldn't possibly understand.

Whether he was *my* Walker or the defendant, I didn't know. But the one obvious thing was, my body remembered something my mind didn't want to. My head was swimming, my skin flushed. I wrapped my hair into a bun and lifted it from the nape of my neck.

Memories began to flood back like a tidal wave. Eyes like spun honey. Cotton candy and stone towers. I took slow, steady breaths, and I reminded myself that I was strong and capable.

I spent so long in the restroom, pacing back and forth, that my aunt came to find me. "Kinsley? What's going on? You've been in here for twenty minutes. Lunch is almost over."

"I'm not hungry."

"Are you sure? Are you feeling all right?"

"Yeah," I said, but my strained voice betrayed me. As soon as Aunt Nora recognized it, I broke down in tears and fell into her arms.

"What's wrong, dear? It's okay."

"It's all so much!"

Aunt Nora let me cry, but only for a moment. "Are you saying you don't want to become an attorney?" she asked.

"Are you serious? This is the worst day of my life!" I laughed, wiping away my tears.

"Really? Because I'm loving it." She had my mother's smile.

"That's because you find pleasure in my pain," I teased.

"And don't you forget it. Now come on. We have to finish this thing. I can feel it. They're going to break soon. Time tests everything."

"Impossible."

I peeked inside the conference room as we passed by. Only one attorney sat at the oval table. Walker was gone. "That's Rushbrooke. He's the attorney causing all the problems today."

Rushbrooke had thinning hair, a bulbous nose, and a red, pitted face.

"He looks mean."

"He's the worst."

As we approached our conference room, Walker and Mr. Barratt were heading back from the lunch area and were caught in an intense discussion. Before our eyes could meet again, I ducked into our room and turned away from the open glass wall. I felt his eyes on my back as their footfalls passed by.

"Very interesting." Aunt Nora rose a brow.

I waited for the second half of the day to begin with a bouncing foot that wouldn't quit and wandering eyes. But as mediation continued, we were informed that the fight had taken a drastic turn, and nobody knew why.

"Well, you're never going to believe it," Walon said.

Aunt Nora and Mr. Brown leaned forward, and I followed their lead, preparing for bad news. "St. James and Attorney Bradley Barratt have demanded that his insurance pay policy limits. I wish I could take credit for this, but in all honesty, I had nothing to do with it."

"Why?" Brown asked. It was the first thing he'd said all day, but we were all thinking it.

Walon spread his open hands and shook his head. The room fell silent as we passed around our confusion. "If I've learned anything in my thirty-nine years of mediation, it's that you don't question a good thing, and you don't argue when you're winning. You see, reality is not just what you make of it—it's also what you dare to dream, and what you are willing to fight for."

"That's why you're the best, Walon," Aunt Nora said, her light tone triumphant.

"I could say the same about you, Ms. Faye."

The mood in our room shifted considerably as we waited for the draft settlement papers to come in. When Walon came back with a proposal, Aunt Nora got her pen ready. She began reading, her finger moving along the words at lightning speed. But then she came to a screeching halt.

"What is it?"

"What is this?" Aunt Nora seethed. I tried to look, but there were about a thousand words on that page. I had to be patient.

"You can't blame him for trying," Walon said with pink cheeks.

"Yes, I can! There's no way in hell I'm signing this. And she won't either!"

"Okay. Okay. Does she want to counter?"

"No counter! This is unacceptable!"

"What is he asking for?" Brown asked. I waited for somebody to tell me what was happening, but it was clear that Aunt Nora was too angry, and Brown was still in the dark.

"Kinsley, one term of the settlement is that you agree to allow St. James to take you to dinner tonight, immediately after mediation."

"What!?"

"He's requesting your company at the steakhouse. I hear it's quite good."

"Can he do that?" I asked, my cheeks heating with embarrassment.

"No!" Aunt Nora snapped.

"Actually, nothing's off the table in mediation. He's allowed to ask for whatever terms he wants. You'd be surprised at what comes across this table."

"She won't do it! We'll walk out of here right now!" Aunt Nora stood, the chair jumping behind her.

"Wait!"

The room grew silent as everybody's eyes fell upon me. My heart thumped in my chest and my throat constricted. "I'll do it."

"Kinsley, no." Aunt Nora shook her head.

"It's okay. It might help me get . . . *closure*. Maybe he wants to apologize," I said. Aunt Nora slowly sat down, and Walon waited patiently. "But I have a counter."

"Yes ma'am. What would you like to counter?"

"I'll go to dinner . . . but I'm driving."

Brown and Walon broke into laughter. Aunt Nora moaned, hiding her face with her hand, and sinking further into her seat. "Your mother's going to kill me," she said beneath her breath.

"Well, you won't have to do that. It's directly across the street," Walon said.

It took several hours for the final version of the

settlement agreement to be drawn up. They awarded me one million from the auto insurance policy, an extra two million from Walker's umbrella insurance policy, and of course, one dinner. I signed on the dotted line, and I knew my life was about to change yet again.

I was a completely different person than I was when I'd gotten into my car on my eighteenth birthday. And whether the time I'd spent falling for Walker was real or not, this contract was between me and a complete stranger. I had no expectations, but I did have hopes of putting the past behind me, getting answers to a few burning questions, and finally moving forward.

While we waited for signatures, I compiled a mental list of things I wanted to ask Walker. I wanted to know what he remembered of the accident. I wanted to align my story with his and finally get a full picture of the accident that had nearly stolen my life. I told myself, beyond that, nothing else mattered. But I knew it was a lie. I was curious about him. About his father, his family, what he'd gone through to recover. And I would be lying if I said there wasn't a piece of me, somewhere inside that dark forgotten corner of my mind, that was aching to know: what did he remember about me?

"I'll wait for you. I'll even eat at the same restaurant to keep an eye on you. And I'll drive you home," Aunt Nora insisted.

"It's okay. I really don't mind. I can call a taxi."

"Kinsley, your mother is going to be *so* mad!"

"Once she hears you got policy limits, I doubt she's going to ask how I got home, where I ate dinner, or who with." Aunt Nora drummed her fingers on the table. It took some time, but she agreed. I *was* legally an adult, after all.

It was dark when we left the conference room. Everyone signed the settlement agreement, and the lawsuit was over. Brown and Walon bantered lightly with my aunt as we walked to the elevator. I stood in the back against the padded wall. The doors began to close as Rushbrooke approached and slammed into the buttons. The doors opened and Brown glanced sideways at Aunt Nora.

My breath hitched as Walker and his two attorneys entered our tightly packed elevator. His amber eyes met mine, and I studied the scar that sliced through his eyebrow. His deep-set dimples were visible in his clenched jaw. He was wildly handsome, and he hadn't taken his eyes off me. I thought I might pass out, hit my head and be rushed to the hospital for a new journey to begin again.

Walker pushed his way to the back of the elevator and stood right by my side. Aunt Nora gave me a quick, protective glance. I nodded to let her know I was okay, but I was pretty sure everybody in the elevator could hear the galloping of my heart that said otherwise.

I didn't know this man, but I wanted to. Something

inside me was drawn to him, and I didn't know if it was his good looks or the idea that dreams do come true. I only hoped that this pull was not caused by a curse, awakened in a distant, far-off land.

The elevator doors closed, and the cabin jerked as we began our descent. I caught a reflection in the steel doors through the tightly packed bodies in the elevator. A girl with dark chestnut hair, brown eyes, and ruby lips stared back at me. A reflection of a girl I both knew and loved. Standing beside me was not a stranger, but somebody I had known for much longer than my conscious mind would allow me to remember.

Walker was so close, I could feel the heat from his skin radiating against the back of my hand. Against all will, my pinky finger sought his. Our flesh touched as I trained my eyes forward, unblinking. Walker wrapped his pinky finger around mine in a small, but monumental gesture.

I froze with bated breath. His finger intertwined with mine for what felt like lifetimes, past and present. Reuniting with Walker brought with it more than just his memory. Within the steel reflection, only our two souls existed. No Aunt Nora. No Mediator Walon. And no lawsuit. No matter which direction I looked, there was only us, standing in an eternal void. A creeping mist enveloped us in its ghostly embrace.

Before I could react, the elevator shuddered to a stop,

and the phantom mist dispelled. The lights brightened, and a cheery bell rang, announcing we'd reached our final destination. I cleared my throat and tried to catch my breath. Walker's hand slipped away from mine as he and his two attorneys exited the elevator.

Aunt Nora checked with me one last time as she ushered me out of the elevator and through the lobby. Once outside in the brisk evening air, I said goodbye to my aunt and thanked her for all she'd done for me. Then Walker and I watched as our attorneys ducked into their cars. We stood silently on the curb as they drove off, parting ways.

Walker placed his hand on the small of my back, as if he'd done it a million times before. We crossed the street, stealing glances at each other and merging in with the crowd. All the black suits hurried on their important business, but Walker and I took our time.

As we approached the steakhouse, I couldn't help but notice the magnificent, ornamental red doors. Three times taller than any regular door, these truly looked like they belonged in a fairy tale. I paused in front of the steakhouse, taking it all in. A moment too precious for me to forget.

Among the bustling crowd, Walker and I stood side-by-side, marveling at the steakhouse store front. Slowly, he turned to me, leaned down and stole my breath away. "I know you," he whispered in my ear.

"Welcome!" the doorkeeper interrupted in a husky

voice. He pulled on the golden handles and opened the luxurious red doors, grand enough to be a real-life portal. And as we stepped inside, I knew that a life I couldn't have imagined in my wildest dreams was about to begin.

The End

I always wanted a scar. Nothing revolting. Just a gash. Something that said I was dangerous . . . or that I could be. I wanted to be mysterious. I got that, and so much more.

Etched into the side of my head was more than just a battle wound. It was a reminder of the pain and suffering it took to become the person I am today. And the gold band on my thumb reminded me of all the unpredictable and enchanting ways our lives could take shape. You see, reality is not just what you make of it—it's also what you dare to dream, and what you are willing to fight for.

Seven years after the accident, I sat in a movie theater on opening night of my first movie. As opening credits illuminated the big screen, Walker pried my white-knuckled hand from the arm rest and together, we took a deep breath and welcomed yet another twist in our remarkable story.

THANK YOU

Thank you for taking the time to read the Phantom Series. **Please take a moment to write a review.**

Want to know what's coming next? Subscribe here: https://www.subscribepage.com/redenbooks

Xoxo,
    Laura

ABOUT THE AUTHOR

I never considered myself a creative person, until a sudden spark of inspiration left me writing my first book. The endless possibilities for creativity and imagination have kept me dedicated to the craft ever since.

I find myself captivated by mixing real life with the unknown, a perspective glimpse on what lies beyond our reality. And driven by deep, unrefined emotions, that are at the heart of life's beauty and tragedy.

If my work has resonated with you, I would be thrilled to hear about it. Please consider leaving a review, subscribing to my email list, or reaching out to me directly. Thank you for reading and I hope to hear from you soon.

If you are interested in staying updated, subscribe to my email list. You will receive opportunities to help name characters, shape stories, get advanced review copies for free, and even have your pet featured in an upcoming novel. **Sign up and get a free ebook download today** https://www.subscribepage.com/redenbooks

Xoxo,

Laura

BB bookbub.com/authors/laura-c-reden

a amazon.com/kindle-dbs/entity/author/B08L1KH3LM

LAURA C. REDEN

DREAMS ARE FICKLE, EMOTIONS ARE BOLD.

THE
PHANTOM SERIES

CAUGHT BETWEEN WORLDS,
KINSLEY WILDE CAN SEE THE DEAD,
MANIFEST HER DREAMS, AND CONJURE HER FEARS.

NOTES FOR BOOK CLUB:

NOTES FOR BOOK CLUB: